PORTERHOUSE BLUE

Tom Sharpe was born in 1928 and educated at Lancing College and at Pembroke College, Cambridge. He did his National Service in the Marines before going to South Africa in 1951, where he did social work before teaching in Natal. He had a photographic studio in Pietermaritzburg from 1957 until 1961, when he was deported. From 1963 to 1972 he was a lecturer in History at the Cambridge College of Arts and Technology. Tom Sharpe is the author of thirteen best-selling novels. His *Porterhouse Blue* and *Blott on the Landscape* were serialised on television and *Wilt* was made into a film. In 1986 he was awarded the XXXIIIème Grand Prix de l'Humour Noir Xavier Forneret. He is married and divides his time between Cambridge England and Northern Spain.

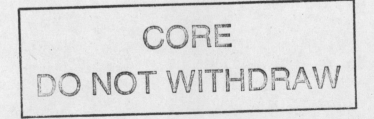

Also by Tom Sharpe

Riotous Assembly
Indecent Exposure
Blott on the Landscape
Wilt
The Great Pursuit
The Throwback
The Wilt Alternative
Ancestral Vices
Vintage Stuff
Wilt on High
Grantchester Grind
The Midden
Wilt in Nowhere
The Gropes

Porterhouse Blue

A Porterhouse Chronicle

Tom Sharpe

arrow books

Published by Arrow Books in 2002

21

Copyright © Tom Sharpe 1974

Tom Sharpe has asserted his right under the Copyright,
Designs and Patents Act, 1988 to be identified as the
author of this work

First published in 1974 by Martin Secker & Warburg Ltd

Arrow Books
The Random House Group Limited
20 Vauxhall Bridge Road, London SW1V 2SA

www.randomhouse.co.uk

Addresses for companies within The Random House Group Limited
can be found at:
www.rbooks.co.uk/environment

The Random House Group Limited Reg. No. 954009

A CIP catalogue record for this book
is available from the British Library

ISBN 9780099435464

Penguin Random House is committed to a sustainable future for
our business, our readers and our planet. This book is made from
Forest Stewardship Council® certified paper.

Printed and bound in Great Britain by Clays Ltd, St Ives plc

To Ivan and Pam Hattingh

1

It was a fine Feast. No one, not even the Praelector who was so old he could remember the Feast of '09, could recall its equal – and Porterhouse is famous for its food. There was Caviar and Soupe à l'Oignon, Turbot au Champagne, Swan stuffed with Widgeon, and finally, in memory of the Founder, Beefsteak from an ox roasted whole in the great fireplace of the College Hall. Each course had a different wine and each place was laid with five glasses. There was Pouilly Fumé with the fish, champagne with the game and the finest burgundy from the College cellars with the beef. For two hours the silver dishes came, announced by the swish of the doors in the Screens as the waiters scurried to and fro, bowed down by the weight of the food and their sense of occasion. For two hours the members of Porterhouse were lost to the world, immersed in an ancient ritual that spanned the centuries. The clatter of knives and forks, the clink of glasses, the rustle of napkins and the shuffling feet of the College servants dimmed the present. Outside the Hall the winter wind swept through the streets of Cambridge. Inside all was warmth and conviviality. Along the tables a hundred candles ensconced in silver candelabra cast elongated shadows of the crouching waiters across the portraits of past Masters that lined the walls. Severe or genial, scholars or politicians, the portraits had one thing in common: they were all rubicund and plump. Porterhouse's kitchen was long established. Only the new Master differed from his predecessors. Seated at the High Table, Sir Godber Evans picked at his swan with a delicate hesitancy that was in marked contrast to the frank enjoyment of the Fellows. A fixed dyspeptic smile lent a grim animation to Sir Godber's pale features as if his mind found relief from the present discomforts of the flesh in some remote and wholly intellectual joke.

'An evening to remember, Master,' said the Senior Tutor sebaceously.

'Indeed, Senior Tutor, indeed,' murmured the Master, his private joke enhanced by this unsought prediction.

'This swan is excellent,' said the Dean. 'A fine bird and the widgeon gives it a certain *gamin* flavour.'

'So good of Her Majesty to give Her permission for us to have swan,' the Bursar said. 'It's a privilege very rarely granted, you know.'

'Very rare,' the Chaplin agreed.

'Indeed, Chaplain, indeed,' murmured the Master and crossed his knife and fork. 'I think I'll wait for the beefsteak.' He sat back and studied the faces of the Fellows with fresh distaste. They were, he thought once again, an atavistic lot, and never more so than now with their napkins tucked into their collars, an age-old tradition of the College, and their foreheads greasy with perspiration and their mouths interminably full. How little things had changed since his own days as an undergraduate in Porterhouse. Even the College servants were the same, or so it seemed. The same shuffling gait, the adenoidal open mouths and tremulous lower lips, the same servility that had so offended his sense of social justice as a young man. And still offended it. For forty years Sir Godber had marched beneath the banner of social justice, or at least paraded, and if he had achieved anything (some cynics doubted even that) it was due to the fine sensibility that had been developed by the social chasm that yawned between the College servants and the young gentlemen of Porterhouse. His subsequent career in politics had been marked by the highest aspirations and the least effectuality, some said, since Asquith, and he had piloted through Parliament a series of bills whose aim, to assist the low-paid in one way or another, had resulted in that middle-class subsidy known as the development grant. His 'Every Home a Bathroom' campaign had led to the sobriquet Soapy and a knighthood, while his period as Minister of Technological Development had been rewarded by an early retirement and the Mastership of Porterhouse. It was one of the ironies of his appointment that he owed it to the very institution for which he professed most abhorrence, royal Patronage, and it was perhaps this knowledge that had led him to the decision to end his career as an initiator of social change by a real alteration in the social character and traditions of his old College. That and the awareness that his appointment had met with the adamant opposition of almost all the Fellows. Only the Chaplain had welcomed him, and that was in all likelihood due to his deafness and a mistaken apprehension of Sir Godber's full name. No, he was Master by default even of his own convictions and by the failure of the Fellows to agree among themselves and choose a new Master by election. Nor had the late Master with his dying breath named his successor, thus exercising the prerogative Porterhouse tradition allows; failing these two expedients it had been left to the Prime Minister, himself in the death throes of an administration, to rid himself of a liability by appointing Sir Godber. In Parliamentary circles, if not in academic ones, the appointment had been greeted with relief. 'Something to get your teeth into at last,' one of his Cabinet colleagues had said to the new Master, a reference less to the excellence of the College cuisine than to the intractable conservatism of Porterhouse. In this respect the College is unique. No other Cambridge college can equal Porterhouse in its adherence to the old traditions and to this day Porterhouse men are distinguished [*sic*] by the cut of their coats and hair and by their steadfast allegiance to gowns. 'County come to Town,' and 'The Squire to School', the other colleges used to sneer in the good old days, and the gibe has an element of truth about it still. A sturdy self-reliance except in scholarship is the mark of the Porterhouse man, and it is an exceptional year when Porterhouse is not Head of the River. And yet the College is not rich. Unlike nearly all the other colleges, Porterhouse has few assets to fall back on. A few terraces of dilapidated houses, some farms in Radnorshire, a modicum of shares in run-down industries, Porterhouse is poor. Its income amounts to less than £50,000 per annum and to this impecuniosity it owes its enduring reputation as the most socially exclusive college in Cambridge. If Porterhouse is poor, its undergraduates are rich. Where other colleges seek academic excellence in their freshmen, Porterhouse more democratically ignores the inequalities of intellect and concentrates upon the evidence of wealth. *Dives In Omnia*, reads the College motto, and the Fellows take it literally when examining the candidates. And in return the College offers social cachet and an enviable diet. True, a few scholarships and exhibitions exist which must be filled by men whose talents do not run to means, but those who last soon acquire the hallmarks of a Porterhouse man.

To the Master the memory of his own days as an undergraduate still had the power to send a shudder through him. A scholar in his day, Sir Godber, then plain G. Evans, had come to Porterhouse from a grammar school in Brierley. The experience had affected him profoundly. From his arrival had dated the sense of social inferiority which more than natural gifts had been the driving force of his ambition and which had spurred him on through failures that would have daunted a more talented man. After Porterhouse, he would remind himself on these occasions, a man has nothing left to fear. And certainly the College had left him socially resilient. To Porterhouse he owed his nerve, the nerve a few years later, while still a Parliamentary Private Secretary to the Minister of Transport, to propose to Mary Lacey, the only daughter of the Liberal Peer, the Earl of Sanderstead: the nerve to repeat the proposal yearly and to accept her annual refusal with a gracelessness that had gradually convinced her of the depth of his feelings. Yes, looking back over his long career Sir Godber could attribute much to Porterhouse and nothing more so than his determination to change once and for all the character of the college that had made him what he was. Looking down the hall at the faces florid in the candlelight and listening to the loud assertions that passed for conversation, he was strengthened in his resolve. The beefsteak and the burgundy came and went, the brandy trifle and the Stilton followed, and finally the port decanter made the rounds. Sir Godber observed and abstained. Only when the ritual of wiping one's forehead with a napkin dipped in a silver bowl had been performed did he make his move. Rapping his knife handle on the table for silence, the new Master of Porterhouse rose to his feet.

*

In the Musicians' Gallery Skullion watched the Feast. Behind him in the darkness the lesser College servants clustered backwardly and gaped at the brilliant scene below them, their pale faces gleaming dankly in the reflected glory of the occasion. As each new dish appeared a muted sigh went up. Their eyes glittered momentarily and glazed again. Only Skullion, the Head Porter, sat surveying the setting with an air of critical propriety. There was no envy in his eyes, only approval at the fitness of the arrangements and the occasional unexpressed rebuke when a waiter spilled the gravy or failed to notice an empty glass waiting to be refilled. It was all as it should be, as it had been since Skullion first came to the College as an under-porter so many years ago. Forty-five Feasts there had been since then and at each Skullion had watched from the Musicians' Gallery just as his ancestors had watched since the College began. 'Skullion, eh? That's an interesting name, Skullion,' old Lord Wurford had said when he first stopped by the lodge in 1928 and saw the new porter there. 'A very interesting name. Skullion. A no nonsense damn-my-soul name. There've been skullions at Porterhouse since the Founder. You take that from me, there have. It's in the first accounts. A farthing to the skullion. You be proud of it.' And Skullion had been proud of it as though he had been newly christened by the old Master. Yes, those were the days and those were the men. Old Lord Wurford, a no nonsense damn-my-soul Master.

He'd have enjoyed a feast like this. He wouldn't have sat up there fiddling with his fork and sipping his wine. He'd have spilt it down his front like he always used to and he'd have guzzled that swan like it was a chicken and thrown the bones over his shoulder. But he'd been a gentleman and a rowing man and he'd stuck to the old Boat Club traditions.

'A bone for the eight in front,' they used to shout.

'What eight? There ain't no eight in front.'

'A bone for the fish in front.' And over their shoulders the bones would go and if it was a good evening there was meat on them still and damned glad we was to get it. And it was true too. There was no eight in front in those days. Only the fish. In the darkness of the Musicians' Gallery Skullion smiled at his memories of his youth. All different now. The young gentlemen weren't the same. The spirit had gone out of them since the war. They got grants now. They worked. Who had ever heard of a Porterhouse man working in the old days? They were too busy drinking and racing. How many of this lot took a cab to Newmarket these days and came back five hundred to the bad and didn't turn a hair? The Honourable Mr Newland had in '33. Lived on Q staircase and got himself killed at Boulogne by the Germans. Skullion could remember a score or more like him. Gentlemen they were. No nonsense damn-my-soul gentlemen.

Presently when the main courses were finished and the Stilton had made its appearance, the Chef climbed the stairs from the kitchen and took his seat next to Skullion.

'Ah, Chef, a fine Feast. As good as any I can remember,' Skullion told him.

'It's good of you to say so, Mr Skullion,' said the Chef.

'Better than they deserve,' said Skullion.

'Someone has to keep up the old traditions, Mr Skullion.'

'True, Chef, very true,' Skullion nodded. They sat in silence watching the waiters clearing the dishes and the port moving ritually round.

'And what is your opinion of the new Master, Mr Skullion?' the Chef asked.

Skullion raised his eyes to the painted timbers of the ceiling and shook his head sadly.

'A sad day for the College, Chef, a sad day,' he sighed.

'Not a very popular gentleman?' the Chef hazarded.

'Not a gentleman,' Skullion pronounced.

'Ah,' said the Chef. Sentence on the new Master had been passed. In the kitchen he would ever be the victim of social obloquy. 'Not a gentleman, eh? And him with his knighthood too.'

Skullion looked at him sternly. 'Gentlemen don't depend on knighthoods, Cheffy. Gentlemen is gentlemen,' Skullion told him, and the Chef, suitably rebuked, nodded. Mr Skullion wasn't somebody you argued with, not about matters of social etiquette, not in Porterhouse. Not if you knew what was good for you. Mr Skullion was a power in the College.

They sat silently mourning the passing of the old Master and the debasement of college life which the coming of a new Master, who was not a gentleman, brought with it.

'Still,' said Skullion finally, 'it was a fine Feast. I can't remember a better.' He said it half-grudgingly, out of respect for the past, and was about to go downstairs when the Master rapped on the High Table for silence and stood up. In the Musicians' Gallery Skullion and the Chef stared in horror at the spectacle. A speech at the Feast? No. Never. The precedence of five hundred and thirty-two Feasts forbade it.

*

Sir Godber stared down at the heads turned towards him so incredulously. He was satisfied. The stunned silence, the stares of disbelief, the tension were what he had wanted. And not a single snigger. Sir Godber smiled.

'Fellows of Porterhouse, members of College,' he began with the practised urbanity of a politician, 'as your new Master I feel that this is a suitable occasion to put before you some new thoughts about the role of institutions such as this in the modern world.' Calculated, every insult delicately calculated, Porterhouse an institution, new, modern, role. The words, the clichés defiled the atmosphere. Sir Godber smiled. His sense of grievance was striking home. 'After such a meal' (in the gallery the Chef shied), 'it is surely not inappropriate to consider the future and the changes that must surely be made if we are to play our part in the contemporary world . . .'

The platitudes rolled out effortlessly, meaninglessly but with effect. Nobody in the hall listened to the words. Sir Godber could have announced the Second Coming without demur. It was enough that he was there, defying tradition and consciously defiling his trust. Porterhouse could remember nothing to equal this. Not even sacrilege but utter blasphemy. And awed by the spectacle, Porterhouse sat in silence.

'And so let me end with this promise,' Sir Godber wound up his appalling peroration, 'Porterhouse will expand. Porterhouse will become what it once was – a house of learning. Porterhouse will change.' He stopped and for the last time smiled and then, before the tension broke, turned on his heel and swept out into the Combination Room. Behind him with a sudden expiration of breath the Feast broke up. Someone laughed nervously, the short bark of the Porterhouse laugh, and then the benches were pushed back and they flooded out of the hall, their voices flowing out before them into the Court, into the cold night air. It had begun to snow. On the Fellows' lawn Sir Godber Evans increased his pace. He had heard that bark and the sounds of the benches and the nervous energy he had expended had left him weak. He had challenged the College deliberately. He had said what he wanted to say. He had asserted himself. There was nothing they could do now. He had risked the stamping feet and the hisses and they had not come but now, with the snow falling round him on the Fellows' lawn, he was suddenly afraid. He hurried on and closed the door of the Master's Lodge with a sigh of relief.

As the hall emptied and as even the Fellows drifted through the door of the Combination Room, the Chaplain rose to say Grace. Deaf to the world and the blasphemies of Sir Godber, the Chaplain gave thanks. Only Skullion, standing alone in the Musicians' Gallery, heard him and his face was dark with anger.

2

In the Combination Room the Fellows digested the Feast dyspeptically. Sitting in their high-backed chairs, each with an occasional table on which stood coffee cups and glasses of brandy, they stared belligerently into the fire. Gusts of wind in the chimney blew eddies of smoke into the room to mingle with the blue cirrus of their cigars. Above their heads grotesque animals pursued in plaster evidently plastered nymphs across a pastoral landscape strangely formal, in which flowers and the College crest, a Bull Rampant, alternated, while from the panelled walls glowered the gross portraits of Thomas Wilkins, Master 1618–39, and Dr Cox, 1702–40. Even the fireplace, itself surrounded by an arabesque of astonishing grapes and well-endowed bananas, suggested excess and added an extra touch of flatulence to the scene. But if the Fellows found difficulty in coming to terms with the contents of their stomachs, the contents of Sir Godber's speech were wholly indigestible.

'Outrageous,' said the Dean, discreetly combining protest with cructation. 'One might have imagined he was addressing an electoral meeting.'

'It was certainly a very inauspicious start,' said the

Senior Tutor. 'One would have expected a greater regard for tradition. When all is said and done we are an old college.'

'All may have been said, though I doubt your optimism,' said the Dean, 'but it has certainly not been done. The Master's infatuation with contemporary fashions of opinion may lead him to suppose that we are flattered by his presence. It is an illusion the scourings of party politics too naturally assume. I for one am unimpressed.'

'I must admit that I find his nomination most curious,' said the Praelector. 'One wonders what the Prime Minister had in mind.'

'The Government's majority is not a substantial one,' said the Senior Tutor. 'I should imagine he was ridding himself of a liability. If this evening's lamentable speech was anything to go by, Sir Godber's statements in the Commons must have raised a good many hackles on the back benches. Besides, his record of achievement is not an enviable one.'

'It still seems odd to me,' said the Praelector, 'that we should have been chosen for his retirement.'

'Perhaps his bark is worse than his bite,' said the Bursar hopefully.

'Bite?' shouted the Chaplain. 'But I've only just finished dinner. Not another morsel, thank you all the same.'

'One must assume that it was a case of any port in a storm,' said the Dean.

The Chaplain looked appalled.

'Port?' he screamed. 'After brandy? I can't think what this place is coming to.' He shuddered and promptly fell asleep again.

'I can't think what the Chaplain is coming to, come to that,' said the Praelector sadly. 'He gets worse by the day.'

'Anno domini,' said the Dean, 'anno domini, I'm afraid.'

'Not a particularly happy expression, Dean,' said the Senior Tutor, who still retained some vestiges of a classical education, 'in the circumstances.'

The Dean looked at him lividly. He disliked the Senior Tutor and found his allusions distinctly trying.

'The year of our Lord,' the Senior Tutor explained. 'I have the notion that our Master sees himself in the role of the creator. We shall have our work cut out preventing him from overexerting himself. We have our faults I daresay but they are not ones I would wish to see Sir Godber Evans remedy.'

'I am sure the Master will allow himself to be guided by our advice,' said the Praelector. 'We have had some obdurate Masters in the past. Canon Bowel had some ill-advised notions about altering the Chapel services, I seem to recall.'

'He wanted compulsory Compline,' said the Dean.

'A fearful thought,' the Senior Tutor agreed. 'It would have interfered with the digestive process.'

'The point was made to him,' the Dean continued,

'after a particularly good dinner. We had had devilled crabs with jugged hare to follow. I think it was the cigars that did it. That and the zabaglione.'

'Zabaglione?' shouted the Chaplain. 'It's a little late but I daresay . . .'

'We were talking about Canon Bowel,' the Bursar explained to him.

The Chaplain shook his head. 'Couldn't abide the man,' he said. 'Used to live on poached cod.'

'He had a peptic ulcer.'

'I'm not surprised,' said the Chaplain. 'With a name like that he should have known better.'

'To return to the present Master,' the Senior Tutor said, 'I am not prepared to sit back and allow him to alter our present admissions policy.'

'I don't see how we can afford to,' the Bursar agreed. 'We are not a rich college.'

'The point will have to be made to him,' the Dean said. 'We look to you, Bursar, to see that he understands it.' The Bursar nodded dutifully. His was not a strong constitution and the Dean overawed him.

'I shall do my best,' he said.

'And as far as the College Council is concerned I think the best policy will be one of . . . er . . . amiable inertia,' the Praelector suggested. 'That has always been one of our strong points.'

'There's nothing like prevarication,' the Dean agreed, 'I have yet to meet a liberal who can withstand the attrition of prolonged discussion of the inessentials.'

'You don't think the Bowel treatment, to coin a phrase?' the Senior Tutor asked.

The Dean smiled and stubbed out his cigar.

'There are more ways of killing a cat than stuffing it with . . .'

'Hush,' said the Praelector, but the Chaplain slept on. He was dreaming of the girls in Woolworths.

They left him sitting there and went out into the Court, their gowns wrapped round them against the cold. Like so many black puddings, they made their way to their rooms. Only the Bursar lived out with his wife. Porterhouse was still a very old-fashioned college.

*

In the Porter's Lodge Skullion sat in front of the gas fire polishing his shoes. A tin of black polish stood on the table beside him and every few minutes he would dip the corner of his yellow duster into the tin and smear the polish on to the toe of his shoe with little circular movements. Round and round his finger would go inside the duster while the toecap dulled momentarily and grew to a new and deeper shine. Every now and then Skullion would spit on the cap and then rub it again with an even lighter touch before picking up a clean duster and polishing the cap until it shone like black japan. Finally he would hold the shoe away from him so that it caught the light and he could see deep in the brilliant polish a dark distorted reflection of himself.

Only then would he put the shoe to one side and start on the other.

It was something he had learnt to do in the Marines so many years ago and the ritual still had the satisfying effect it had had then. In some obscure way it seemed to ward off the thought of the future and all the threats implicit in that future, as if tomorrow was always a regimental sergeant-major and an inspection and change could be propitiated by a gleaming pair of boots. All the time his pipe smoked out of the corner of his mouth and the mantles of the gas fire darkened or glowed in the draught and the snow fell outside. And all the time Skullion's mind, protected by the ritual and the artefacts of habit, digested the import of the Master's speech. Change? There was always change and what good did it do? Skullion could think of nothing good in change. His memory ranged back over the decades in search of certainty and found it only in the assurance of men. Men no longer living or, if not dead, distant and forgotten, ignored by a world in search of effervescent novelty. But he had seen their assurance in his youth and had been infected by it so that now, even now, he could call it up like some familiar from the past to calm the seething uncertainties of the present. Quality, he had called it, this assurance that those old men had. Quality. He couldn't define it or fix it to particulars. They had had it, that was all, and some of them had been fools or blackguards come to that but when they'd spoken there'd been a harshness in their voices as if they didn't give a damn for anything. No doubts, that's what they'd had, or if they had them kept them to themselves instead of spreading their uncertainties about until you were left wondering who or where you were. Skullion spat on his shoe in memory of such men and their assurance and polished his reflection by the fire. Above him the tower clock whirred and rumbled before striking twelve. Skullion put on his shoes and went outside. The snow was falling still and the Court and all the College roofs were white. He went to the postern gate and looked outside. A car slushed by and all the way up King's Parade the lamps shone orange through the falling snow. Skullion went in and shut the door. The outside world was none of his affair. It had a bleakness that he didn't want to know.

He went back into the Porter's Lodge and sat down again with his pipe. Around him the paraphernalia of his office, the old wooden clock, the counter, the rows of pigeonholes, the keyboard and the blackboard with 'Message for Dr Messmer' scrawled on it, were reassuring relics of his tenure and reminders that he was still needed. For forty-five years Skullion had sat in the Lodge watching over the comings and goings of Porterhouse until it seemed he was as much a part of the College as the carved heraldic beasts on the tower above. A lifetime of little duties easily attended to while the world outside stormed by in a maelstrom of change had bred in Skullion a devotion to the changelessness of Porterhouse traditions. When he'd first come there'd been an Empire, the greatest Empire that the world had known, a Navy, the greatest Navy in the world, fifteen battleships, seventy cruisers, two hundred destroyers, and Skullion had been a keyboard sentry on the *Nelson* with her three for'ard turrets and her arse cut off to meet the terms of some damned treaty. And now there was nothing left of that. Only Porterhouse was still the same. Porterhouse and Skullion, relics of an old tradition. As for the intellectual life of the College, Skullion neither knew nor cared about it. It was as incomprehensible to him as the rigmarole of a Latin mass to some illiterate peasant. They could say or think what they liked. It was the men he worshipped, some at least and fewer these days, their habits and the trappings he associated with that old assurance. The Dean's, 'Good morning, Skullion,' Dr Huntley's silk shirts, the Chaplain's evening stroll around the Fellows' Garden, Mr Lyons' music evening every Friday, the weekly parcel from the Institute for Dr Baxter. Chapel, Hall, the Feast, the meeting of the College Council, all these occasions like internal seasons marked the calendar of Skullion's life and all the time he looked for that assurance that had once been the hallmark of a gentleman.

Now sitting there with the gas fire hissing before him he searched his mind for what it was those old men signified. It wasn't that they were clever. Some were, but half were stupid, more stupid than the young men coming up these days. Money? Some had a lot and others hadn't. That wasn't what had made the difference. To him at least. Perhaps it had to them. A race apart they were. Helpless half of them. Couldn't make their beds, or wouldn't. And arrogant. 'Skullion this and Skullion that.' Oh, he'd resented it at the time and done it all the same and hadn't minded afterwards because . . . because they'd been gentlemen. He spat into the fire affectionately and remembered an argument he'd had once with a young pup in a pub who'd heard him going on about the good old days.

'What gentlemen?' the lad had said. 'A lot of rich bastards with nothing between their ears who just exploited you.'

And Skullion had put down his pint and said, 'A gentleman stood for something. It wasn't what he was. It was what he knew he ought to be. And that's something you will never know.' Not what they were but what they ought to be, like some old battle standard that you followed because it was a symbol of the best. A ragged tattered piece of cloth that stood for something and gave you confidence and something to fight for.

He got up and walked across the Court and through the Screens and down the Fellows' Garden to the back gate. Everywhere the snow had submerged the details of the garden. Skullion's feet on the gravel path were soundless. In a few rooms lights still burned. The Dean's windows were still alight.

'Brooding on the speech,' Skullion thought and glanced reproachfully at the Master's Lodge where all was dark. At the back gate he stood looking up at the rows of iron spikes that topped the wall and the gate. How often in the old days he had stood there in the shadow of the beech-trees watching young gentlemen negotiate those spikes only to step out and take their names. He could remember a good many of those names still and see the startled faces turned towards his as he stepped out into the light.

'Good morning, Mr Hornby. Dean's report in the morning, sir.'

'Oh damn you, Skullion. Why can't you go to bed sometimes?'

'College regulations, sir.'

And they had gone off to their rooms cursing cheerfully. Now no one climbed in. Instead they knocked you up at all hours. Skullion didn't know why he bothered to come and look at the back wall any more. Out of habit. Old habit. He was just about to turn and trudge back to his bed in the Lodge when a scuffling noise stopped him in his tracks. Someone in the street was trying to climb in.

*

Zipser walked down Free School Lane past the black clunch walls of Corpus. The talk on 'Population Control in the Indian Subcontinent' had gone on longer than he had expected, partly due to the enthusiasm of the speaker and partly to the intractable nature of the problem itself. Zipser had not been sure which had been worse, the delivery, if that was an appropriate word to use about a speech that concerned itself with abortion, or the enthusiastic advocacy of vasectomy which had prolonged the talk beyond its expected limits. The speaker, a woman doctor with the United Nations Infant Prevention Unit in Madras, who seemed to regard infant mortality as a positive blessing, had disparaged the coil as useless, the pill as expensive, female sterilization as complicated, had described vasectomy so seductively that Zipser had found himself crossing and recrossing his legs and wishing to hell that he hadn't come. Even now as he walked back to Porterhouse through the snow-covered streets he was filled with foreboding and a tendency to waddle. Still, even if the world seemed doomed to starvation, he had had to get out of Porterhouse for the evening. As the only research graduate in the College he found himself isolated. Below him the undergraduates pursued a wild promiscuity which he envied but dared not emulate, and above him the Fellows found compensation for their impotence in gluttony. Besides he was not a Porterhouse man, as the Dean had pointed out when he had been accepted. 'You'll have to live in College to get the spirit of the place,' he had said, and while in other colleges research graduates lived in cheap and comfortable digs, Zipser found himself occupying an exceedingly expensive suite of rooms in Bull Tower and forced to follow the regime of an undergraduate. For one thing he had to be in by twelve or face the wrath of Skullion and the indelicate inquiries next morning of the Dean. The whole system was anachronistic and Zipser wished he had been accepted by one of the other colleges. Skullion's attitude he found particularly unpleasant. The Porter seemed to regard him as an interloper, and lavished a wealth of invective on him normally reserved for tradesmen. Zipser's attempts to mollify him by explaining that Durham was a university and that there had been a Durham College in Oxford in 1380 had failed hopelessly. If anything, the mention of Oxford had increased Skullion's antipathy.

'This is a gentleman's college,' he had said, and Zipser, who didn't claim to be even a putative gentleman, had been a marked man ever since. Skullion had it in for him.

As he crossed Market Hill he glanced at the Guildhall clock. It was twelve thirty-five. The main gate would be shut and Skullion in bed. Zipser slackened his pace. There was no point in hurrying now. He might just as well stay out all night now. He certainly wasn't going to knock Skullion up and get cursed for his pains. It wouldn't have been the first time he had wandered about Cambridge all night. Of course there was Mrs Biggs the bedder to be taken care of. She came to wake him every morning and was supposed to report him if his bed hadn't been slept in but Mrs Biggs was accommodating. 'A pound in the purse is worth a flea in the ear,' she had explained after his first stint of night wandering, and Zipser had paid up cheerfully. Mrs Biggs was all right. He was fond of her. There was something almost human about her in spite of her size.

Zipser shivered. It was partly the cold and partly the thought of Mrs Biggs. The snow was falling heavily now and it was obvious he couldn't stay out all night in this weather. It was equally clear that he wasn't going to wake Skullion. He would have to climb in. It was an undignified thing for a graduate to do but there was no alternative. He crossed Trinity Street and went past Caius. At the bottom he turned right and came to the back gate in the lane. Above him the iron spikes on top of the wall looked more threatening than ever. Still, he couldn't stay out. He would probably freeze to death if he did. He found a bicycle in front of Trinity Hall and dragged it up the lane and put it against the wall. Then he climbed up until he could grasp the spikes with his hands. He paused for a moment and then with a final kick he was up with one knee on the wall and his foot under the spikes. He eased himself up and swung the other leg over, found a foothold and jumped. He landed softly in the flowerbed and scrambled to his feet. He was just moving off down the path under the beech-tree when something moved in the shadow and a hand fell on his shoulder. Zipser reacted instinctively. With a wild flurry he struck out at his attacker and the next moment a bowler hat was in mid-air and Zipser himself, ignoring the College rules which decreed that only

Fellows could walk on the lawns, was racing across the grass towards New Court. Behind him on the gravel path Skullion lay breathing heavily. Zipser glanced over his shoulder as he dashed through the gate into the Court and saw his dark shape on the ground. Then he was in O staircase and climbing the stairs to his rooms. He shut the door and stood in the darkness panting. It must have been Skullion. The bowler hat told him that. He had assaulted a College porter, bashed his face and chopped him down. He went to the window and peered out and it was then that he realized what a fool he had been. His footsteps in the snow would give him away. Skullion would follow them to the Bull Tower. But there was no sign of the Porter. Perhaps he was still lying out there unconscious. Perhaps he had knocked him out. Zipser shuddered at this fresh indication of his irrational nature, and its terrible consequences for mankind. Sex and violence, the speaker had said, were the twin poles of the world's lifeless future, and Zipser could see now what she had meant.

Anyway, he could not leave Skullion lying out there to freeze to death even if going down to help him meant that he would be sent down from the University for 'assaulting a college porter', his thesis on The Pumpernickel as A Factor in the Politics of Sixteenth-Century Westphalia uncompleted. He went to the door and walked slowly downstairs.

*

Skullion got to his feet and picked up his bowler, brushed the snow off it and put it on. His waistcoat and jacket were covered with patches of snow and he brushed them down with his hands. His right eye was swelling. Young bastard had caught him a real shiner. 'Getting too old for this job,' he muttered, muddled feelings of anger and respect competing in his mind. 'But I can still catch him.' He followed the footsteps across the lawn and down the path to the gate into New Court. His eye had swollen now so that he could hardly see out of it, but Skullion wasn't thinking about his eye. He wasn't thinking about catching the culprit. He was thinking back to the days of his youth. 'Fair's fair. If you can't catch 'em, you can't report 'em,' old Fuller, the Head Porter at Porterhouse had said to him when he first came to the College and what was true then was true now. He turned left at the gate and went down the Cloister to the Lodge and went through to his bedroom. 'A real shiner,' he said examining the swollen eye in the mirror behind the door. It could do with a bit of beefsteak. He'd get some from the College kitchen in the morning. He took off his jacket and was unbuttoning his waistcoat when the door of the Lodge opened. Skullion buttoned his waistcoat again and put on his jacket and went out into the office.

*

Zipser stood in the doorway of O staircase and watched Skullion cross the Court to the Cloisters. Well, at least he wasn't lying out in the snow. Still he couldn't go back to his room without doing something. He had better go down and see if he was all right. He walked across the Court and into the Lodge. It was empty and he was about to turn away and go back to his room when the door at the back opened and Skullion appeared. His right eye was black and swollen and his face, old and veined, had a deformed lopsided look about it.

'Well?' Skullion asked out of the side of his mouth. One eye peered angrily at Zipser.

'I just came to say I'm sorry,' Zipser said awkwardly.

'Sorry?' Skullion asked as if he didn't understand.

'Sorry about hitting you.'

'What makes you think you hit me?' The lopsided face glared at him.

Zipser scratched his forehead.

'Well, anyway I'm sorry. I thought I had better see if you were all right.'

'You thought I was going to report you, didn't you?' Skullion asked contemptuously. 'Well, I'm not. You got away.'

Zipser shook his head.

'It wasn't that. I thought you might be . . . well . . . hurt.'

Skullion smiled grimly.

'Hurt? Me hurt? What's a little hurt matter?' He turned and went back into the bedroom and shut the

door. Zipser went out into the Court. He didn't understand. You knocked an old man down and he didn't
mind. It wasn't logical. It was all so bloody irrational.
He walked back to his room and went to bed.

3

The Master slept badly. The somatic effects of the Feast and the psychic consequences of his speech had combined to make sleep difficult. While his wife slept demurely in her separate bed, Sir Godber lay awake reliving the events of the evening with an insomniac's obsessiveness. Had he been wise to so offend the sensibilities of the College? It had been a carefully calculated decision and one which his political eminence had seemed to warrant. Whatever the Fellows might say about him, his reputation for moderate and essentially conservative reform would absolve him of the accusation that he was the advocate of change for change's sake. As the Minister who had made the slogan 'Alteration without Change' so much a part of the recent tax reforms, Sir Godber prided himself on his conservative liberalism or, as he had put it in a moment of self-revelation, authoritarian permissiveness. The challenge he had thrown down to Porterhouse had been deliberate and justified. The College was absurdly old-fashioned. Out of touch with the times, and to a man whose very life had been spent keeping in touch with the times there could be no greater dereliction. An advocate of comprehensive education at no matter what cost, chairman of the Evans Committee on Higher Education which had introduced Sixth Form Polytechnics for the Mentally Retarded, Sir Godber prided himself on the certain knowledge that he knew what was best for the country, and he was supported in this by Lady Mary, his wife, whose family, now staunchly Liberal, still retained the Whig traditions enshrined in the family motto *Laisser Mieux*. Sir Godber had taken the motto for his own, and associating it with Voltaire's famous dictum had made himself the enemy of the good wherever he found it. 'Be good, sweet maid, and let who will be clever' had no appeal for Sir Godber's crusading imagination. What sweet maids required was a first-rate education and what sleeping dogs needed was a kick up the backside. This was precisely what he intended to administer to Porterhouse.

Lying awake through the still hours of the night listening to the bells of the College clocks and the churches toll the hours, a sound he found medieval and unnecessarily premonitory, Sir Godber planned his campaign. In the first instance he would order a thorough inventory of the College's resources and make the economies needed to finance the alterations he had in mind. In themselves such economies would effect some changes in Porterhouse. The kitchen staff could well do with some thinning out and since so much of the ethos of Porterhouse emanated from the kitchen and the men, a careful campaign of retrenchment there would do much to alter the character of the College. And such savings would be justified by the building programme and the expansion of numbers. With the experience of hundreds of hours in committees behind him, the Master anticipated the arguments that would be raised against him by the Fellows. Some would object to any change in the kitchen. Others would deny the need for expansion in numbers. In the darkness Sir Godber smiled happily. It was precisely on such divisions of opinion that he thrived. The original issue would get lost in argument and he would emerge as the arbiter between divided factions, his role as the initiator of dissension quite forgotten. But first he would need an ally. He ran through the Fellows in search of a weak link.

The Dean would oppose any increase in the numbers of undergraduates on the specious grounds that it would destroy the Christian community which he supposed Porterhouse to be and, more accurately, would make discipline difficult to impose. Sir Godber put the Dean to one side. There was no help to be found there except indirectly from the very obduracy of his conservatism, which irritated some of the other Fellows. The Senior Tutor? A more difficult case to assess. A rowing man in his day, he might be inclined to favour a large intake on the grounds that it would add weight to the College boat and improve Porterhouse's chances in the Bumps. On the other hand he would oppose any changes in the kitchen for fear that the diet of the Boat Club might be diminished. The Master decided a compromise was in order. He would give an absolute assurance that the Boat Club would continue to get its quota of beefsteak no matter what other economies were made in the kitchen. Yes, the Senior Tutor could be persuaded to support expansion. Sir Godber balanced him against the Dean and turned his attention to the Bursar. Here was the key, he thought. If the Bursar could be enlisted on the side of change, his assistance would be invaluable. His advocacy of the financial benefits to be gained from an increase of undergraduate contributions, his demand for frugality in the kitchens, would carry immense weight. Sir Godber considered the Bursar's character and, with that insight into his own nature which had been the cornerstone of his success, recognized opportunism when he saw it. The Bursar, he had no doubt, was an ambitious man and unlikely to be content with the modest attainments of College. The opportunity to serve on a Royal Commission – Sir Godber's retirement from the Cabinet was sufficiently recent for him to know of several pending – would give him a chance to put this nonentity at the service of the public and give him the recognition which would make amends for his lack of achievement. Sir Godber had no doubt that he could arrange his invitation. There was always a place for a man of the Bursar's contingent character on Royal Commissions. He would concentrate his attention on the Bursar. Satisfied with this plan of campaign, the Master turned on his side and fell asleep.

At seven he was woken by his wife whose insistence that early to bed and early to rise makes a man healthy, comfortably off and wise had never ceased to irritate him. As she bustled about the bedroom with a lack of concern for the feelings of other people which characterized her philanthropy, Sir Godber studied once more those particulars of his wife which had been such a spur to his political ambitions. Lady Mary was not an attractive woman. Her physical angularity made manifest the quality of her mind.

'Time to get up,' she said, spotting Sir Godber's open eye.

'Ours not to reason why, ours but to do or die,' thought the Master, sitting up and fumbling for his slippers.

'How did the Feast go?' Lady Mary asked, adjusting the straps of her surgical corset with a vigour that reminded Sir Godber of a race meeting.

'Tolerably, I suppose,' he said with a yawn. 'We had swan stuffed with some sort of duck. Very indigestible. Kept me awake half the night.'

'You should be more careful about what you eat.' Lady Mary sat down and swung one leg over the other to put on her stockings. 'You don't want to have a stroke.'

'It's called Porterhouse Blue.'

'What is?'

'A stroke,' said Sir Godber.

'I thought it was something you got for rowing,' said

Lady Mary. 'That, or a cheese. Something on the order of a Stilton – blue and veined—'

Sir Godber lowered his eyes from her legs. 'Well, it isn't,' he said hurriedly, 'it's an apoplectic fit brought on by overindulgence. An old College tradition, and one I intend to eradicate.'

'And about time too,' said Lady Mary. 'I think it's utterly disgraceful in this day and age that all this good food should go to waste just to satisfy the greed of some old men. When I think of all those . . .'

Sir Godber went into the bathroom and shut the door and turned the tap on in the hand basin. Dimly through the door and through the noise of running water he could hear his wife lamenting starving children in India. He looked at himself in the mirror and sighed. Just like the bloody cockcrow, he thought. Starts the day with a dirge. Wouldn't be happy if someone wasn't dying of starvation or drowning in a hurricane or dropping dead of typhus.

He shaved and dressed and went down to breakfast. Lady Mary was reading the *Guardian* with an avidity that suggested a natural disaster of considerable magnitude. Sir Godber refrained from enquiring what it was and contented himself with reading one or two bills.

'My dear,' he said when he had finished, 'I shall be seeing the Bursar this morning and I was thinking of inviting him to dinner on Wednesday.'

Lady Mary looked up. 'Wednesday's no good. I have a meeting on. Thursday would be better,' she said. 'Do you want me to invite anyone else? He's a rather common little man, isn't he?'

'He has his good points,' said the Master. 'I'll see if Thursday suits him.' He went to his study with *The Times*. There were days when his wife's moral intensity seemed to hang like a pall over his existence. He wondered what the meeting on Wednesday was about. Battered babies probably. The Master shuddered.

*

In the Bursar's office the telephone rang.

'Ah, Master. Yes, certainly. No, not at all. In five minutes then.' He put down the phone with a smile of quiet satisfaction. The bargaining was about to begin and the Master had not invited anyone else. The Bursar's office overlooked the Fellows' Garden and nobody else had taken the path under the beech-trees to the Master's Lodge. As he left his office and walked across the lawn the Bursar reviewed the strategy he had decided on during the night. He had been tempted to put himself at the head of the Fellows in their opposition to any change. There were after all advantages to be gained in the climate of the seventies from adherence to the principles of strict conservatism, and in the event of the Master's retirement or early death the Fellows might well elect him Master in his place out of gratitude. The Bursar rather fancied not. He lacked the carnivorous bonhomie that Porterhouse sought in its Masters. Old Lord Wurford for instance, Skullion's touchstone, or Canon Bowel, whose penchant for Limburger cheese and rugby fanaticism had in a sinister way been interrelated. No, the Bursar could not see himself among their number. It was wiser to follow in his Master's footsteps. He knocked on the door of the Master's Lodge and was admitted by the French au pair.

'Ah, Bursar, so good of you to come,' said the Master, rising from his chair behind the large oak desk that stood in front of the fire. 'Some Madeira? Or would you prefer something a little more contemporary?' The Master chuckled. 'A Campari, for instance. Something to keep the cold out.' In the background the radiators gurgled gently. The Bursar considered the question.

'I think something contemporary would be fitting, Master,' he said at last.

'So do I, Bursar, so I do indeed,' said the Master, and poured the drinks.

'Now then,' he said when the Bursar had seated himself in an armchair, 'to business.'

'To business,' said the Bursar raising his glass in the mistaken belief that a toast had been proposed. The Master eyed him cautiously.

'Yes. Well,' he said, 'I've asked you here this morning to discuss the College finances. I understand from the Praelector that you and I share responsibility in this matter. Correct me if I am wrong?'

'Quite right, Master,' said the Bursar.

'But of course as Bursar you are the real power. I

quite appreciate that,' the Master continued. 'I have no desire to impinge upon your authority in these matters, let me assure you of that.' He smiled genially on the Bursar.

'My purpose in asking you here this morning was to reassure you that the changes I spoke of last night were of a purely general nature. I seek no alterations in the administration of the College.'

'Quite,' said the Bursar, nodding with approval. 'I entirely agree.'

'So good of you to say so, Bursar,' said the Master. 'I had the impression that my little sally had a not altogether unmixed reception from the less . . . er . . . contemporary Senior Fellows.'

'We are a very traditional college, Master,' said the Bursar.

'Yes, so we are, but some of us, I suspect, are rather less traditional than others, eh, Bursar?'

'I think it's fair to say so, Master,' the Bursar assented.

Like two elderly dogs they circled warily in search of the odour of agreement, sniffing each hesitation for the nuance of complicity. Change was inevitable. Indeed, indeed. The old order. Quite so. Quite so. Those of us in authority. Ah yes. Ah yes. On the mantelpiece the alabaster clock ticked on. It was an hour before the preliminary skirmishes were done and with a second, larger Campari Sir Godber relaxed the role of Master.

'It's the sheer animality of so many of our undergraduates I object to,' he told the Bursar.

'We tend to attract the less sensitive, I must admit.' The Bursar puffed his cigar contentedly.

'Academically our results are deplorable. When did we last get a first?'

'In 1956,' said the Bursar.

The Master raised his eyes to heaven.

'In Geography,' said the Bursar, rubbing salt in the wound.

'In Geography. One might have guessed.' He got up and stood looking out of the French windows at the garden covered in snow. 'It is time to change all that. We must return to the Founder's intentions, "studiously to engage in learning". We must accept candidates who have good academic records instead of the herd of illiterates we seem to cater for at present.'

'There are one or two obstacles to that,' the Bursar sighed.

'Quite so. The Senior Tutor for one. He is in charge of admissions.'

'I was thinking rather of our, how shall I say, dependence on the endowment subscriptions,' said the Bursar.

'The endowment subscriptions? I've never heard of them.'

'Very few people have, Master, except of course the parents of our less academic undergraduates.'

Sir Godber frowned and stared at the Bursar. 'Do you mean to say that we accept candidates without academic qualifications if their parents subscribe to an endowment fund?' he asked.

'I'm afraid so. Frankly, the College could hardly continue without their contributions,' the Bursar told him.

'But this is monstrous. Why, it's tantamount to selling degrees.'

'Not tantamount, Master. Identical.'

'But what about the Tripos examinations?'

The Bursar shook his head. 'Ah I'm afraid we don't aspire to such heights. Specials are more our mark. Ordinary degrees. Just good plain old-fashioned BAs. We put up the names and they're accepted without question.'

Sir Godber sat down dumbfounded.

'Good God, and you mean to tell me that without these . . . er . . . contributions . . . dammit, these bribes, the College couldn't carry on?'

'In a nutshell, Master,' said the Bursar. 'Porterhouse is broke.'

'But why? What do other colleges do?'

'Ah,' said the Bursar, 'well that's rather different. Most of them have enormous resources. Shrewd investments over the years. Trinity, for instance, is to the best of my knowledge the third largest landowner in the country. Only the Queen and the Church of England exceed Trinity's holdings. King's had Lord Keynes as

Bursar. We unfortunately had Lord Fitzherbert. Where Keynes made a fortune, Fitzherbert lost one. You've heard of the man who broke the bank at Monte Carlo?'

The Master nodded miserably.

'Lord Fitzherbert,' said the Bursar.

'But he must have made a fortune,' said the Master.

The Bursar shook his head. 'It wasn't the bank of Monte Carlo he broke, Master, but the bank at Monte Carlo, our bank, the Anglian Lowland Bank. Two million on the spin of the wheel. Never recovered from the blow.'

'I'm not in the least surprised,' said the Master, 'I wonder he didn't blow his brains out on the spot.'

'The bank, Master, not Lord Fitzherbert. He came back and eventually was elected Master,' said the Bursar.

'Elected Master? It seems an odd thing to elect a man who has bankrupted the place. I should have thought he'd have been lynched.'

'Frankly, the College had to depend on him for some time. The revenue from his estate saw us through bad times, I'm told.' The Bursar sighed. 'So you see, Master, while I support you in principle, I'm afraid the . . . er . . . exigencies of our financial position do impose certain restraints in the way of effecting the changes you have in mind. A case of cutting our coats to suit our cloth.' The Bursar finished his Campari and stood up. The Master sat staring out into the garden. It had started to snow again but the Master was not aware of it. His mind was on other things. Looking back over his long career, he was suddenly conscious that the situation he was now facing was a familiar one. The Bursar's arguments had been those of the Treasury and the Bank of England. Sir Godber's ideals had always foundered on the rocks of financial necessity. This time it would be different. The frustrations of a lifetime had come to a head. Sir Godber had nothing left to lose. Porterhouse would change or bust. Inspired by the example of Lord Fitzherbert, Sir Godber stood up and turned to the Bursar. But the Bursar was no longer there. He had tiptoed from the room and could be seen waddling gently across the Fellows' Garden.

4

Zipser overslept. His exertions, both mental and physical, had left him exhausted. By the time he woke, Mrs Biggs was already busy in his outer room, moving furniture and dusting. Zipser lay in bed listening to her. Like something out of Happy Families, he thought. Mrs Biggs the Bedder. Skullion the Head Porter. The Dean. The Senior Tutor. Relics of some ancient childish game. Everything about Porterhouse was like that. Masters and Servants.

Lying there listening to the ponderous animality of Mrs Biggs' movements, Zipser considered the curious turn of events that had forced him into the role of a master while Mrs Biggs maintained an aggressive servility quite out of keeping with her personality and formidable physique. He found the relationship peculiar, and further complicated by the sinister attractions she held for him. It must be that in her fullness Mrs Biggs retained a natural warmth which in its contrast to the artificiality of all else in Cambridge made its appeal. Certainly nothing else could explain it. Taken in her particulars, and Zipser couldn't think of any other way of taking her, the bedder was quite remarkably without attractions. It wasn't simply the size of her appendages

that was astonishing but the sheer power. Mrs Biggs'
walk was a thing of menacing maternity, while her face
retained a youthfulness quite out of keeping with her
volume. Only her voice declared her wholly ordinary.
That and her conversation, which hovered tenuously
close to the obscene and managed to combine servility
with familiarity in a manner he found unanswerable.
He got out of bed and began to dress. It was one of the
ironies of life, he thought, that in a college that prided
itself on its adherence to the values of the past, Mrs
Biggs' manifest attractions should go unrecognized. In
palaeolithic times she would have been a princess and
he was just wondering at what particular moment of
history the Mrs Biggses had ceased to represent all that
was finest and fairest in womanhood when she knocked
on the door.

'Mr Zipser, are you decent?' she called.

'Hang on. I'm coming,' Zipser called back.

'I shouldn't be at all surprised,' Mrs Biggs muttered
audibly.

Zipser opened the door.

'I haven't got all day,' Mrs Biggs said brushing past
him provocatively.

'I'm sorry to have kept you,' said Zipser sarcastically.

'Kept me indeed. Listen to who's talking. And what
makes you think I'd mind being kept?'

Zipser blushed. 'That's hardly what I meant,' he said
hotly.

'Very complimentary I'm sure,' said Mrs Biggs,

regarding him with arch disapproval. 'Got out of bed the wrong side this morning, did we?'

Zipser noted the plural with a delicious shudder and lowered his eyes. Mrs Biggs' boots, porcinely tight, entranced him.

'Mr Skullion's got a black eye this morning,' the bedder continued. 'A right purler. Not before time either. I says to him, "Somebody's been taking a poke at you." You know what he says?' Zipser shook his head. 'He says, "I'll thank you to keep your comments to yourself, Mrs Biggs." That's what he says. Silly old fool. Don't know which century he's living in.' She went into the other room and Zipser followed her. He put a kettle on to make coffee while Mrs Biggs bustled about picking things up and putting them down again in a manner which suggested that a great deal of work was being done but which merely helped to emphasize her feelings. All the time she rattled on with her daily dose of inconsequential information while Zipser dodged about the room like a toreador trying to avoid a talkative bull. Each time she brushed past him he was aware of an animal magnetism that overrode consider-ations of taste and that aesthetic sensibility his edu-cation was supposed to have given him. Finally he stood in the corner, hardly able to contain himself, and watched her figure as it walloped about the room. Her words lost all meaning, became mere soothing sounds, waves of accompaniment to the surge of her thighs and the great rollers of her buttocks dimpled and shimmering

Tom Sharpe

beneath her skirt. 'Well I says, "You know what you can do ..."' Mrs Biggs' voice echoed Zipser's terrible thought. She bent over to plug in the vacuum-cleaner and her breasts plunged in her blouse and undulated with a force of attraction Zipser found almost irresistible. He felt himself moved out of his corner like a boxer urged forward by unnatural passion for an enormous opponent. Words crowded into his mouth. Unwanted words. Unspeakable words.

'I want you,' he said and was saved the final embarrassment by the vacuum-cleaner which roared into life.

'What's that you said?' Mrs Biggs shouted above the din. She was holding the suction pipe against a cushion on the armchair. Zipser turned purple.

'Nothing,' he bawled, and fell back into his corner.

'Bag's full,' said Mrs Biggs, and switched the machine off.

In the silence that followed Zipser leant against the wall, appalled at his terrible avowal. He was about to make a dash for the door when Mrs Biggs bent over and undid the clips on the back of the vacuum-cleaner. Zipser stared at the backs of her knees. The boots, the creases, the swell of her thighs, the edge of her stockings, the crescent ...

'Bag's full,' Mrs Biggs said again. 'You can't get any suction when the bag's full.'

She straightened up holding the bag grey and swollen ... Zipser shut his eyes. Mrs Biggs emptied the bag into the wastepaper basket. A cloud of grey dust billowed up into the room.

'Are you feeling all right, dearie?' she asked, peering at him with motherly concern. Zipser opened his eyes and stared into her face.

'I'm all right,' he managed to mutter trying to take his eyes off her lips. Mrs Biggs' lipstick gleamed thickly. 'I didn't sleep well. That's all.'

'Too much work and not enough play makes Jack a dull boy,' said Mrs Biggs holding the bag limply. To Zipser the thing had an erotic appeal he dared not analyse. 'Now you just sit down and I'll make you some coffee and you'll feel better.' Mrs Biggs' hand grasped his arm and guided him to a chair. Zipser slumped into it and stared at the vacuum-cleaner while Mrs Biggs, bending once again and even more revealingly now that Zipser was sitting down and closer to her, inserted the bag into the back of the machine and switched it on. A terrible roar, and the bag was sucked into the interior with a force which corresponded entirely to Zipser's feelings. Mrs Biggs straightened up and went through to the gyp room to make coffee while Zipser shifted feebly in the chair. He couldn't imagine what was happening to him. It was all too awful. He had to get away. He couldn't go on sitting there while she was in the room. He'd do something terrible. He couldn't control himself. He'd say something. He was about to get up and sneak out when Mrs Biggs came back with two cups of coffee.

'You do look funny,' she said, putting a cup into his hand. 'You ought to go and see a doctor. You might be going down with something.'

'Yes,' said Zipser obediently. Mrs Biggs sat down opposite him and sipped her coffee. Zipser tried to keep his eyes off her legs and found himself gazing at her breasts.

'Do you often get taken queer?' Mrs Biggs enquired.

'Queer?' said Zipser, shaken from his reverie by the accusation. 'Certainly not.'

'I was only asking,' said Mrs Biggs. She took a mouthful of coffee with a schlurp which was distinctly suggestive. 'I had a young man once,' she continued, 'just like you. Got took queer every now and then. Used to throw himself about and wriggle something frightful. Took me all my time to hold him down, it did.'

Zipser stared at her frenziedly. The notion of being held down while wriggling by Mrs Biggs was more than he could bear. With a sudden lurch that spilt his coffee Zipser hurled himself out of the chair and dashed from the room. He rushed downstairs and out into the safety of the open air. 'I've got to do something. I can't control myself. First Skullion and now Mrs Biggs.' He walked hurriedly out of Porterhouse and through Clare towards the University Library.

Alone in Zipser's room, Mrs Biggs switched on the vacuum-cleaner and poked the handle round the room. As she worked she sang to herself loudly, 'Love me

tender, love me true.' Her voice, raucously off key, was
drowned by the roar of the Electrolux.

*

The Dean spent the morning writing letters to members
of the Porterhouse Society. As the Society's secretary
he attended the annual dinners in London and Edin-
burgh and corresponded regularly with members, a
great many of whom lived in Australia or New Zealand,
and for whom the Dean's letters formed a link with
their days at Porterhouse on which they had traded
socially ever since. For the Dean himself the very
remoteness of most of his correspondents, and particularly their tendency to assume that nothing had changed
since their undergraduate days, was a constant reassur-
ance. It allowed him to pretend to an omnipotent
conservatism that had little connection with reality.
After the new Master's speech it was not easy to
maintain that pretence, and the Dean's pen held in his
mottled hand crawled slowly across the paper like some
literate but decrepit tortoise. Every now and then he
would lift his head and look for inspiration into the
clear-cut features of the young men whose photographs
cluttered his desk and stared with sepia arrogance from
the walls of his room. The Dean recalled their athleticism and youthful indiscretions, the shopgirls they had
compromised, the tailors they had bilked, the exams
they had failed, and from his window he could look

down on to the fountain where they had ducked so many homosexuals. It had all been so healthy and naturally violent, so different from the effete aestheticism of today. They hadn't fasted for the good of the coolies in India or protested because an anarchist was imprisoned in Brazil or stormed the Garden House Hotel because they disapproved of the government in Greece. They'd acted in high spirits. Wholesomely. The Dean sat back in his chair remembering the splendid riot on Guy Fawkes Night in 1948. The bomb that blew the Senate House windows out. The smoke bomb down the lavatory in Market Square that nearly killed an old man with high blood pressure. The lamp glass littering the streets. The bus being pushed backwards. The coppers' helmets flying. The car they'd overturned in King's Parade. There'd been a pregnant woman in it, the Dean recalled, and afterwards they'd all chipped in to pay her for the damage. Good-hearted lads. They didn't make them like that any more. Quickened by the recollection, his pen scrawled swiftly across the page. It would take more than Sir Godber Evans to change the character of Porterhouse. He'd see to that. He had just finished a letter and was addressing the envelope when there was a knock on the door.

'Come in,' the Dean called. The door opened and Skullion came in, holding his bowler hat in one hand.

'Morning, sir,' Skullion said.

'Good morning, Skullion,' the Dean said. The ritual of twenty years, the porter's daily report, always began with pleasantries. 'Heavy fall of snow during the night.'

'Very heavy, sir. Three inches at least.'

The Dean licked the envelope and fastened it down.

'Nasty eye you've got there, Skullion.'

'Slipped on the path, sir. Icy,' Skullion said. 'Very slippery.'

'Slippery? Got away, did he?' the Dean asked.

'Yes, sir.'

'Good for him,' said the Dean. 'Nice to know there are still some undergraduates with spirit about. Nothing else to report?'

'No, sir. Nothing to report. Nothing except Cheffy, sir.'

'Cheffy? What's the matter with him?'

'Well, it's not just him, sir. It's all of us. Very upset about the Master's speech,' Skullion said carefully, treading the tightrope between speaking out of turn and rightful protest. There were things you could say to the Dean and there were things you couldn't. Reporting the Chef's sense of outrage seemed a safe way of expressing his own feelings.

The Dean swung his chair round and looked out of the window to evade the difficulty. He relied on Skullion's information but there was always the danger of condoning insubordination or at least encouraging a familiarity detrimental to good discipline. But Skullion wasn't the man to take advantage of the situation. The Dean trusted him.

'You can tell the Chef there'll be no changes,' he said finally. 'The Master was just feeling his way. He'll learn.'

'Yes, sir,' said Skullion doubtfully. 'Very upsetting that speech, sir.'

'Thank you, Skullion,' said the Dean dismissively.

'Thank you, sir,' Skullion said and left the room.

The Dean swung his chair round to his desk and took up his pen again. Skullion's resentment had inspired him with a new determination to block Sir Godber's schemes. There were all the OPs, for instance. Their opinion and influence could be decisive properly organized. It might be as well to inform that opinion now.

*

Skullion went back to the Lodge and sorted out the second mail. His conversation with the Dean had only partially restored his confidence. The Dean was getting old. His voice didn't carry the same weight any more in the College Council. It was the Bursar who was listened to, and Skullion had his doubts about *him*. He took the *New Statesman* and the *Spectator* and read *The Times*, not the *Telegraph* like the other dons. 'Neither fish, flesh, fowl nor good red herring,' Skullion summed him up with his usual political acumen. If the Master got at him there was no saying which way he'd jump. Skullion began to think it might be time for him to pay a visit to General Sir Cathcart D'Eath at Coft. He usually went there on the first Tuesday of every month, a ritual visit with news of the College and also to have a word with a reliable stable boy in Sir Cathcart's racing stables whose information had in the past done much to supplement Skullion's meagre income. Sir Cathcart had been one of Skullion's Scholars and the debt had never been wholly repaid. 'Taking the afternoon off,' he told Walter the under-porter when he finished sorting the mail and Walter had put Dr Baxter's weekly issue of *The Boy* back into its plain envelope.

'What? Going fishing?' Walter asked.

'Never you mind where I'm going,' Skullion told him. He lit his pipe and went into the back room to fetch his coat and presently was cycling with due care and attention over Magdalene Bridge towards Coft.

*

Zipser sat on the third floor of the north wing of the University Library trying to bring his mind to bear on The Influence of Pumpernickel on the Politics of 16th-Century Osnabruck but without success. He no longer cared that it had been known as *bonum paniculum* and his interest in Westphalian local politics had waned. The problem of his feelings for Mrs Biggs was more immediate.

He had spent an hour in the stacks browsing feverishly through textbooks of clinical psychology in search of a medical explanation of the symptoms of irrational violence and irrepressible sexuality which had manifested themselves in his recent behaviour. From what

Tom Sharpe

he had read it had begun to look as if he were suffering from a multitude of different diseases. On the one hand his reaction to Skullion suggested paranoia, 'violent behaviour as a result of delusions of persecution', while the erotic compulsion of his feelings for Mrs Biggs was even more alarming and seemed to indicate schizophrenia with sado-masochistic tendencies. The combination of the two diseases, paranoid schizophrenia, was apparently the worst possible form of insanity and quite incurable. Zipser sat staring out of the windows at the trees in the garden beyond the footpath and contemplated a lifetime of madness. He couldn't imagine what had suddenly occasioned the outbreak. The textbooks implied that heredity had a lot to do with it, but apart from an uncle who had a passion for concrete dwarves in his front garden and who his mother had said was a bit touched in the head, he couldn't think of anyone in the family who was actually and certifiably insane.

The explanation had to lie elsewhere. His feelings for the bedder deviated from every known norm. So for that matter did Mrs Biggs. She bulged where she should have dimpled and bounced when she should have been still. She was gross, vulgar, garrulous and, Zipser had no doubt in his mind, thoroughly insanitary. To find himself irresistibly attracted to her was the worst thing he could think of. It was perfectly all right to be queer. It was positively fashionable. To have constant and insistent sexual desires for French au pair girls, Swedish language students, girls in Boots, even undergraduates at Girton, was normality itself, but Mrs Biggs came into the category of the unmentionable. And the knowledge that but for the fortuitous intervention of the vacuum-cleaner he would have revealed his true feelings for her threw him into a panic. He left his table and went downstairs and walked back into town.

As he reached Great St Mary's the clock was striking twelve. Zipser stopped and studied the posters on the railings outside the church which announced forthcoming sermons.

CHRIST AND THE GAY CHRISTIAN Rev. F. Leaney.

HAS SALT LOST ITS SAVOUR? Anglican attitudes to disarmament. Rev. B. Tomkins.

JOB, A MESSAGE FOR THE THIRD WORLD Right Reverend Sutty, Bishop of Bombay.

JESUS JOKES Fred Henry by permission of ITA & the management of the Palace Theatre, Scunthorpe.

BOMBS AWAY A Christian's attitude to Skyjacking by Flight Lieutenant Jack Piggett, BOAC.

Zipser stared at the University Sermons with a sudden sense of loss. What had happened to the old Church, the Church of his childhood, the friendly Vicar and the helping hand? Not that Zipser had ever been to church, but he had seen them on television and had been comforted by the knowledge that they were still there in *Songs of Praise* and *Saints Alive* and *All Gas and Gaiters*. But now when he needed help there was only this pale parody of the daily paper with its mishmash of politics and sensationalism. Not a word about evil and how to cope with it. Zipser felt betrayed. He went back into Porterhouse in search of help. He'd go and see the Senior Tutor. There was just time before lunch. Zipser climbed the stairs to the Tutor's rooms and knocked on the door.

*

'The trouble with the Feast,' said the Dean, munching a mouthful of cold beef, 'is that it does tend to run on. Cold beef today. Cold beef tomorrow. Cold beef on Thursday. After that I suppose we'll have stewed beef on Friday and Saturday and cottage pie on Sunday. By next week we should be getting back to normal.'

'Difficult to eat an entire ox at one sitting,' said the Bursar. 'One suspects our predecessors had, shall we say, grosser appetites.'

'I always said it was a mistake to make him Prime Minister,' said the Chaplain.

The Senior Tutor took his place at table. He was looking more than usually austere.

'Talking of gross appetites,' he said grimly. 'I have the gravest doubts about some of our younger members. I have just had a visit from a young man who claims to be under some compulsion to sleep with his bedder.' He helped himself to horseradish.

The Bursar sniggered. 'Which one?' he asked.

'Zipser,' said the Senior Tutor.

'Which bedder?'

'I didn't enquire,' said the Senior Tutor. 'It didn't seem a particularly relevant question.'

The Bursar considered the problem.

'Isn't he in the Tower?' he asked the Dean.

'Who?'

'Zipser.'

'Yes. I think he is,' said the Dean.

'Then it must be Mrs Biggs.'

The Senior Tutor, who had been debating what to do with a long piece of gristle, swallowed it.

'Dear me. Mrs Biggs. I must say I did young Zipser an injustice,' he said with alarm.

'Impossible to do an injustice to anyone with such depraved taste,' said the Dean firmly.

'Mrs Biggs hardly comes within the category of forbidden fruit,' tittered the Bursar.

'Thank you,' answered the Chaplain, 'I think I will have an apple.'

'Mrs Biggs,' muttered the Tutor. 'No wonder the poor fellow imagined he was going mad.'

'Not really,' said the Chaplain. 'This one is all right at any rate.'

'What advice did you give him?' the Bursar asked.

The Senior Tutor looked at him disbelievingly. 'Advice?' he asked. 'It is hardly my position to offer advice on such questions. I am the Senior Tutor, not a

Marriage Guidance Counsellor. As a matter of fact I advised him to see the Chaplain.'

'It's a noble calling,' said the Chaplain, helping himself to a pear. The Senior Tutor sighed and finished his cold beef.

'It only goes to show what happens when you open the doors of the College to research graduates. In the old days such a thing would have been unheard of,' said the Dean.

'Unheard of perhaps but not I think unknown,' said the Bursar.

'With bedders?' the Dean asked angrily. 'With *bedders*? Maintain some sense of proportion, I beg you.'

'No thank you, Dean. I've had quite enough already,' the Chaplain replied.

The Dean was about to say something about old fools when the Senior Tutor intervened. 'In the case of Mrs Biggs,' he said, 'it is precisely the question of proportion that is at stake.'

'We had that last night,' said the Chaplain.

'Oh for God's sake,' the Senior Tutor snarled. 'How the hell can one conduct a serious discussion with him around.'

'My dear fellow,' the Praelector sighed, 'that is a question that has been bothering me for years.'

They finished the meal in silence, each occupied with his own thoughts. It was only when they were assembled in the Combination Room for coffee and the Chaplain had been persuaded to go to his room to write a note inviting Zipser to tea that the discussion began again.

'I think that we should view this matter in the wider context,' the Dean said. 'The Master's speech last night indicated only too clearly that he has in mind an extension of precisely that permissiveness of which this latest incident is indicative. I understand, Bursar, that you had a *tête-à-tête* with Sir Godber this morning.'

The Bursar looked at him unpleasantly. 'The Master phoned to ask me to discuss the College finances with him,' he said. 'I think you might give me credit for having done my best to disabuse him of the changes his speech suggested.'

'You explained that our resources do not allow us to indulge in the liberal extravagances of King's or Trinity?' the Senior Tutor asked. The Bursar nodded.

'And was the Master satisfied?' the Dean asked.

'Stunned, I think, would be the more accurate description of his reaction,' said the Bursar.

'Then we are all agreed that whatever he suggests at the meeting of the College Council tomorrow we shall oppose on principle,' said the Dean.

'I think it would be best to wait to hear what he proposes before deciding on a definite policy,' the Praelector said.

The Senior Tutor nodded. 'We must not appear too inflexible. An appearance of open-mindedness has in my experience a tendency to disarm the radical left. They seem to feel the need to reciprocate. I've often wondered why but it has worked to keep the country on the right lines for years.'

'Unfortunately this time we are dealing with a politician,' the Dean objected. 'I have a shrewd idea the Master is rather more experienced in these affairs than we give him credit for. I still think an undivided front is the best policy.'

They finished their coffee and went about their business. The Senior Tutor went down to the Boathouse to coach the first boat, the Dean slept until teatime, and the Bursar spent the afternoon doodling in his office wondering if he had been wise to tell Sir Godber about the endowment subscriptions. There had been a strength of feeling in the Master's reaction that had surprised the Bursar and had made him wonder if he had gone too far. Perhaps he had misjudged Sir Godber and the vehemence of his ideals.

5

Skullion cycled out along the Barton Road towards
Coft. His bowler hat set squarely on his head, his cycle
clips and his black overcoat buttoned against the cold
gave him an intransigently episcopalian air in the snow-
covered landscape. He cycled slowly but relentlessly,
his thoughts as dark as his habit and as bitter as the
wind blowing unchecked from the Urals. The few
bungalows he passed looked insubstantial beside him,
transient and rootless in contrast to the black figure on
the bicycle in whose head centuries of endured servitude had bred a fierce bigotry nothing would easily
remove. Independence he called it, this hatred for
change whether for better or worse. In Skullion's view
there was no such thing as change for the better. That
came under the heading of improvement. He was
prepared to give his qualified approval to improvements
provided there was no suggestion that it was the past
that had been improved upon. That was clearly out of
the question and if at the back of his mind he recognized the illogicality of his own argument, he refused
to admit it even to himself. It was one of the mysteries
of life which he accepted as unquestioningly as he did
the great metal spiders' webs strung out across the fields

beside the road to catch the radio evidence of stars that had long since ceased to exist. The world of Skullion's imagination was as remote as those stars but it was enough for him that, like the radio telescopes, he was able to catch echoes of it in men like General the Honourable Sir Cathcart D'Eath, KCMG, DSO.

The General had influence in high places and Royalty came to stay at Coft Castle. Skullion had once seen a queen mother dawdling majestically in the garden and had heard royal laughter from the stables. The General could put in a good word for him and more importantly a bad one for the new Master and, as an undergraduate, the then just Hon. Cathcart D'Eath had been one of Skullion's Scholars.

Skullion never forgot his Scholars and there was little doubt that though they might have liked to, none of them forgot him. They owed him too much. It had been Skullion who had arranged the transactions and had acted as intermediary. On the one hand idle but influential undergraduates like the Hon. Cathcart and on the other impecunious research graduates eking out a living giving supervision and grateful for the baksheesh Skullion brought their way. The weekly essay regularly handed in and startlingly original for undergraduates so apparently ill-informed. Two pounds a week for an essay had served to subsidize some very important research. More than one doctorate owed everything to those two pounds. And finally Tripos by proxy, with Skullion's Scholars lounging in a King

Street pub while in the Examination School their substitutes wrote answers to the questions with a mediocrity that was unexceptional. Skullion had been careful, very careful. Only one or two a year and in subjects so popular that there would be no noticing an unfamiliar face in the hundreds writing the exams. And it had worked. 'No one will be any the wiser,' he had assured the graduate substitutes to allay their fears before slipping five hundred, once a thousand, pounds into their pockets. And no one had been any the wiser. Certainly the Honourable Cathcart D'Eath had gone down with a II.ii in History with his ignorance of Disraeli's influence on the Conservative Party unimpaired in spite of having to all appearances written four pages on the subject. But what he had gained on the roundabout he had also gained on the swings and the study of horseflesh he had undertaken during those three years at Newmarket served him well in the future. His use of cavalry in the Burmese jungle had unnerved the Japanese by its unadulterated lunacy and, combined with his name, had suggested a kamikaze element in the British Army they had never suspected. Sir Cathcart had emerged from the campaign with twelve men and a reputation so scathed that he had been promoted to General to prevent the destruction of the entire army and the loss of India. Early retirement and his wartime experience of getting horses to attempt the impossible had encouraged Sir Cathcart to return to his first love and to take up training. His stables at Coft were world-famous. With what appeared to be a magical touch but owed in fact much to Skullion's gift for substitution, Sir Cathcart could transform a broken-winded nag into a winning two-year-old and had prospered accordingly. Coft Castle, standing in spacious grounds, was surrounded by a high wall to guard against intruding eyes and cameras and by an ornate garden in a remote corner of which was a small canning factory where the by-products of the General's stables were given discreet anonymity in Cathcart's Tinned Catfood. Skullion dismounted at the gate and knocked on the lodge door. A Japanese gardener, a prisoner of war, whom Sir Cathcart kept carefully ignorant of world news and who was, thanks to the language barrier, incapable of learning it for himself, opened the gate for him and Skullion cycled on down the drive to the house.

In spite of its name there was nothing remotely ancient about Coft Castle. Staunchly Edwardian, its red brick bespoke a lofty disregard for style and a concern for comfort on a grand scale. The General's Rolls-Royce, RIP I, gleamed darkly on the gravel outside the front door. Skullion dismounted and pushed his bicycle round to the servants' entrance.

'Come to see the General,' he told the cook. Presently he was ushered into the drawing-room where Sir Cathcart was lolling in an armchair before a large coal fire.

'Not your usual afternoon, Skullion,' he said as Skullion came in, bowler hat in hand.

'No, sir. Came special,' said Skullion. The General waved him to a kitchen chair the cook brought in on these occasions and Skullion sat down and put his bowler hat on his knees.

'Carry on smoking,' Sir Cathcart told him. Skullion took out his pipe and filled it with black tobacco from a tin. Sir Cathcart watched him with grim affection.

'That's filthy stuff you smoke, Skullion,' he said as blue smoke drifted towards the chimney. 'Must have a constitution like an elephant to smoke it.'

Skullion puffed at his pipe contentedly. It was at moments like this, moments of informal subservience, that he felt happiest. Sitting smoking his pipe on the hard kitchen chair in Sir Cathcart D'Eath's drawing-room he felt approved. He basked in the General's genial disdain.

'That's a nice black eye you've got there,' Sir Cathcart said. 'You look as if you've been in the wars.'

'Yes, sir,' said Skullion. He was quite pleased with that black eye.

'Well, out with it, man, what have you come about?' Sir Cathcart said.

'It's the new Master. He made a speech at the Feast last night,' Skullion told him.

'A speech? At the Feast?' Sir Cathcart sat up in his chair.

'Yes, sir. I knew you wouldn't like it.'

'Disgraceful. What did he say?'

'Says he's going to change the College.'

Sir Carthcart's eyes bulged in his head. 'Change the College? What the devil does he mean by that? The damned place has been changed beyond all recognition already. Can't go in the place without seeing some long-haired lout looking more like a girl than a man. Swarming with bloody poofters. Change the College? There's only one change that's needed and that's back to the old ways. The old traditions. Cut their hair off and duck them in the fountain. That's what's needed. When I think what Porterhouse used to be and see what it's become, it makes my blood boil. It's the same with the whole damned country. Letting niggers in and keeping good white men out. Gone soft, that's what's happened. Soft in the head and soft in the body.' Sir Cathcart sank back in his chair limp from his denunciation of the times. Skullion smiled inwardly. It was just such bitterness he had come to hear. Sir Cathcart spoke with an authority Skullion could never have but which charged his own intransigence with a new vigour.

'Says he wants Porterhouse to be an open college,' he said, stoking the embers of the General's fury.

'Open college?' Sir Cathcart responded to the call. 'Open? What the devil does he mean by that? It's open enough already. Half the scum of the world in as it is.'

'I think he means more scholars,' Skullion said.

Sir Cathcart grew a shade more apoplectic.

'Scholars? That's half the trouble with the world today, scholarship. Too many damned intellectuals about who think they know how things should be done.

Academics, bah! Can't win a war with thinking. Can't run a factory on thought. It needs guts and sweat and sheer hard work. If I had my way I'd kick every damned scholar out of the College and put in some athletes to run the place properly. Anyone would think Varsity was some sort of school. In my day we didn't come up to learn anything, we came up to forget all the damned silly things we'd had pumped into us at school. My God, Skullion, I'll tell you this, a man can learn more between the thighs of a good woman than he ever needs to know. Scholarship's a waste of time and public money. What's more, it's iniquitous.' Exhausted by his outburst, Sir Cathcart stared belligerently into the fire.

'What's Fairbrother say?' he asked finally.

'The Dean, sir? He doesn't like it any more than you do, sir,' Skullion said, 'but he's not as young as he used to be, sir.'

'Don't suppose he is,' Sir Cathcart agreed.

'That's why I came to tell you, sir,' Skullion continued. 'I thought you'd know what to do.'

Sir Cathcart stiffened. 'Do? Don't see what I can do,' he said presently. 'I'll write to the Master, of course, but I've no influence in the College these days.'

'But you have outside, sir,' Skullion assured him.

'Well perhaps,' Sir Cathcart assented. 'All right. I'll see what I can do. Keep me informed, Skullion.'

'Yes, sir. Thank you, sir.'

'Get Cook to give you some tea before you go,' Sir Cathcart told him and Skullion went out with his chair and took it back to the kitchen. Twenty minutes later he cycled off down the drive, spiritually resuscitated. Sir Cathcart would see there were no more changes. He had influence in high places. There was only one thing that puzzled Skullion as he rode home. Something Sir Cathcart had said about learning more between the thighs of a good woman than ... but Sir Cathcart had never married. Skullion wondered how an unmarried man got between the thighs of a good woman.

*

Zipser's interview with the Senior Tutor had left him with a sense of embarrassment that had unnerved him completely. His attempt to explain the nature of his compulsion had been fraught with difficulties. The Senior Tutor kept poking his little finger in his ear and wriggling it around and examining the end of it when he took it out while Zipser talked, as if he held some waxy deposit responsible for the flow of obscene information that was reaching his brain. When he finally accepted that his ears were not betraying him and that Zipser was in fact confessing to being attracted by his bedder, he had muttered something to the effect that the Chaplain would expect him for tea that afternoon and that, failing that, a good psychiatrist might help. Zipser had left miserably and had spent the early part of the afternoon in his room trying to concentrate on his thesis without success. The image of Mrs Biggs, a cross between a cherubim in menopause and a booted succubus, kept intruding. Zipser turned for escape to a book of photographs of starving children in Nagaland but in spite of this mental flagellation Mrs Biggs prevailed. He tried Hermitsch on *Fall Out & the Andaman Islanders* and even *Sterilization, Vasectomy and Abortion* by Allard, but these holy writs all failed against the pervasive fantasy of the bedder. It was as if his social conscience, his concern for the plight of humanity at large, the universal and collective pity he felt for all mankind, had been breached in some unspeakably personal way by the inveterate triviality and egoism of Mrs Biggs. Zipser, whose life had been filled with a truly impersonal charity – he had spent holidays from school working for SOBB, the Save Our Black Brothers campaign – and whose third worldliness was impeccable, found himself suddenly the victim of a sexual idiosyncrasy which made a mockery of his universalism. In desperation he turned to *Syphilis, the Scourge of Colonialism*, and stared with horror at the pictures. In the past it had worked like a charm to quell incipient sexual desires while satisfying his craving for evidence of natural justice. The notion of the Conquistadores dying of the disease after raping South American Indians no longer had its old appeal now that Zipser himself was in the grip of a compulsive urge to rape Mrs Biggs. By the time it came for him to go to the Chaplain's rooms for tea, Zipser had exhausted the resources of his theology. So too, it seemed, had the Chaplain.

'Ah my boy,' the Chaplain boomed as Zipser nego-
tiated the bric-à-brac that filled the Chaplain's sitting-
room. 'So good of you to come. Do make yourself
comfortable.' Zipser nudged past a gramophone with a
papier-mâché horn, circumvented a brass-topped table
with fretsawed legs, squeezed beneath the fronds of a
castor-oil plant and finally sat down on a chair by the
fire. The Chaplain scuttled backwards and forwards
between his bathroom and the tea table muttering
loudly to himself a liturgy of things to fetch. 'Teapot
hot. Spoons. Milk jug. You do take milk?' 'Yes, thank
you,' said Zipser. 'Good. Good. So many people take
lemon, don't they? One always forgets these things.
Tea-cosy. Sugar basin.' Zipser looked round the room
for some indication of the Chaplain's interests but the
welter of conflicting objects, like the addition of random
numbers to a code, made interpretation impossible.
Apart from senility the furnishings had so little in
common that they seemed to indicate a wholly catholic
taste.

'Crumpets,' said the Chaplain scurrying out of the
bathroom. 'Just the thing. You toast them.' He speared
a crumpet on the end of a toasting-fork and thrust the
fork into Zipser's hand. Zipser poked the crumpet at
the fire tentatively and felt once again that dissociation
from reality that seemed so much a part of life in
Cambridge. It was as if everyone in the College sought
to parody himself, as if a parody of a parody could
become itself a new reality. Behind him the Chaplain

stumbled over a footrest and deposited a jar of honey with a boom on the brass-topped table. Zipser removed the crumpet, blackened on one side and ice cold on the other, and put it on a plate. He toasted another while the Chaplain tried to spread butter on the one he had half done. By the time they had finished Zipser's face was burning from the fire and his hands were sticky with a mixture of melted butter and honey. The Chaplain sat back in his chair and filled his pipe from a tobacco jar with the Porterhouse crest on it.

'Do help yourself, my dear boy,' said the Chaplain, pushing the jar towards him.

'I don't smoke.'

The Chaplain shook his head sadly. 'Everyone should smoke a pipe,' he said. 'Calms the nerves. Puts things in perspective. Couldn't do without mine.' He leant back, puffing vigorously. Zipser stared at him through a haze of smoke.

'Now then where were we?' he asked. Zipser tried to think. 'Ah yes, your little problem, that's right,' said the Chaplain finally. 'I knew there was something.'

Zipser stared into the fire resentfully.

'The Senior Tutor said something about it. I didn't gather very much but then I seldom do. Deafness, you know.'

Zipser nodded sympathetically.

'The affliction of the elderly. That and rheumatism. It's the damp, you know. Comes up from the river. Very unhealthy living so close to the Fens.' His pipe percolated gently. In the comparative silence Zipser tried to think what to say. The Chaplain's age and his evident physical disabilities made it difficult for Zipser to conceive that he could begin to understand the problem of Mrs Biggs.

'I really think there's been a misunderstanding,' he began hesitantly and stopped. It was evident from the look on the Chaplain's face that there was no understanding at all.

'You'll have to speak up,' the Chaplain boomed. 'I'm really quite deaf.'

'I can see that,' Zipser said. The Chaplain beamed at him.

'Don't hesitate to tell me,' he said. 'Nothing you say can shock me.'

'I'm not surprised,' Zipser said.

The Chaplain's smile remained insistently benevolent. 'I know what we'll do,' he said, hopping to his feet and reaching behind his chair. 'It's something I use for confession sometimes.' He emerged holding a loud-hailer and handed it to Zipser. 'Press the trigger when you're going to speak.'

Zipser held the thing up to his mouth and stared at the Chaplain over the rim. 'I really don't think this is going to help,' he said finally. His words reverberated through the room and set the teapot rattling on the brass table.

'Of course it is,' shouted the Chaplain, 'I can hear perfectly.'

'I didn't mean that,' Zipser said desperately. The fronds of the castor-oil plant quivered ponderously. 'I meant I don't think it's going to help to talk about . . .' He left the dilemma of Mrs Biggs unspoken.

The Chaplain smiled in absolution and puffed his pipe vigorously. 'Many of the young men who come to see me,' he said, invisible in a cloud of smoke, 'suffer from feelings of guilt about masturbation.'

Zipser stared frantically at the smoke screen. 'Masturbation? Who said anything about masturbation?' he bawled into the loudhailer. It was apparent someone had. His words, hideously amplified, billowed forth from the room and across the Court outside. Several undergraduates by the fountain turned and stared up at the Chaplain's windows. Deafened by his own vociferousness, Zipser sat sweating with embarrassment.

'I understood from the Senior Tutor that you wanted to see me about a sexual problem,' the Chaplain shouted.

Zipser lowered the loudhailer. The thing clearly had disadvantages.

'I can assure you I don't masturbate,' he said.

The Chaplain looked at him incomprehendingly. 'You press the trigger when you want to speak,' he explained. Zipser nodded dumbly. The knowledge that to communicate with the Chaplain at all he had to announce his feelings for Mrs Biggs to the world at large presented him with a terrible dilemma made no less intolerable by the Chaplain's shouted replies.

'It often helps to get these things into the open,' the Chaplain assured him. Zipser had his doubts about that. Admissions of the sort he had to make broadcast through a loudhailer were not likely to be of any help at all. He might just as well go and propose to the wretched woman straightaway and be done with it. He sat with lowered head while the Chaplain boomed on.

'Don't forget that anything you tell me will be heard in the strictest confidence,' he shouted. 'You need have no fears that it will go any further.'

'Oh sure,' Zipser muttered. Outside in the Court a small crowd of undergraduates had gathered by the fountain to listen.

Half an hour later Zipser left the room, his demoralization quite complete. At least he could congratulate himself that he had revealed nothing of his true feelings and the Chaplain's kindly probings, his tentative questions, had elicited no response. Zipser had sat silently through a sexual catechism only bothering to shake his head when the Chaplain broached particularly obscene topics. In the end he had listened to a lyrical description of the advantages of au pair girls. It was obvious that the Chaplain regarded foreign girls as outside the sexual canons of the Church.

'So much less danger of a permanently unhappy involvement,' he had shouted, 'and after all I often think that's what they come here for. Ships that pass in the night and not on one's own doorstep you know.' He paused and smiled at Zipser salaciously. 'We all have to sow our wild oats at some time or other and it's much better to do it abroad. I've often thought that's what Rupert Brooke had in mind in that line of his about some corner of a foreign field. Mind you, one can hardly say that he was particularly healthy, come to think of it, but there we are. That's my advice to you, dear boy. Find a nice Swedish girl, I'm told they're very good, and have a ball. I believe that's the modern idiom. Yes, Swedes or French, depending on your taste. Spaniards are a bit difficult, I'm told, and then again they tend to be rather hairy. Still, buggers can't be choosers as dear old Sir Winston said at the queer's wedding. Ha, ha.'

Zipser staggered from the room. He knew now what muscular Christianity meant. He went down the dark staircase and was about to go out into the Court when he saw the group standing by the fountain. Zipser turned and fled up the stairs and locked himself in the lavatory on the top landing. He was still there an hour later when First Hall began.

6

Sir Godber dined at home. He was still recovering from the gastric consequences of the Feast and in any case the Bursar's revelations had disinclined him to the company of the Fellows until he had formulated his plans more clearly. He had spent the afternoon considering various schemes for raising money and had made several telephone calls to financial friends in the City to ask their advice and to put up proposals of his own but without success. Blomberg's Bank had been prepared to endow several Research Fellowships in Accountancy but even Sir Godber doubted if such generosity would materially alter the intellectual climate of Porterhouse. He had even considered offering the American Phosgene Corp. facilities for research into nerve gas, facilities they had been denied by all American universities, in return for a really large endowment but he suspected that the resultant publicity and student protest would destroy his already tenuous liberal reputation. Publicity was much on his mind. At five o'clock the BBC phoned to ask if he would appear on a panel of leading educationalists to answer questions on financial priority in Education. Sir Godber was sorely tempted to agree but refused on the grounds that he had hardly acquired much experience. He put the phone down reluctantly and wondered what effect his announcement to several million viewers that Porterhouse College was in the habit of selling degrees to rich young layabouts would have had. It was a pleasing thought and gave rise in the Master's mind to an even more satisfying conclusion. He picked up the phone again and spoke to the Bursar.

'Could we arrange a College Council meeting for tomorrow afternoon? Say two-thirty?' he asked.

'It's rather short notice, Master,' the Bursar replied.

'Good. Two-thirty it is then,' Sir Godber said with iron geniality and replaced the receiver. He sat back and began to draw up a list of innovations. Candidates to be chosen by academic achievement only. The kitchen endowment to be cut by three-quarters and the funds reallocated to scholarships. Women undergraduates to be admitted as members. Gate hours abolished. College playing fields open to children from the town. Sir Godber's imagination raced on compiling proposals with no thought for the financial implications. They would have to find the money somewhere and he didn't much care where. The main thing was that he had the Fellows over a barrel. They might protest but there was nothing they could do to stop him. They had placed a weapon in his hands. He smiled to himself at the thought of their faces when he explained the alternatives tomorrow. At six-thirty he went through to the drawing-room where Lady Mary, who had been chairing a committee on Teenage Delinquency, was writing letters.

'Be with you in a minute,' she said when Sir Godber asked her if she would like a sherry. He looked at her dubiously. There were times when he wondered if his wife was ever with him. Her mind followed a wholly independent course and was ever concentrated on the more distressing aspects of other people's lives. Sir Godber poured himself a large whisky.

'Well, I think I've got them by the short hairs,' he said when she finally stopped tapping at her typewriter.

Lady Mary's lean tongue lubricated the flap of an envelope. 'Non-specific urethritis is reaching epidemic proportions among school-leavers,' she said. Sir Godber ignored the interjection. He couldn't for the life of him see what it had to do with the College. He pursued his own topic. 'I'm going to show them that I'm not prepared to be a cipher.'

'Surveys show that one in every five children has . . .'

'I haven't ended my career in politics only to be pushed into a sinecure,' Sir Godber contended.

'That's not the problem,' Lady Mary agreed.

'What isn't?' Sir Godber asked, momentarily interested by her assertion.

'Cure. Easy enough. What we've got to get at is the moral·delinquency . . .'

Sir Godber drank his whisky and tried not to listen. There were times when he wondered if he would ever have succeeded as a politician without the help of his

wife. Without her incessant preoccupation with unsavoury statistics and sordid social problems, late-night
sittings in the House might have had less appeal and
committees less utility. Would he have made so many
passionate speeches or spoken with such urgency if
Lady Mary had been prepared to listen to one word he
said at home? He rather doubted it. They went into
dinner and Sir Godber passed the time as usual by
counting the number of times she said Must and Our
Duty. The Musts won by fifty-four to forty-eight. Not
bad for the course.

*

After he had heard the Chaplain go down to Hall,
Zipser slipped out of the lavatory and went to his room.
There was no sign of the little crowd of undergraduates
who had been gathered in the Court when he first went
down and he hoped no one would find out who had
been talking, if that was the right word, to the Chaplain.
The tendency he shared with the Master's wife to think
in wholly impersonal terms about world issues had
quite deserted him. During his hour in the lavatory he
had taken the Chaplain's advice and had attempted to
interpose the image of a Swedish girl between himself
and Mrs Biggs. Every time Mrs Biggs intruded he
concentrated on the slim buttocks and breasts of a
Swedish actress he had seen once in *Playboy* and to
some extent the practice had worked. Not entirely.
The Swede tended to swell and to assume unnatural

proportions until she was displaced by a smiling Mrs Biggs, but the series of little respites was encouraging and suggested that a substantial Swede might be even more effective. He would take the Chaplain's advice and find an au pair girl or a language student and . . . and . . . well . . . and. Zipser's lack of sexual experience prevented him from formulating at all clearly what he would do then. Well, he would copulate with her. Having arrived at this neat if somewhat abstract conclusion he felt better. It was certainly preferable to raping Mrs Biggs, which seemed the only alternative. As usual Zipser had no doubts about rape. It was a brutal, violent act of assertive masculinity, a loosening of savage instinctual forces, passionate and bestial. He would hurl Mrs Biggs to the floor and thrust himself . . . With an effort of will he dragged his imagination back from the scene and thought aseptically about copulating with a Swede.

A number of difficulties immediately presented themselves. First and foremost he knew no Swedes, and secondly he had never copulated with anyone. He knew a great many intense young women who shared his concern for the fate of mankind and who were prepared to talk about birth control into the early hours of the morning but they were all English and their preoccupation with mankind's problems had seemed to preclude any interest in him. In any case Zipser had scruples on aesthetic grounds about asking any of them to act as a substitute Mrs Biggs, and rather doubted their efficacy in the role. It would have to be a Swede. With the abstract calculation that was implicit in his whole approach Zipser decided that he would probably be able to find a promiscuous Swede in the Cellar Bar. He wrote it down and put as an alternative the Ali Baba Discothèque. That dealt with the first problem. He would fill her up with wine, Portuguese white would do, and bring her back to his room. All quite simple. With her cooperation the sexual spectre of Mrs Biggs would lose its force. He went to bed early having set the alarm for seven o'clock so as to be up and out before the bedder arrived – and before he fell asleep realized that he had forgotten an important detail. He would need some contraceptives. He'd go and have his hair cut in the morning and get some.

*

Skullion sat in front of the gas fire in the Porter's Lodge and smoked his pipe. His visit to Coft Castle had eased his mind. The General would use his influence to see that the Master didn't make any changes. You could rely on the General. One of the old brigade, and rich too. The sort that always gave you a big tip at the end of term. Skullion had had some big tips in his time and he had put them all away in his bank with the shares old Lord Wurford had left him in his will and had never touched them. He lived off his salary and what he earned on his night off as a steward at the Fox Club. There had been some big takings there too in his time;

the Maharajah of Indpore had once given him fifty quid after a day at the races, when a tip from Sir Cathcart's stable-boy had paid off. Skullion considered the Maharajah quite a gent, a compliment he paid to few Indians, but then a Maharajah wasn't a proper Indian, was he? Maharajahs were Princes of the Empire and as far as Skullion was concerned wogs in the Empire were quite different from wogs outside it and wogs in the Fox Club wasn't wogs at all or they wouldn't be members. The intricate system of social classification in Skullion's mind graded everyone. He could place a man within a hair's breadth in the social scale by the tone of his voice or even the look in his eye. Some people thought you could depend on the cut of a man's coat but Skullion knew better. It wasn't externals that mattered, it was something much more indefinable, an inner quality which Skullion couldn't explain but which he recognized immediately. And responded to. It had something to do with assurance, a certainty of oneself which nothing could shake. There were lots of intermediate stages between this ineffable superiority and the manifest inferiority of, say, the kitchen staff, but Skullion could sense them all and put them in the right place. There was money by itself, brash and full of itself but easily deflated. There was two-generation money with a bit of land. Usually a bit pompous, that was. There was County rich and poor. Skullion noted the distinction but tended to ignore it. Some of the best families had come down in the world and so long as the confidence was there, money didn't count, not in Skullion's eyes anyway. In fact confidence without money was preferable, it indicated a genuine quality and was accordingly revered. Then there were various degrees of uncertainty, nuances of self-doubt that went unnoticed by most people but which Skullion spotted immediately. Flickers of residual deference immediately suppressed – but too late to be missed by Skullion. Doctors' and lawyers' sons. Professional classes and treated respectfully. Still public school anyway, and graded from Eton and Winchester downwards. Below public school Skullion lost all interest, according only slight respect if there was money in it for him. But at the top of the scale above all these distinctions there was an assurance so ineffable that it seemed almost to merge into its opposite. Real quality, Skullion called it, or even the old aristocracy to distinguish it from mere titular nobility. These were the saints of his calendar, the touchstone against which all other men were finally judged. Even Sir Cathcart was not of their number. In fact Skullion had to admit that he was fundamentally of the fourth rank, though near the top of it, and that was high praise considering how many ranks Skullion had in his mind. No, the real quality were without Sir Cathcart's harshness. There was often an unassuming quality about the saints which less perceptive porters than Skullion mistook for timidity and social insecurity but which he knew to be a sign of breeding, and not to be taken advantage of. It accorded his servility the highest accolade, this helplessness that was quite unforced, and gave him the sure knowledge that he was needed. Under the cover of that helplessness Skullion could have moved mountains, and frequently had to in the way of luggage and furniture, humping it up staircases and round corners and arranging it first here and then there while its owner, graciously indecisive, tried to make up what there was of his mind where it would look best. From such expeditions Skullion would emerge with a temporary lordliness as if touched by grace and would recall such services rendered in years to come with the feeling that he had been privileged to attend an almost spiritual occasion. In Skullion's social hagiography two names stood out as the epitome of the effeteness he worshipped. Lord Pimpole and Sir Launcelot Gutterby, and at moments of contemplation Skullion would repeat their names to himself like some repetitive prayer. He was in the process of this incantation and had reached his twentieth 'Pimpole and Gutterby' when the Lodge door opened and Arthur, who waited at High Table, came in.

'Evening, Arthur,' said Skullion condescendingly.

'Evening,' said Arthur.

'Going off home?' Skullion enquired.

'Got something for you,' Arthur told him, leaning confidentially over the counter.

Skullion looked up. Arthur's attendance at High Table was a source of much of his information about the College. He rose and came over to the counter. 'Oh ah,' he said.

'They're in a tizz-whizz tonight,' Arthur said. 'Proper tizz-whizz.'

'Go on,' said Skullion encouragingly.

'Bursar come in to dinner all flushed and flummoxy and the Dean's got them high spots on his cheeks he gets when his gander's up and the Tutor don't eat his soup. Not like him to turn up his soup,' Arthur said. Skullion grunted his agreement. 'So I know something's up.' Arthur paused for effect. 'Know what it is?' he asked.

Skullion shook his head. 'No. What is it?' he said.

Arthur smiled. 'Master's called a College Council for tomorrow. The Bursar said it wasn't convenient and the Master said to call it just the same and they don't like it. They don't like it at all. Put them off their dinner it did, the new Master acting all uppity like that, telling them what to do just when they thought they'd got him where they wanted him. Bursar said he'd told the Master they hadn't got the money for all the changes he has in mind and the Master seemed to have taken it, but then he rings the Bursar up and tells him to call the meeting.'

'Can't call a College Council all of a sudden,' Skullion said, 'Council meets on the first Thursday of every month.'

'That's what the Dean said and the Tutor. But the

Master wouldn't have it. Got to be tomorrow. Bursar rang him up and said Dean and Tutor wouldn't attend like they'd told him and Master said that was all right with him but that the meeting would be tomorrow whether they were there or not.' Arthur shook his head mournfully over the Master's wilfulness. 'It ain't right all this telling people what to do.'

Skullion scowled at him. 'The Master come to dinner?' he asked.

'No,' said Arthur, 'he don't stir from the Lodge. Just telephones his orders to the Bursar.' He glanced significantly at the switchboard in the corner. Skullion nodded pensively.

'So he's going ahead with his changes,' he said at last. 'And they thought they'd got him where they wanted him, eh?'

'That's what they said,' Arthur assured him. 'Bursar said he wasn't going to do nothing and then he suddenly calls the meeting.'

'What's the Dean say to all this?' Skullion asked.

'Says they've all got to stick together. Mind you, he didn't have much to say tonight. Too upset by the look of him. But that's what he's said before.'

'Don't suppose the Tutor agrees with him,' Skullion suggested.

'He do now. Didn't before but this being told to attend the meeting has got him on the raw. Don't like that at all, the Tutor don't.'

Skullion nodded. 'Ah well, that's something,' he said. 'It isn't like him to side with the Dean. Bursar agree?'

'Bursar says he does but you never can tell with him, can you?' Arthur said. 'He's a slippery sod, he is. One moment this, the next moment something else. You can't rely on him.'

'Got no bottom, the Bursar,' said Skullion, drawing on the language of the late Lord Wurford for his judgement.

'Ah, is that what it is?' Arthur said. He gathered up his coat. 'Got to be getting along now.'

Skullion saw him to the door. 'Thank you, Arthur,' he said. 'Very useful that is.'

'Glad to be of service,' Arthur said, 'besides I don't want any changes in the College any more than you do. Too old for changes, I am. Twenty-five years I've waited at High Table and fifteen years before that I was . . .'

Skullion shut the door on old Arthur's reminiscences and went back to the fire. So the Master was going ahead with his plans. Well, it wasn't a bad thing he'd ordered the College Council for tomorrow. It had got the Dean and the Senior Tutor to agree for the first time in years. That was something in itself. They had hated one another's guts for years, ever since the Dean had preached a sermon on the text, 'Many that are first shall be last', when the Tutor had first begun to coach the Porterhouse Boat. Skullion smiled to himself at the memory. The Tutor had come storming out of Chapel with his gown billowing behind him like the wrath of God and had worked the eight so hard they were past their peak by the time of the May Bumps. Porterhouse had been bumped three times that year and had lost the Head of the River. He'd never forgiven the Dean that sermon. Never agreed with him about anything since and now the Master had got their backs up. Well, it was an ill wind that blew no good. And anyway there was always Sir Cathcart in the wings to put his oar in if the Master went too far. Skullion went out and shut the gate and went to bed. Outside it was snowing again. Damp flakes flicked against the windows and ran in runnels of water down the panes. 'Pimpole and Gutterby,' murmured Skullion for the last time, and fell asleep.

*

Zipser slept fitfully and was awake before the alarm clock went off at seven. He dressed and made himself some coffee before going out and he was just cutting himself some bread in the gyp room when Mrs Biggs arrived.

'You're up early for a change,' she said, easing herself through the door of the tiny gyp room.

'What are you doing here now?' Zipser demanded belligerently. 'You shouldn't come till eight.'

Mrs Biggs, fulsome in a red mackintosh, smiled dreadfully. 'I can come any time I want to,' she said with quite unnecessary emphasis. Zipser needed no telling. He writhed against the sink and stared helplessly into the acres of her smile. Mrs Biggs unbuttoned her mac slowly with one hand like a gargantuan stripper and Zipser's eyes followed her down. Her breasts swarmed in her blouse as she slipped the mac over her shoulders. Zipser's eyes salivated over them.

'Here, help me with the arms,' Mrs Biggs said, wedging herself round so that she had her back to him. Zipser hesitated a moment and then, impelled by a fearful and uncontrollable urge, lunged forward.

'Here,' said Mrs Biggs somewhat surprised by the frenzy of his assistance and the unusual whinnying sounds Zipser was making, 'the arms I said. What do you think you're doing?' Zipser floundered in the folds of her mac unable to think at all let alone what he was doing. His mind was ablaze with overwhelming desire. As he thrust himself into the red inferno of Mrs Biggs' raincoat, the bedder hunched herself and then heaved. Zipser fell back against the sink and Mrs Biggs issued into the hall. Between them on the gyp-room floor, like the plastic afterbirth of some terrible delivery, the disputed raincoat slowly subsided.

'Goodness gracious me,' said Mrs Biggs recovering her composure, 'you want to be more careful. You might give people the wrong idea.'

Zipser, huddled in the corner of the gyp room breathing heavily, hoped desperately that Mrs Biggs didn't get the right idea.

'I'm sorry,' he mumbled, 'I must have slipped. Don't know what came over me.'

'Wonder you didn't come all over me,' Mrs Biggs said coarsely. 'Throwing yourself about like that.' She plummeted over and picked up the raincoat and, trailing it behind her like a bull fighter's cape, marched into the other room. Zipser stared at her boots with a fresh surge of longing and hurried downstairs. The need for a girl his own age to take his body off the bedder had become imperative. He had to do something to escape the temptation presented by Mrs Biggs' extensive charms or he would find himself before the Dean. Zipser could think of nothing worse than being sent down from Porterhouse for 'the attempted rape of a bedder'. Or only one thing. The successful accomplishment of rape. That would be a police-court matter. He would kill himself sooner than face that humiliation.

'Good morning, sir,' Skullion called out as he passed the Lodge.

'Good morning,' said Zipser and went out of the gate. He had over an hour to wait before the barbers' shops opened. He walked along the river to kill time and envied the ducks, sleeping on the banks, their uncomplicated existence.

*

Mrs Biggs tucked the sheets under the mattress of Zipser's bed with a practised hand and plumped his pillow with a mitigated force that was almost tender.

She was feeling rather pleased with herself. It had been some years since Mr Biggs had passed on, consigned to an early grave by his wife's various appetites, and even longer since anyone had paid her the compliment of finding her attractive. Zipser's clumsy advances had not escaped her attention. The fact that he followed her about from room to room as she worked and that his eyes were seldom off her were signs too obvious to be ignored. 'Poor boy misses his mum,' she had thought at first and had noted Zipser's solitariness as an indication of homesickness. But his recent behaviour had suggested less remote causes for his interest. The bedder's fancy ignored the weather and lumbered to thoughts of love. 'Don't be silly,' she told herself. 'What would he see in you?' But the notion remained and Mrs Biggs' sense of propriety began to adapt itself to the incongruities of the situation. She had begun to dress accordingly and to pay more attention to her looks and even, as she went from room to room and bed to bed, to indulge her imagination a little. The episode in the gyp room had confirmed her best suspicions. 'Fancy now,' she said to herself, 'and him such a nice young fellow too. Who'd have guessed?' She looked at herself in the mirror and primped her hair with a heavy hand.

*

At nine-fifteen Zipser took his seat in the barber's chair.

'Just a trim,' he told the barber.

The man looked at his head doubtfully.

'Wouldn't like a nice short back and sides, I don't suppose?' he asked mournfully.

'Just a trim, thank you,' Zipser told him.

The barber tucked the sheet into his collar. 'Don't know why some of you young fellows bother to have your hair cut at all,' he said. 'Seem determined to put us out of business.'

'I'm sure you still get lots of work,' Zipser said.

The barber's scissors clicked busily round his ears. Zipser stared at himself in the mirror and wondered once again at the disparity between his innocent appearance and the terrible passion which surged inside him. His eyes moved sideways to the rows of bottles, Eau de Portugal, Dr Linthrop's Dandruff Mixture, Vitalis, a jar of Pomade. Who on earth used Pomade? Behind him the barber was chattering on about football but Zipser wasn't listening. He was eyeing the glass case to his left where a box in one corner suggested the reason for his haircut. He couldn't move his head so that he wasn't sure what the box contained but it looked the right sort of box. Finally when the man moved forward to pick up the clippers Zipser turned his head and saw that he had been eyeing with quite pointless interest a box of razor blades. He turned his head further and scanned the shelves. Shaving creams, razors, lotions, combs, all were there in abundance but not a single carton of contraceptives.

Zipser sat on in a trance while the clippers buzzed on his neck. They must keep the damned things somewhere. Every hairdresser had them. His face in the mirror assumed a new uncertainty. By the time the barber had finished and was powdering his neck and waving a handmirror behind him, Zipser was in no mood to be critical of the result. He got out of the chair and waved the barber's brush away impatiently.

'That'll be thirty pence, sir,' the barber said, and made out a ticket. Zipser dug into his pocket for the money. 'Is there anything else?' Now was the moment he had been waiting for. The open invitation. That 'anything else' of the barber had covered only too literally a multitude of sins. In Zipser's case it was hopelessly inadequate not to say misleading.

'I'll have five packets of Durex,' Zipser said with a strangled bellow.

'Afraid we can't help you,' said the man. 'Landlord's a Catholic. It's in the lease we're not allowed to stock them.'

Zipser paid and went out into the street, cursing himself for not having looked in the window to see if there were any contraceptives on display. He walked into Rose Crescent and stared into a chemist's shop but the place was full of women. He tried three more shops only to find that they were all either full of housewives or that the shop assistants were young females. Finally he went into a barber's shop in Sidney Street where the window display was sufficiently broad-minded.

Two chairs were occupied and Zipser stood uncertainly just inside the door waiting for the barber to attend to him. As he stood there the door behind him opened and someone came in. Zipser stepped to one side and found himself looking into the face of Mr Turton, his supervisor.

'Ah, Zipser, getting your hair cut?' It seemed an unnecessarily inquisitive remark to Zipser. He felt inclined to tell the wretched man to mind his own business. Instead he nodded dumbly and sat down.

'Next one,' said the barber. Zipser feigned politeness.

'Won't you . . .?' he said to Mr Turton.

'Your need is greater than mine, my dear fellow,' the supervisor said and sat down and picked up a copy of *Titbits*. For the second time that morning Zipser found himself in a barber's chair.

'Any particular way?' the barber said.

'Just a trim,' said Zipser.

The barber bellied the sheet out over his knees and tucked it into his collar.

'If you don't mind my saying so, sir,' he said, 'but I'd say you'd already had your hair cut this morning.'

Zipser, staring into the mirror, saw Mr Turton look up and his own face turn bright red.

'Certainly not,' he muttered. 'What on earth makes you think that?' It was not a wise remark and Zipser regretted it before he had finished mumbling.

'Well, for one thing,' the barber went on, responding to this challenge to his powers of observation, 'you've still got powder on your neck.' Zipser said shortly that he'd had a bath and used talcum powder.

'Oh quite,' said the barber sarcastically, 'and I suppose all these clipper shavings . . .'

'Listen,' said Zipser conscious that Mr Turton had still not turned back to *Titbits* and was listening with interest, 'if you don't want to cut my hair . . .' The buzz of the clippers interrupted his protest. Zipser stared angrily at his reflection in the mirror and wondered why he was being dogged by embarrassing situations. Mr Turton was eyeing the back of his head with a new interest.

'I mean,' said the barber putting his clippers away, 'some people like having their hair cut.' He winked at Mr Turton and in the mirror Zipser saw that wink. The scissors clicked round his ears and Zipser shut his eyes to escape the reproach he saw in them in the mirror. Everything he did now seemed tinged with catastrophe. Why in God's name should he fall in love with an enormous bedder? Why couldn't he just get on with his work, read in the library, write his thesis and go to meetings of CUNA?

'Had a customer once,' continued the barber remorselessly, 'who used to have his hair cut three times a week. Mondays, Wednesdays and Fridays. Regular as clockwork. I asked him once, when he'd been coming for a couple of years mind you, I said to him, "Tell me, Mr Hattersley, why do you come and have your hair cut so often?" Know what he said? Said it was the one place he could think. Said he got all his best ideas in the barber's chair. Weird when you think about it. Here I stand all day clipping and cutting and right in front of me, under my hand you might say, there's all those thoughts going on unbeknown to me. I mean I must have cut the hair on over a hundred thousand heads in my time. I've been cutting hair for twenty-five years now and that's a lot of customers. Stands to reason some of them must have been having some pretty peculiar thoughts at the time. Murderers and sex maniacs, I daresay. I mean there would be, wouldn't there, in all that number? Stands to reason.'

Zipser shrank in the chair. Mr Turton had lost all interest in *Titbits* now.

'Interesting theory,' he said encouragingly. 'I suppose statistically you're right. I've never thought of it that way before.'

Zipser said it took all sorts to make a world. It seemed the sort of trite remark the occasion demanded. By the time the barber had finished, he had given up all thought of asking for contraceptives. He paid the thirty pence and staggered out of the shop. Mr Turton smiled and took his place in the chair.

It was almost lunchtime.

7

'I think we can dispense with formalities,' the Master said, sitting forward in his chair and looking down the long mahogany table. On his left the Bursar fiddled with his pen while on his right the Chaplain, accorded this position by virtue of his deafness, nodded his agreement. Down the long table the faces of the Council reflected their displeasure at this sudden meeting.

'It would appear to me,' said the Dean, 'that we have already dispensed with such formalities as we are used to. I can see no virtue in ridding ourselves of the few that are left.'

The Master regarded him closely. 'Bear with me, Dean,' he said, aware that he was relapsing from his carefully rehearsed down-to-earth manner into the vernacular of academic bitchiness. He pulled himself up. 'I have called this meeting,' he continued with a nasty smile, 'to discuss in detail the changes in the College I mentioned in my speech on Tuesday night. I shan't keep you long. When I have finished you can go away and think about my suggestions.' A ripple of indignation at the effrontery of his remark ran round the table. The Dean in particular lost his cool.

'The Master seems to be under some misapprehension as to the purpose of the College Council,' he said. 'May I remind him that it is the governing body of the College. We have been summoned here this afternoon at short notice and we have come at considerable inconvenience to ourselves ...' The Master yawned. 'Quite so. Quite so,' he murmured. The Dean's face turned a deeper shade of puce. A virtuoso in the art of the discourteous aside, he had never been subjected to such disrespect.

'I think,' said the Senior Tutor stepping into the breach, 'that it should be left to the Council to decide whether or not the Master's proposals merit discussion this afternoon.' He smiled unctuously at the Master.

'As you wish,' said Sir Godber. He looked at his watch. 'I shall be here until three. If after that you have things you wish to discuss, you will have to do so without me.' He paused. 'We can meet again tomorrow or the next day. I shall be available in the afternoon.'

He looked down the table at the suffused faces of the Fellows and felt satisfied. The atmosphere was just what he had wanted for the announcement of his plans. They would react predictably and with a violence that would disarm them. Then when it would appear to be all over he would nullify all their protests with a threat. It was a charming prospect made all the more pleasing by the knowledge that they would misinterpret his motives. They would, they would. Obtuse men, small men for whom Porterhouse was the world and Cambridge the universe. Sir Godber despised them, and it showed.

'If we are all agreed, then,' he continued, ignoring the titubation of the Dean who had been nerving himself to protest at the Master's incivility and leave the meeting, 'let me outline the changes I have in mind. In the first place, as you are all aware, Porterhouse's reputation has declined sadly since . . . I believe the rot set in in 1933. I have been told there was a poor intake of Fellows in that year. Correct me if I'm wrong.'

It was the turn of the Senior Tutor to stiffen in his seat. 1933 had been the year of his election.

'Academically our decline seems to have set in then. The quality of our undergraduates has always seemed to me to be quite deplorable. I intend to change all that. From now on, from this year of Grace, we shall accept candidates who possess academic qualifications alone.' He paused to allow the information to sink in. When the Bursar ceased twitching in his chair, he continued. 'That is my first point. The second is to announce that the College will become a co-educational institution from the beginning of the forthcoming academic year. Yes, gentlemen, from the beginning of next year there will be women living in Porterhouse.' A gasp, almost a belch of shock, broke from the Fellows. The Dean buried his face in his hands and the Senior Tutor put both his hands on the edge of the table to steady himself. Only the Chaplain spoke.

'I heard that,' he bellowed, his face radiant as if with

divine revelation. 'I heard it. Splendid news. Not before time either.' He relapsed into silence. The Master beamed. 'I accept your approval, Chaplain,' he said, 'with thanks. It is good to know that I have support from such an unexpected quarter. Thirdly . . .'

'I protest,' shouted the Senior Tutor, half rising to his feet. Sir Godber cut him short.

'Later,' he snapped and the Senior Tutor dropped back into his seat. 'Thirdly, the practice of dining in Hall will be abandoned. A self-service canteen run by an outside catering firm will be established in the Hall. There will be no High Table. All forms of academic segregation will disappear. Yes Dean . . .?'

But the Dean was speechless. His face livid and congested he had started to protest only to slump in his chair. The Senior Tutor hurried to his side while the Chaplain, always alert to the possibilities provided by a stricken audience, bellowed words of comfort into the insensible Dean's ear. Only the Master remained unmoved.

'Not, I trust, another Porterhouse Blue,' he said audibly to the Bursar, and looked at his watch, with calculated unconcern. To the Dean Sir Godber's manifest lack of interest in his demise came as a stimulant. His face grew pale and his breathing less sibilant. He opened his eyes and stared with loathing down the table at the Master.

'As I was saying,' continued Sir Godber, picking up the threads of his speech, 'the measures I have proposed will transform Porterhouse at a stroke.' He paused and smiled at the appositeness of the phrase. The Fellows stared at this fresh evidence of gaucherie. Even the Chaplain, imbued with the spirit of goodwill and deaf to the world's wickedness, was appalled by the Master's sang-froid.

'Porterhouse will regain its rightful place in the forefront of colleges,' the Master went on in a manner now recognizably political. 'No longer will we stumble on hamstrung by the obsolescence of outmoded tradition and class prejudice, by the limitations of the past and the cynicism of the present, but inspired by confidence in the future we shall prove ourselves worthy of the great trust that has been bequeathed us.' He sat down, inspired by his own brief eloquence. It was clear that nobody else present shared his enthusiasm for the future. When at last someone spoke it was the Bursar.

'There do appear to be one or two problems involved in this . . . er . . . transformation,' he pointed out. 'Not insuperable, I daresay, but nevertheless worth mentioning before we all become too enthusiastic.'

The Master surfaced from his reverie. 'Such as?' he said shortly.

The Bursar pursed his lips. 'Quite apart from the foreseeable difficulties of getting this . . . er . . . legislation accepted by the Council, I use the term advisedly you understand, there is the question of finance to consider. We are not a rich college . . .' He hesitated. The Master had raised an eyebrow.

'I am not unused to the argument,' he said urbanely. 'In a long career in government I had heard it put forward on too many occasions to be wholly convinced that the plea of poverty is as formidable as it sounds. It is precisely the rich who use it most frequently.'

The Bursar was driven to interrupt. 'I can assure you . . .' he began but the Master overrode him.

'I can only invoke the psalmist and say Cast thy bread upon the waters.'

'Not to be taken literally,' snapped the Senior Tutor.

'To be taken how you wish,' Sir Godber snapped back. The members of the Council stared at him with open belligerence.

'It is precisely that we have no bread to throw,' said the Bursar, trying to pour oil on troubled waters.

The Senior Tutor ignored his efforts. 'May I remind you,' he snarled at the Master, 'that this Council is the governing body of the College and . . .'

'The Dean reminded me earlier in the meeting,' the Master interrupted.

'I was about to say that policy decisions affecting the running of the College are taken by the Council as a whole,' continued the Senior Tutor. 'I should like to make it quite clear that I for one have no intention of accepting the changes outlined in the proposals that the Master has submitted to us. I think I can speak for the Dean,' he glanced at the speechless Dean before continuing, 'when I say we are both adamantly opposed to any changes in College policy.' He sat back. There were murmurs of agreement from the other Fellows. The Master leant forward and looked round the table.

'Am I to understand that the Senior Tutor has expressed the general feelings of the meeting?' he asked. There was a nodding of heads round the table. The Master looked crestfallen.

'In that case, gentlemen, there is little I can say,' he said sadly. 'In the face of your opposition to the changes in College policy that I have proposed, I have little choice but to resign the Mastership of Porterhouse.' A gasp came from the Fellows as the Master rose and gathered his notes. 'I shall announce my resignation in a letter to the Prime Minister, an open letter, gentlemen, in which I shall state the reasons for my resignation, namely that I am unable to continue as Master of a college that augments its financial resources by admitting candidates without academic qualifications in return for large donations to the Endowment Subscription Fund and selling degrees.' The Master paused and looked at the Fellows who sat stunned by his announcement. 'When I was nominated by the Prime Minister, I had no idea that I was accepting the Mastership of an academic auction-room nor that I was ending a career marked, I am proud to say, by the utmost adherence to the rules of probity in public life by becoming an accessory to a financial scandal of national proportions. I have the facts and figures here, gentlemen, and I shall include them in my letter to the Prime Minister, who will doubtless pass them on to the Director of Public Prosecutions. Good afternoon, gentlemen.'

The Master turned and stalked out of the room. Behind him the Fellows of Porterhouse sat rigid like embalmed figures round the table, each absorbed in calculating his own complicity in a scandal that must bring ruin to them all. It took little imagination to foresee the public outcry that would follow Sir Godber's resignation and the publication of his open letter, the wave of indignation that would sweep the country, the execrations that would fall on their heads from the other colleges in Cambridge, the denunciations of the other, newer universities. The Fellows of Porterhouse had little imagination but they could foresee all this and more, the demand for public accountability, possibly even prosecutions, even perhaps an enquiry into the sources and size of College funds. What would Trinity and King's say to this? The Fellows of Porterhouse knew the odium they could expect for having precipitated a public enquiry that could put, would put, in jeopardy the vast wealth of the other colleges and they shrank from the prospect. It was the Dean who first broke the silence with a strangled cry.

'He must be stopped,' he gurgled.

The Senior Tutor nodded sympathetically. 'We have little alternative.'

'But how?' demanded the Bursar, who was desperately trying to banish from his mind the knowledge that he had inadvertently provided the Master with the information he was now threatening to disclose. If the other Fellows should ever learn who had provided Sir Godber with this material for blackmail his life in College would not be worth living.

'At all costs the Master must be persuaded to stay on,' said the Senior Tutor. 'We simply cannot afford the scandal that would ensue from the publication of his letter of resignation.'

The Praelector looked at him vindictively. 'We?' he asked. 'I beg not to be included in the list of those responsible for this disgraceful disclosure.'

'And what precisely do you mean by that?' asked the Senior Tutor.

'I should have thought that it was obvious,' said the Praelector. 'Most of us have had nothing to do with the administration of College finances nor with the admissions procedure. We cannot be held responsible for . . .'

'We are all responsible for College policy,' shouted the Senior Tutor.

'You are responsible for admissions,' the Praelector shouted back. 'You are responsible for the choice of candidates. You are . . .'

'Gentlemen,' the Bursar interposed, 'let us not bicker about individual responsibilities. We are all responsible as members of the Council for the running of the College.'

'Some of us are more responsible than others,' the Praelector pointed out.

'And we shall all share the blame for the mistakes that have been made in the past,' continued the Bursar.

'Mistakes? Who said anything about mistakes?' demanded the Dean breathlessly.

'I think that in the light of the Master's . . .' began the Senior Tutor.

'Damn the Master,' the Dean snarled, struggling to his feet. 'Damn the man. Let us stop talking about mistakes. I said he must be stopped. I didn't say we had to surrender to the swine.' He waddled to the head of the table, portly, belligerent and stubborn, like some crimson toad and with all that creature's resilience to the challenges of climate. The Senior Tutor hesitated in the face of his colleague's revitalized obstinacy. 'But . . .' he began. The Dean raised a hand for silence.

'He must be stopped,' he said. 'For the time being perhaps we must accept his proposals, but for the time being only. In the short run we must use the tactics of delay, but only in the short run.'

'And then?' the Senior Tutor asked.

'We must buy time,' continued the Dean. 'Time to bring influence to bear upon Sir Godber and time to subject his own career to the scrutiny he has seen fit to apply to the customs and traditions of the College. No man who has spent as long as Sir Godber Evans in public life is wholly without fault. It is our business to discover the extent of his weaknesses.'

'Are you saying that we should . . .' the Praelector began.

'I am saying that the Master is vulnerable,' the Dean went on, 'that he is corrupt and that he is open to influence from the powers that be. The tactics he has used this afternoon, tactics of blackmail, are a symptom of the corruption I am referring to. And let us not forget that we have powerful friends.'

The Senior Tutor pursed his lips and nodded. 'True. Very true, Dean.'

'Yes, Porterhouse can justly claim its share of eminent men. The Master may dismiss our protests but we have powerful allies,' said the Dean.

'And in the meantime we must eat humble pie and ask the Master to reconsider his resignation in the light of our acceptance of the changes he has proposed?' said the Senior Tutor.

'Precisely.' The Dean looked round the table at the Fellows for a sign of hesitancy. 'Has anyone here any doubts as to the wisdom of the course I have proposed?' he asked.

'We seem to be left with little choice,' said the Bursar.

'We have no choice at all,' the Dean told him.

'And if the Master refuses to withdraw his resignation?' the Praelector asked.

'There is no possible reason why he should,' the Dean said. 'I propose that we go now in a body to the Master's Lodge and ask him to reconsider.'

'In a body? Is that really wise? Wouldn't it look . . . rather . . . well . . . obsequious?' the Senior Tutor asked doubtfully.

'I don't think this is any time to be thinking about appearances,' said the Dean. 'I am only concerned with results. Humble pie, you said yourself. Very well, if Sir Godber requires humble pie to retract his threat he shall have it. I shall see to it that he eats it himself later on. Besides I should not like him to think that we are in any way divided.' He stared fiercely at the Bursar. 'At a time of crisis it is vital that we present a united front. Don't you agree, Bursar?'

'Oh yes. Absolutely, Dean,' the Bursar assured him.

'Very well, let us go,' said the Dean and led the way out of the Council Chamber. The Fellows trooped after him into the cold.

*

Skullion listened to their footsteps on the floor above his head and climbed off the chair he had been standing on. It was hot in the boiler-room, hot and dusty, a dry heat that had irritated his nose and made it difficult not to sneeze while he stood on the chair with his ear pressed to a pipe listening to the voices raised in anger in the Council Chamber. He brushed the dust off his sleeve and spread an old newspaper on the seat of the chair and sat down. It wouldn't do to be seen coming out of the boiler-room just yet and besides he wanted to think.

The central heating system wasn't the best conductor of conversations in the world, it tended to parenthesize its own gurgles at important moments, but Skullion had heard enough to startle him. The Master's threat to resign he had greeted with delight, only to feel the sting in its tail with an alarm that equalled that of the Fellows. His thoughts flew to his Scholars and the threat that public exposure of the sort Sir Godber was proposing would do to them. Sir Cathcart must hear this new danger at once – but then the Dean had proposed his own solution and Skullion's heart had warmed to the old man. 'There's life in the old Dean yet,' he said to himself and chuckled at the thought of Sir Godber retracting his resignation only to find that he had been outsmarted. Powerful allies, the Dean had said and Skullion wondered if the old man knew just how powerful some of those allies were, or what a threat the Master's disclosure would pose to them. Cabinet ministers ranked among Skullion's Scholars, cabinet ministers, civil servants, directors of the Bank of England, eminent men indeed. It began to dawn on Skullion that the Master was in a stronger position than he knew. A public enquiry into the academic antecedents of so many public figures would have appalling consequences, and the powerful allies the Dean evidently had in mind were hardly likely to put up more than token opposition to the changes at Porterhouse the Master wanted, if the alternative was a national scandal in which they would figure so prominently. The Dean was barking up the wrong tree after all, and Skullion's premature optimism gave way to a deep melancholy. At this rate there would be women in

Porterhouse before the year was out. It was a prospect that infuriated him. 'Over my dead body,' he muttered darkly, and pondered ways and means of frustrating Sir Godber.

8

Zipser was drunk. Eight pints of bitter, each drunk in a different pub, had changed his outlook on life. The narrow confines of his compulsion had given way to a brighter, broader, more expansive frame of mind. True, his haircuts had left him short and practically bald and with an aversion for the company of barbers which would last him a lifetime, but his eyes sparkled, his cheeks had a ruddier, rosier look, and he was in a mood to run the gauntlet of a hundred middle-aged house-wives and to face the disapproval of as many chemists in search of an immaculate misconception. In any case a flash of inspiration had robbed him of the need to publicize his requirements. As he had wandered up Sidney Street after his second haircut he had suddenly recalled having seen a contraceptive dispenser in the lavatory of a pub in Bermondsey, and while Bermond-sey was rather too far to go in search of a discreet anonymity, it occurred to him that Cambridge pubs must surely offer a similarly sophisticated service for lovers caught as it were on the hop. Zipser's spirits rose with the thought. He went into the first pub he came to and ordered a pint. Ten minutes later he left that pub empty-handed and found another only to be similarly disappointed. By the time he had been to six pubs and had drunk six pints of bitter he was in a mood to point out the deficiency of their service to the bartenders. At the seventh pub he struck gold. Waiting until two elderly men had finished a protracted pee Zipser fumbled with his change and put two coins into the machine. He was about to pull the handle when an undergraduate came in. Zipser went out and finished his seventh pint keeping an eagle eye on the door of the Gents. Two minutes later he was back and tugging at the handle. Nothing happened. He pulled and pushed but the dispenser refused to dispense. He peered into the Money Returned slot and found it empty. Finally he put two more coins in and pulled the handle again. This time his money dropped into the slot and Zipser took it out and looked at it. The damned dispenser was empty. Zipser went back to the bar and ordered an eighth pint.

'That machine in the toilet,' he said conspiratorially to the barman.

'What about it?' the barman asked.

'It's empty,' said Zipser.

'That's right,' said the barman. 'It's always empty.'

'Well, it's got some of my money in it.'

'You don't say.'

'I do say.'

'A gin and tonic,' said a man with a moustache next to Zipser.

'Coming up,' said the barman. Zipser sipped his pint

while the barman poured a gin and tonic. Finally when the man with the moustache had taken his drink back to a table by the window, Zipser raised the subject of faulty dispensers again. He was beginning to feel distinctly belligerent.

'What are you going to do about my money?' he asked.

The barman looked at him warily.

'How do I know you put any in?' he asked. 'How do I know you're not just trying it on?'

Zipser considered the question.

'I don't see how I can,' he said finally. 'I haven't got it.'

'Very funny,' said the barman. 'If you've got any complaints to make about that dispenser, you take them to the suppliers.' He reached under the bar and produced a card and handed it to Zipser. 'You go and tell them your problems. They stock the machines. I don't. All right?' Zipser nodded and the man went off down the other end of the counter to serve a customer. Zipser left the pub with the card and went down the road. He found the suppliers in Mill Road. There was a young man with a beard behind the counter. Zipser went in and put the card down in front of him.

'I've come from the Unicorn,' he said. 'The dispenser is empty.'

'What, already?' the man said. 'Don't know what happens to them, they go so quickly.'

'I want . . .' Zipser began thickly but the young man had disappeared through a door to the back. Zipser was beginning to feel distinctly light-headed. He tried to think what he was doing discussing wholesale contraceptive sales with a young man with a beard in an office in Mill Road.

'Here you are. Two gross. Sign here,' said the clerk reappearing from the back with two cartons which he plonked on the counter. Zipser stared at the cartons, and was about to explain that he had merely come to ask for his money back when a woman came in. Zipser suddenly felt sick. He picked up the ballpen and signed the slip and then, clutching the two cartons, stumbled from the shop.

By the time he got back to the Unicorn the pub was shut. Zipser tried knocking on the door without result and finally gave it up and went back to Porterhouse.

He weaved his way past the Porter's Lodge and headed across the Court towards his staircase. Ahead of him a line of black figures emerged from the door of the Council Chamber in solemn processional and moved towards him. At the head of them waddled the Dean. Zipser hiccupped and tried to focus on them. It was very difficult. Almost as difficult as trying to stop the world going round. Zipser hiccupped again and was sick on the snow as the column of figures advanced on him.

'Beg your pardon,' he said. 'Shouldn't have done that. Had too much to drink.'

The column stopped and Zipser peered down into the Dean's face. It kept going in and out of focus alarmingly.

'Do you . . . do you . . . know how red your face is?'
he asked, waving his head erratically at the Dean.
'Shouldn't have a red face, should you?'

'Out of the way,' snapped the Dean.

'Schertainly,' said Zipser and sat down in the snow.
The Dean loomed over him menacingly.

'You, sir, are drunk. Disgustingly drunk,' he said.

'Quite right,' said Zipser. 'Full marks for perspic . . .
perspicac . . . ity. Hit the nail on the head firsht time.'

'What is your name?'

'Zhipsher, shir, Zhipsher.'

'You're gated for a week, Zipser,' snarled the
Dean.'

'Yesh,' said Zipser happily, 'I am gated for a week.
Shertainly, shir.' He struggled to his feet, still clutching
his cartons, and the column of dons moved on across
the Court. Zipser wobbled off to his room and collapsed
on the floor.

*

Sir Godber watched the deputation of Fellows from his
study window. 'Canossa,' he thought to himself as the
procession trudged through the snow to the front door
and rang the bell. For a moment it crossed his mind to
let them wait but better judgement prevailed. Pope
Gregory's triumph had after all been a temporary one.
He went out into the hall and let them in.

'Well, gentlemen,' he said when they had filed into
his study, 'and what can I do for you now?'

The Dean shuffled forward. 'We have reconsidered our decision, Master,' he said.

Behind him the members of the College Council nodded obediently. Sir Godber looked round their faces and was satisfied. 'You wish me to remain as Master?'

'Yes, Master,' the Dean said.

'And this is the general wish of the Council?'

'It is.'

'And you accept the changes in the College that I have proposed without any reservations?' the Master asked.

The Dean mustered a smile. 'Naturally, we have reservations,' he said. 'It would be asking rather much to expect us to abandon our . . . er . . . principles without retaining the right to have private reservations, but in the interest of the College as a whole we accept that there may be need for compromise.'

'My conditions are final,' said the Master. 'They must be accepted as they stand. I am not prepared to attenuate them. I think I should make that plain.'

'Quite so, Master. Quite so.' The Dean smiled weakly.

'In that case I shall postpone my decision,' said Sir Godber, 'until the next meeting of the College Council. That will give us all time to consider the matter at our leisure. Shall we say next Wednesday at the same time?'

'As you wish, Master,' said the Dean. 'As you wish.'

They trooped out and Sir Godber, having seen them

to the door, stood at the window watching the dark procession disappear into the winter evening with a new sense of satisfaction. 'The iron fist in the iron glove,' he murmured to himself, conscious that for the first time in a long career of political manoeuvring and compromise he had at long last achieved a clear-cut victory over an apparently intransigent opposition. There had been no doubting the Fellows' obeisance. They had crawled to him and Sir Godber indulged himself in the recollection before going on to consider the implications of their surrender. No one – and who should know better than Sir Godber – crawled quite so submissively without good reasons. The Fellows' obeisance had been too complete to be without ulterior motive. It was not enough to suppose that his threat had been utter. It had been sufficient to force them to come to heel but there had been no need for the Dean, of all people, to wag his tail so obsequiously. Sir Godber sat down by the fire and considered the character of the Dean for a hint of his motive. And the more he thought the less cause he found for premature self-congratulation. Sir Godber did not underestimate the Dean. The man was an ignorant bigot, with all the persistence of bigotry and all the cunning of the ignorant. 'Buying time,' he thought shrewdly, 'but time for what?' It was an unpleasant notion. Not for the first time since his arrival at Porterhouse Sir Godber felt uneasy, aware, if only subliminally, that the facile assumptions about human nature upon which his liberal ideas were founded were somehow threatened by a devious scholasticism whose origins were less rational and more obscure than he preferred to think. He got up and stared out into the night at the medieval buildings of the College silhouetted against the orange sky. It had begun to snow again and the wind had risen, blowing the snowflakes hither and thither in sudden ungovernable flurries. He pulled the curtains to shut out the sight of nature's lack of symmetry and settled himself in his chair with his favourite author, Bentham.

*

At High Table the Fellows dined in moody silence. Even the Chef's poached salmon failed to raise their spirits, dampened by the obduracy of the Master and the memory of their capitulation. Only the Dean remained undaunted, shovelling food into his mouth as if to fuel his determination and mouthing imprecations on Sir Godber simultaneously, his forehead greasy and his eyes bright with the cunning Sir Godber had recognized.

In the Combination Room, as they took their coffee, the Senior Tutor broached the topic of their next move. 'It would appear that we have until Wednesday to circumvent the Master's proposals,' he said, sipping brandy fastidiously.

'A relatively short time, if you don't mind my saying so.'

'Short but enough,' said the Dean tersely.

'I must say I find your confidence a little surprising, Dean,' said the Bursar nervously.

The Dean looked at him with a sudden ferocity. 'No more surprising than I find your lack of discretion, Bursar,' he snapped. 'I hardly imagine that this unfortunate turn of events would have occurred without your disclosure of the financial state of the College.'

The Bursar reddened. 'I was simply trying to point out to the Master that the changes he was proposing would place an intolerable strain on our resources,' he protested. 'If my memory serves me right you were the first to suggest that the finances should be brought to his attention.'

'Certainly I suggested that. I didn't however suggest that he should be made privy to the details of our admissions policy,' the Dean retorted.

'Gentlemen,' said the Senior Tutor, 'the mistake has been made. Nothing is to be gained by post-mortem. We are faced by an urgent problem. It is not in our best interest to apportion blame for past mistakes. If it comes to that we are all culpable. Without the divisions that prevented the election of Dr Siblington as Master, we should have avoided the nomination of Sir Godber.'

The Dean finished his coffee. 'There is some truth in that,' he admitted, 'and a lesson to be learnt. We must remain united in the face of the Master. In the meantime I have already made a move. I have arranged a meeting with Sir Cathcart D'Eath for this evening. His car should be waiting for me now.' He rose to his feet and gathered his gown about him.

'May one inquire the purpose of this meeting?' the Praelector asked. The Dean looked down at the Bursar. 'I should not like to think that our plans are likely to reach Sir Godber's ears,' he said deliberately.

'I can assure you . . .' began the Bursar.

'I have requested this meeting because Sir Cathcart as you all know is President of the OPs. I think he should know what changes the Master proposes. Furthermore I think he should know the manner in which the Master has conducted himself in the matter. I fancy that there will be an extraordinary meeting of the Porterhouse Society next Tuesday to discuss the situation and I have high hopes that at that meeting a resolution will be passed censoring Sir Godber for the dictatorial attitude he has adopted in his dealings with the College Council and calling for his immediate resignation from the Mastership.'

'But, Dean, surely that is most unwise,' protested the Senior Tutor, thoroughly alarmed. 'If a motion of that sort is passed, the Master is bound to resign and to publish his confounded letter. I really don't see what that is going to accomplish.'

The Bursar put down his coffee-cup with unwonted violence. 'For God's sake, Dean,' he said, 'consider what you are doing.'

The Dean smiled grimly. 'If Sir Godber can threaten us,' he said, 'we can threaten him.'

'But the scandal, think of the scandal. It will involve us all,' muttered the Bursar desperately.

'It will also involve Sir Godber. That is precisely the point of the exercise. We shall get in first by demanding his resignation. The force of his letter to the PM will be dulled by the fact that the College authorities and the Porterhouse Society have both demanded his resignation on the grounds of incompetence and his letter to the press with its so-called disclosures will have the appearance of being the action of a slighted and bitter man. Besides I rather think you overestimate Sir Godber's political courage. Faced with the ultimatum we shall present at the Council meeting on Wednesday I doubt if he will risk a further confrontation.'

'But if the call for his resignation has already been published . . .'

'It won't have been. The motion will have been passed, I trust unanimously, but its publication will be dependent on Sir Godber's attitude. If he persists in demanding the changes in the College, then we shall publish.'

'And if he resigns without warning?'

'We shall publish all the same,' said the Dean. 'We shall muddy the issue until it is uncertain whether we forced his resignation or not. Oh, we shall stir the pot, gentlemen. Have no fear of that. If there must be dirt let there be lots of it.' The Dean turned and went out, his gown billowing darkly behind him. In the Combination Room the Fellows looked at one another ruefully. Whatever changes the Master proposed appeared minor by comparison with the uproar the Dean seemed bent on provoking.

It was the Chaplain who broke the silence. 'I must say,' he shouted, 'that the Chef excelled himself tonight. That soufflé was delicious.'

Outside the main gate Sir Cathcart's Rolls-Royce waited ostentatiously as the Dean, swaddled in a heavy coat and wearing his blackest hat, hurried past the Porter's Lodge.

Skullion opened the car door for him.

'Good evening, Skullion.'

'Good evening to you, sir,' Skullion murmured humbly.

The Dean clambered in and the car moved off, its wheels slushing through the snow. In the back the Dean stared through the window at the flurries of snowflakes and the passers-by with their heads bent against the driving wind. He felt warm and contented, with none of the uneasy feelings that had driven the Master to his Bentham. This was weather he appreciated, cold bitter weather with the river rising and the biting wind creating once again the divisions of his youth, that hierarchy of rich and poor, good and bad, the comfort and the misery which he longed to preserve and which Sir Godber would destroy in his search for soulless uniformity. 'The old order changeth,' he muttered to himself, 'but damned slowly if I have anything to do with it.'

*

Skullion went back into the Porter's Lodge.

'Going to supper,' he told the under-porter and trudged across the Court to the kitchen. He went down the stone stairs to the kitchen where the Chef had laid a table for two in his pantry. It was hot and Skullion took off his coat before sitting down.

'Snowing again they tell me,' said the Chef, taking his seat.

Skullion waiting until a young waiter with a gaping mouth had brought the dishes before saying anything.

'Dean's gone to see the General,' he said finally.

'Has he now?' said the Chef, helping himself to the remains of the poached salmon.

'Council meeting this afternoon,' Skullion continued.

'So I heard.'

Skullion shook his head.

'You aren't going to like this,' he said. 'The Master's changes aren't going to suit your book, I can tell you.'

'Never supposed they would, Mr Skullion.'

'Worse than I expected, Chef, much worse.' Skullion took a mouthful of Ockfener Herrenberg 1964 before going on.

'Self-service in Hall,' he said mournfully.

The Chef put down his knife and fork. 'Never,' he growled.

'It's true. Self-service in Hall.'

'Over my dead body,' said the Chef. 'Over my bloody dead body.'

'Women in College too.'

'What? Living in College?'

'That's it. Living in College.'

'That's unnatural, Mr Skullion. Unnatural.'

'You don't have to tell me that, Chef. You don't have to tell me. Unnatural and immoral. It isn't right, Chef, it's downright wicked.'

'And self-service in Hall,' the Chef muttered. 'What's the world coming to? You know, Mr Skullion, when I think of all the years I've been Chef to the College and all the dinners I've cooked for them, I sometimes wonder what's the meaning of it all. They've got no right to do it.'

'It's not them that's doing it,' Skullion told him. 'It's him that says it's got to change.'

'Why don't they stop him? They're the Council. He can't do it without their say-so.'

'They can't stop him. Threatened to resign if they didn't agree.'

'Why didn't they let him? Good riddance to bad rubbish.'

'Threatened to write to the papers and tell them we've been selling degrees,' Skullion said.

The Chef looked at him with alarm.

'You don't mean he knows about your . . .'

'I don't know what he knows and what he don't,' Skullion said. 'I don't think he knows about them. I think he's talking about the ones they let in because they've got no money. I think that's what he means.'

'But we've a right to let in who we like,' the Chef protested. 'It's our college. It's not anyone else's.'

'That's not the way he sees it,' Skullion said. 'He's threatened them with a national scandal if they don't toe the line and they've agreed.'

'What did the Dean say? He must have said something.'

'Said they'd got to buy time by seeming to agree. He's gone to see the General now. They'll think of something.'

Skullion finished his wine and smiled to himself. 'He don't know what he's tackled,' he said more cheerfully.

'Thinks he's dealing with the pipsqueaks in Parliament, he does. Wordmongers, that's what MPs are. Think you've only got to say a thing for it to be there next day. They don't know nothing about doing and they don't have nothing to lose, but the Dean's a different kettle of fish. He and the General, they'll do him down. See if they don't.' He grinned knowingly and winked his unblacked eye. The Chef nibbled a grape moodily.

'Don't see how they can,' he said.

'Digging for dirt,' said Skullion. 'Digging for dirt in his past, that's what the Dean said.'

'Dirt? What sort of dirt?'

'Women,' said Skullion.

'Ah,' said the Chef. 'Disreputable women.'

'Precisely, Chef, them and money.'

The Chef pushed his hat back on his head. 'He wasn't what you might call a rich undergrad, was he?'

'No,' said Skullion, 'he wasn't.'

'And he's rich now.'

'Married it,' Skullion told him. 'Lacey money, that's what it is. Lady Mary's money. That's the sort of man he is, Sir Godber.'

'Bony woman. Not my cup of tea,' said the Chef. 'Like something with a bit more meat to it myself. Wouldn't be surprised it he hadn't got a fancy woman somewhere.'

Skullion shook his head doubtfully. 'Not him. Not enough guts,' said Skullion.

'You don't think they'll find anything, then?'

'Not that sort of thing. They'll have to bring pressure. Influential friends the College has got, the Dean said. They'll use them.'

'They'd better use something. I'm not staying on to run a self-service canteen and have women in my Hall,' said the Chef.

Skullion got up from the table and put on his coat. 'The Dean'll see to it,' he said and climbed the stairs to the Screens. The wind had blown snow on to the steps and Skullion turned up the collar of his coat. 'Got no right to change things,' he grumbled to himself, and went out into the night.

*

At Coft Castle the Dean and Sir Cathcart sat in the library, a decanter of brandy half empty on the table beside them and their thoughts bitter with memories of past greatness.

'England's ruin, damned Socialists,' growled Sir Cathcart. 'Turned the country into a benevolent society. Seem to think you can rule a nation with good intentions. Damned nonsense. Discipline. That's what the country needs. A good dose of unemployment to bring the working classes to their senses.'

'Doesn't seem to work these days,' said the Dean with a sigh. 'In the old days a depression seemed to have a very salutary effect.'

'It's the dole. Man can earn more not working than he can at his job. All wrong. A bit of genuine starvation would soon put that right.'

'I suppose the argument is that the wives and children suffer,' said the Dean.

'Can't see much harm in that,' the General continued. 'Nothing like a hungry woman to put some pep into a man. Reminds me of a painting I saw once. Lots of fellows sitting round a table waiting for their dinner and the lady of the house comes in and lifts the cover of the dish. Spur inside, what? Sensible woman. Fine painting. Have some more brandy?'

'That's very kind of you,' said the Dean, proffering his glass.

'Trouble with this Godber Evans fellow is he comes from poor stock,' continued Sir Cathcart when he had filled their glasses. 'Doesn't understand men. Hasn't got generations of county stock behind him. No leadership qualities. Got to have lived with animals to understand men, working men. Got to train them properly. A whack on the arse if they do something wrong and a pat on the head if they get it right. No use filling their heads with a whole lot of ideas they can't use. Bloody nonsense, half this education lark.'

'I quite agree,' said the Dean. 'Educating people above their station has been one of the great mistakes of this century. What this country requires is an educated elite. What it's had in fact, for the past three hundred years.'

'Three meals a day and a roof over his head and the average man has nothing to grumble about. Stout fellows. The present system is designed to create layabouts. Consumer society indeed. Can't consume what you don't make. Damned tommyrot.'

The Dean's head nodded on his chest. The fire, the brandy and the ubiquitous central heating in Coft Castle mingled with the warmth of Sir Cathcart's sentiments to take their toll of his concentration. He was dimly aware of the rumble of the General's imprecations, distant and receding like some tide going out across the mudflats of an estuary where once the fleet had lain at anchor. All empty now, the ships gone, dismantled, scrapped, the evidence of might deplenished, only a sandpiper with Sir Godber's face poking its beak into the sludge. The Dean was asleep.

9

Zipser stirred on the floor of his room. His face in contact with the carpet felt sore and his head throbbed. Above all he was cold and stiff. He turned on his side and stared at the window, where an orange glow from the sky over Cambridge shone dimly through the falling snow. Slowly he gathered himself together and got to his feet. Feeling distinctly weak and sick he went to the door and turned on the light and stood blinking at the two large cartons on the floor. Then he sat down hurriedly in a chair and tried to remember what had happened to him and why he was the possessor of two gross of guaranteed electronically tested three-teat vending machine pack contraceptives. The details of the day's events slowly returned to him and with them the remembrance of his misunderstanding with the Dean. 'Gated for a week,' he murmured and realized the implications of his predicament. He couldn't deliver the beastly things to the Unicorn now and he had signed the slip at the wholesale office. Enquiries would be made. The barman at the Unicorn would identify him. So would the wretched clerk at the wholesale office. The police would be informed. There would be a search. He'd be arrested. Charged with being in felon-

Porterhouse Blue

ious possession of two gross of . . . Zipser clutched his
head in his hands and tried to think what to do. He'd
have to get rid of the things. He looked at his watch.
Eleven o'clock. Got to hurry. Burn them? He looked at
the gas fire and gave up the idea. Out of the question.
Flush them down the lavatory? Better idea. He threw
himself at the cartons and began to open them. First
the outer carton, then the inner one, then the packet
itself and finally the foil wrapper. It was a laborious job.
He'd never do it. He'd got to do it.

Beside him on the carpet a pile of empty packets
slowly grew and with it a pile of foil and a grotesque
arrangement of latex rings looking like flattened and
translucent button mushrooms. Lubricated with sensitol, his hands were sticky, which made it even more
difficult to tear the foil. Finally after an hour he had
emptied one carton. It was twelve o'clock. He gathered
the contraceptives up and took a handful out on to the
landing and into the lavatory. He dropped them into
the pan and pulled the chain. A rush of water, swirls,
bubbles, gone? The water subsided and he stared down
at two dozen rubber rings floating defiantly in the pan.
'For God's sake,' said Zipser desperately and waited
until the cistern had filled again. He waited a minute
after the water had stopped running and pulled the
chain again. Two dozen contraceptives smiled up at
him. One or two had partially unfurled and were filled
with air. Zipser stared at the things frantically. Got to
get them to go down somehow. He reached behind the

pan and grabbed the cleaning brush and shoved it down on them. One or two disappeared round the U bend but for the most part they resisted his efforts. Three even had the audacity to adhere to the brush itself. Zipser picked them off with fastidious disgust and dropped them back into the water. By this time the cistern had filled again, gurgling gently and ending with a final swish. Zipser tried to think what to do. If buying the damned things had been fraught with appalling difficulties, getting rid of them was a nightmare.

He sat down on the lavatory seat and considered the intractability of matter. A tin of lavatory cleanser caught his attention. He picked it up and wondered if it would dissolve rubber. Then he got off the seat and emptied the contents on to the rings floating in the water. Whatever chemical action the cleanser promised failed altogether. The contraceptives remained unaffected. Zipser grabbed the brush again and plunged it into the pan. Wafts of disinfectant powder irritated his nose. He sneezed loudly and clutched the chain. For the third time the cistern flushed and Zipser was just studying the subsidence and counting the six contraceptives which remained immune to chemistry and the rush of water when someone knocked on the door.

'What the hell's going on in there?' a voice asked. It was Foxton, who lived in the room next door.

Zipser looked hauntedly at the door. 'Got diarrhoea,' he said weakly.

'Well, must you pull the bloody chain so often?'

Foxton asked. 'Making a bloody awful noise and I'm trying to sleep.' He went back to his room and Zipser turned back to the pan and began fishing for the six contraceptives with the lavatory brush.

Twenty minutes later he was still searching for some method of disposing of his incriminating evidence. He had visited six lavatories on neighbouring staircases and had found a method of getting the things to disappear by first filling them with water from a tap and tying the ends. It was slow and cumbersome and above all noisy and when he had tried six at a time on J staircase he had to spend some time unblocking the U pipe. He went back to his room and sat shivering with cold and anxiety. It was one o'clock and so far he had managed to rid himself of thirty-eight. At this rate he would still be flushing lavatories all over the College when Mrs Biggs arrived in the morning. He stared at the pile of foil and the packets. Got to get rid of them too. Put them behind the gas fire and burn them he thought and he was just wrestling with the gas fire and trying to make space behind it when the howling draught in the chimney gave him a better idea. He went to the window and looked out into the night. In the darkness outside snowflakes whirled and scattered while the wind battered at the window pane. Zipser opened the window and poked his head out into the storm before wetting his finger and holding it up to the wind. 'Blowing from the east,' he muttered and shut the window with a smile of intense satisfaction. A moment later he was kneeling beside the gas fire and undoing the hose of his gas ring and five minutes afterwards the first of 250 inflated contraceptives bounced buoyantly against the sooty sides of the medieval chimney and disappeared into the night sky above. Zipser rushed to the window and gazed up for a glimpse of the winsome thing as it whirled away carrying its message of abstinence far away into the world, but the sky was too dark and there was nothing to see. He went back and fetched a torch and shone it up the chimney but apart from one or two errant snowflakes the chimney was clear. Zipser turned cheerfully back to the gas ring and inflated five more. Once again the experiment was entirely successful. Up the chimney they floated, up and away. Zipser inflated twenty and popped them up the chimney with equal success. He was just filling his hundredth when the gas gave out, and with a hideous wheeze the thing deflated. Zipser rummaged in his pockets for a shilling and finally found one. He put it into the meter and the contraceptive assumed a new and satisfactory shape. He tied the end and stuffed it up the chimney. The night wore on and Zipser acquired a wonderful dexterity. On to the tube, gas on, gas off, a knot in the end and up the chimney. Beside him on the floor the cartons filled with discarded foil and Zipser was just wondering if there were schoolchildren who collected used contraceptive containers like milk-bottle tops when he became aware that something had gone wrong in the chimney. The bloated and strangulated rear of his last contraceptive was hanging suspended in the fireplace. Zipser gave it a shove of encouragement but the poor thing merely bulged dangerously. Zipser pulled it out and peered up the chimney. He couldn't peer very far. The chimney was crowded with eager contraceptives. He extracted another, smeared with soot, and put it down on the floor. He extracted a third and thrust it behind him. Then a fourth and a fifth, both deeply encrusted with soot. After that he gave up. The rest were too high to reach. He clambered out of the fireplace and sat on the floor wondering what to do. At least he had disposed of all two gross, even if some were lodged in the chimney stack. They were well hidden there – or would be once he had put the gas fire back in place. He would think of some way of disposing of them in the morning. He was too tired to think of anything now. He turned to reach for the five he had managed to extract only to find that they had disappeared. 'I put them down on the carpet. I'm sure I did,' he muttered lightheadedly to himself and was about to look under the bookcase when his eye caught sight of a movement on the ceiling. Zipser looked up. Five sooty contraceptives had lodged themselves in a corner by the door. Little bits of soot marked the ceiling where they had touched.

Zipser got wearily to his feet and climbed on to a chair and reached up. He could just manage to get his fingers on to the belly of one of the things but the sensitol made it impossible to get a grip. Zipser squeezed and with a coy squeak the contraceptive evaded his grasp and lumbered away across the room, leaving a track of soot behind it. Zipser tried again on another with the same result. He moved the chair across the room and reached up. The contraceptive waddled gently into the corner by the window. Zipser moved the chair again but the contraceptive rolled away. Zipser climbed down and stared maniacally at his ceiling. It was covered in delicate black trails as if some enormous snail had called after a stint of coal-heaving. The self-control Zipser had been exercising began to slip. He picked up a book and lobbed it at a particularly offensive-looking contraceptive, but apart from driving it across the room to join the flock in the corner by the door the gesture was futile. Zipser crossed to the desk and pushed it over to the door. Then he fetched the chair and stood it on the desk and climbed precariously up and seized a contraceptive by its knotted tail. He climbed down and thrust it up the chimney. Five minutes later all five were back in place and although the last one still protruded below the lintel, when he pushed the gas fire back into position it was invisible. Zipser collapsed on to his sofa and stared at the ceiling. All that remained was to clean the soot off the plaster. He went out into the gyp room and fetched a duster and spent the next half hour pushing his desk round the room and climbing on to it to dust the ceiling. Traces of soot still remained but they were less noticeable now. He pushed the desk back into its corner and looked round the room. Apart from a noticeable smell of gas and the more intransigent stains on the ceiling there was nothing to connect him with two gross of contraceptives fraudulently obtained from the wholesalers. Zipser opened the window to clear the room of gas and went through to his bedroom and went to bed. In the eastern sky the first light of dawn was beginning to appear, but Zipser had no eyes for the beauties of nature. He fell into a restless sleep haunted by the thought that the logjam in his chimney might break during the coming day to issue with shocking ebullience above the unsuspecting College. He need not have worried. Porterhouse was already infested. The falling snow had seen to that. As each porcine sensitol-lubricated protective had emerged from the chimney stack the melting snow had ended its night flight almost abruptly. Zipser had not foreseen the dangers of icing.

*

The Dean arrived back at Porterhouse in Sir Cathcart's Rolls-Royce at two o'clock. He was spiritually restored though physically taxed by the day's excitements and Sir Cathcart's brandy. He knocked on the main gate and Skullion, who had been waiting up obediently for him, opened the postern and let him in.

'Need any help, sir?' Skullion asked as the Dean tottered through.

'Certainly not,' said the Dean thickly and set off across the Court. Skullion followed him at a distance like a good dog and saw him through the Screens before turning back to his Porter's Lodge and bed. He had already shut the door and gone through into his backroom when the Dean's strangled cry sounded from the New Court. Skullion heard nothing. He took off his collar and tie and climbed between the sheets. 'Drunk as a lord,' he thought fondly, and closed his eyes.

*

The Dean lay in the snow and cursed. He tried to imagine what he had slipped on. It certainly wasn't the snow. Snow didn't squash like that. Snow certainly didn't explode like that and even in these days of air pollution snow didn't smell of gas like that. The Dean eased himself on to a bruised hip and peered into the darkness. A strange rustling sound in which a sort of wheeze and the occasional squeak were intermingled came from all sides. The Court seemed to be alive with turgid and vaguely translucent shapes which gleamed in the starlight. The Dean reached out tentatively towards the nearest one and felt it bounce delicately away from him. He scrambled to his feet and kicked another. A ripple of rustling, squeaking, jostling shapes issued across the Court. 'That damned brandy,' muttered the Dean. He waded through the mass to the door of his staircase and stumbled upstairs. He was feeling distinctly ill. 'Must be my liver,' he thought, and slumped into a chair with the sudden resolution to leave brandy well alone in future. After a bit he got up and went to the window and looked out. Seen from above the Court looked empty, white with snow but otherwise normal. The Dean shut the window and turned back into the room. 'I could have sworn there were . . .' He tried to think just what he could have sworn the Court was filled with, but couldn't think of anything appropriate. Balloons were as near as he could get, but balloons didn't have that awful translucent ectoplasmic quality about them.

He went into his bedroom and undressed and put on his pyjamas and got into bed but sleep was impossible. He had dozed too long at Sir Cathcart's, and besides, he was haunted by his recent experience. After an hour the Dean got out of bed again and put on his dressing-gown and went downstairs. At the bottom he peered out into the Court. There was the same indelicate squeaking sound but apart from that the night was too dark to see anything clearly. The Dean stepped out into the Court and banged into one of the objects. 'They *are* there after all,' he muttered and reached down to pick whatever it was up. The thing had a soft vaguely oily feel about it and scuttled away as soon as the Dean's fingers tightened on it. He tried another and missed and it was only at the third attempt that he managed to obtain a grip. Holding the thing by its tail the Dean took it into the lighted doorway and looked at it with a growing sense of disgust and outrage. He held it head down and the thing righted itself and turned head up.

Holding it thus he went out into the Court and through the Screens to Old Court and the Porter's Lodge.

*

To Skullion, emerging sleepily from his backroom, the sight of the Dean in his dressing-gown holding the knotted end of an inflated contraceptive had about it a nightmare quality that deprived him of his limited amount of speech. He stood staring wild-eyed at the Dean while on the periphery of his vision the contraceptive wobbled obscenely.

'I have just found this in New Court, Skullion,' said the Dean, suddenly conscious that there was a certain ambiguity about his appearance.

'Oh ah,' said Skullion in the tone of one who has his private doubts. The Dean let go of the contraceptive hurriedly.

'As I was saying . . .' he began only to stop as the thing slowly began to ascend. Skullion and the Dean watched it, hypnotized. The contraceptive reached the ceiling and hovered there. Skullion lowered his eyes and stared at the Dean.

'There seem to be others of that ilk,' continued the Dean.

'Oh ah,' said Skullion.

'In the New Court,' said the Dean. 'A great many others.'

'In the New Court?' said Skullion slowly.

'Yes,' said the Dean. In the face of Skullion's evident

doubts he was beginning to feel rather heated. So was the contraceptive. The draught from the door had nudged it next to the light bulb in the ceiling and as the Dean opened his mouth to say that the New Court was alive with the things, the one above their heads touched the bulb and exploded. In fact there were three explosions. First the contraceptive blew. Then the bulb, and finally and most alarmingly of all the gas ignited. Blinded momentarily by the flash and bereft of the light of the bulb, the Dean and Skullion stood in darkness while fragments of glass and rubber descended on them.

'There are more where that one came from,' said the Dean finally, and led the way out into the night air. Skullion groped for his bowler and put it on. He reached behind the counter for his torch and followed the Dean. They passed through the Screens and Skullion shone his torch into New Court.

Huddled like so many legless animals, some two hundred contraceptives gleamed in the torchlight. A light dawn breeze had risen and with it some of the more inflated contraceptives, so that it seemed as though they were attempting to mount their less active neighbours while the whole mass seethed and rippled. One or two were to be seen nudging the windows on the first floor.

'Gawd,' said Skullion irreverently.

'I want them cleared away before it gets light, Skullion,' said the Dean. 'No one must hear about this. The College reputation, you understand.'

Tom Sharpe

'Yes, sir,' said Skullion. 'I'll clear them away. Leave it to me.'

'Good, Skullion,' said the Dean and with one last disgusted look at the obscene flock went up the stairs to his rooms.

*

Mrs Biggs had a bath. She had poured bath salts into the water and the pink suds matched the colour of her frilly shower cap. Bath night for Mrs Biggs was a special occasion. In the privacy of her bathroom she felt liberated from the constraints of commonsense. Standing on the pink bath mat surveying her reflection in the steamed-up mirror it was almost possible to imagine herself young again. Young and fancy free, and she fancied Zipser. There was no doubt about it and no doubt too that Zipser fancied her. She dried herself lovingly and put on her nightdress and went through to her bedroom. She climbed into bed and set the alarm clock for three. Mrs Biggs wanted to be up early. She had things to do.

In the early hours she left the house and cycled across Cambridge. She locked the bicycle by the Round Church and made her way on foot down Trinity Street to the side entrance of Porterhouse and let herself in with a key she had used in the old days when she had bedded for the Chaplain. She passed through the passage by the Buttery and came out by the Screens and was about to make her way across New Court when a strange sound stopped her in her tracks. She peered round the archway. In the early morning light Skullion was chasing balloons. Or something. Not chasing. Dancing seemed more like it. He ran. He leapt. He cavorted. His outstretched arms reached yearningly towards whatever it was that floated jauntily beyond his reach as if to taunt the Porter. Backwards and forwards across the ancient court the strange pursuit continued until just as it seemed the thing was about to escape over the wall into the Fellows' Garden there was a loud pop and whatever it was or had been hung limp and tatterdemalion upon the branches of a climbing rose like some late-flowering bloom. Skullion stopped, panting, and stared up at the object of his chase and then, evidently inspired by its fate, turned and hurried towards the Screens. Mrs Biggs retreated into the darkness of the Buttery passage as Skullion hurried by and then, when she could see him heading for the Porter's Lodge, emerged and tiptoed through the contraceptives to the Bull Tower. Around her feet the contraceptives squeaked and rustled. Mrs Biggs climbed the staircase to Zipser's room with a fresh sense of sexual excitement brought on by the presence of so many prophylactics. She couldn't remember when she had seen so many. Even the American airmen with whom she had been so familiar in the past had never been quite so prolific with their rubbers, and they'd been generous enough in all conscience if her memory served her aright. Mrs Biggs let herself into Zipser's room and sported the oak. She had no intention of being disturbed. She crossed to Zipser's bedroom and went inside. She switched on the bedside light.

Zipser awoke from his troubled sleep and blinked. He sat up in bed and stared at Mrs Biggs brilliant in her red coat. It was evidently morning. It didn't feel like morning but there was Mrs Biggs so it must be morning. Mrs Biggs didn't come in the middle of the night. Zipser levered himself out of bed.

'Sorry,' he mumbled groping for his dressing-gown. 'Must have overslept.' Zipser's eye caught the alarm clock. It seemed to indicate half-past three. Must have stopped.

'Shush,' said Mrs Biggs with a terrible smile. 'It's only half-past three.'

Zipser looked at the clock again. It certainly said half-past three. He tried to equate the time with Mrs Biggs' arrival and couldn't. There was something terribly wrong with the situation.

'Darling,' said Mrs Biggs, evidently sensing his dilemma. Zipser looked up at her open-mouthed. Mrs Biggs was taking off her coat. 'Don't make any noise,' she continued, with the same extraordinary smile.

'What the hell is going on?' asked Zipser. Mrs Biggs went into the other room.

'I'll be with you in a minute,' she called out in a hoarse whisper.

Zipser stood up shakily. 'What are you doing?' he asked.

There was a rustle of clothes in the other room. Even to Zipser's befuddled mind it was evident that Mrs Biggs was undressing. He went to the door and peered out into the darkness.

'For God's sake,' he said, 'you mustn't do that.'

Mrs Biggs emerged from the shadows. She had taken off her blouse. Zipser stared at her enormous brassière.

'Darling,' she said. 'Go back to bed. You mustn't stand and watch me. It's embarrassing.' She gave him a push which sent him reeling on to the bed. Then she shut the door. Zipser sat on his bed shaking. The sudden emergence of Mrs Biggs at half-past three in the morning from the shadows of his own private fantasies into a real presence terrified him. He tried to think what to do. He couldn't shout or scream for help. Nobody would believe he hadn't invited her to . . . He'd be sent down. His career would be finished. He'd be disgraced. They'd find the French letters up the chimney. Oh God. Zipser began to weep.

In the front room Mrs Biggs divested herself of her bra and panties. It was terribly cold. She went to the window to shut it when a faint popping noise from below startled her. Mrs Biggs peered out. Skullion was running round the Court with a stick. He appeared to be spearing the contraceptives. 'That'll keep him busy,' Mrs Biggs thought happily, and shut the window. Then she crossed to the gas fire and lit it. 'Nice to get dressed in the warm,' she thought, and went into the bedroom.

Zipser had got back into bed and had switched off the light.

'Wants to spare me,' Mrs Biggs thought tenderly and climbed into bed. Zipser shrank from her but Mrs Biggs had no sense of his reluctance. Grasping him in her arms she pressed him to her vast breasts. In the darkness Zipser squeaked frantically and Mrs Biggs' mouth found his. To Zipser it seemed that he was in the grip of a great white whale. He fought desperately for air, surfaced for a moment and was engulfed again.

*

Skullion, who had returned from the Porter's Lodge armed with a broom handle to which he had taped a pin, hurled himself into the shoal and struck about him with a fury that was only partially explained by having to work all night. It was rather the effrontery of the things that infuriated him. Skullion had little use for contraceptives at the best of times. Unnatural, he called them, and placed them in the lower social category of things along with elastic-sided boots and made-up bow ties. Not the sort of attire for a gentleman. But even more than their humble origins, he was infuriated by the insult to Porterhouse that the presence of so great and so inflated a number represented. The Dean's admonition that news of the infestation must not leak out was wasted on Skullion. He needed no telling. 'We'd be the laughing-stock of the University,' he thought, lancing a particularly large one. By the time dawn broke over Cambridge Skullion had cleared New Court. One or two had escaped into the Fellows' Garden and he went through the archway in the wall and began spiking the remainder. Behind him the Court was littered with tattered latex, almost invisible against the snow. 'I'll wait until it's a bit lighter to pick them up,' he muttered. 'Can't see them now.' He had just run a small but agile one to earth in the rose garden when a full rumbling noise at the top of the Tower made him turn and look up. Something was going on in the old chimney. The chimney pot at the top was shaking. The brickwork silhouetted against the morning sky appeared to be bulging. The rumbling stopped, to be succeeded by an almighty roar as a ball of flame issued from the chimney and billowed out before ascending above the College. Below it the chimney toppled sideways, crashed on to the roof of the Tower and with a gradually increasing rumble of masonry the fourteenth-century building lost its entire façade. Behind it the rooms were clearly visible, their floors tilted horribly and sagging. Skullion stood mesmerized by the spectacle. A bed on the first floor slid sideways and dropped on to the masonry below. Desks and chairs followed suit. There were shouts and screams. People poured out of doorways and windows opened all round the Court. Skullion ignored the screams for help. He was busy chasing the last few remaining contraceptives when the Master, clad in his dressing-gown, emerged from the Master's Lodge and hurried to the scene of the disaster. As he rushed across the garden he found Skullion trying to spear a contraceptive floating in the fishpond.

'Go and open the main gates,' the Master shouted at him.

'Not yet,' said Skullion taciturnly.

'What do you mean, not yet?' the Master demanded. 'The ambulance men and the fire brigade will want to get in.'

'Not having any strangers in College till I've cleared these things up. Wouldn't be right,' said Skullion.

The Master stared at the floating contraceptive furiously. Skullion's obstinacy enraged him. 'There are injured people in there,' he screamed.

'So there are,' said Skullion, 'but there's the College reputation to be thought of too.' He leant across the pond and burst the floating bubble. Sir Godber turned and ran on to the scene of the accident. Skullion turned and followed him slowly. 'Got no sense of tradition,' he said sadly, and shook his head.

10

'These sweetbreads are delicious,' said the Dean at dinner. 'The coroner's inquest has given me a considerable appetite.'

'Very tactfully handled,' said the Senior Tutor. 'I must admit I had anticipated a less magnanimous verdict. As it is, suicide never hurt anyone.'

'Suicide?' shouted the Chaplain. 'Did I hear someone say suicide?' He looked up expectantly. 'Now there's a topic we could well consider.'

'The Coroner has already done so at some length, Chaplain,' the Bursar bawled in his ear.

'Very good of him too,' said the Chaplain.

'The Senior Tutor has just made that point,' the Bursar explained.

'Has he now? Very interesting,' said the Chaplain, 'and about time too. Haven't had a decent suicide in College for some years now. Most regrettable.'

'I must say I can't see why the decline of the fashion should be so regrettable, Chaplain,' said the Bursar.

'I think I'll have a second helping of sweetbreads,' said the Dean.

The Chaplain leant back in his chair and looked at them over his glasses. 'In the old days hardly a week went by without some poor fellow taking the easy way out. When I first came here as Chaplain I used to spend half my time attending inquests. Come to think of it, there was a time when we were known as the Slaughterhouse.'

'Things have changed for the better since then,' said the Bursar.

'Nonsense,' said the Chaplain. 'The fall in the number of suicides is the clearest indication of the decline of morality. Undergraduates don't seem to be as conscience-stricken as they were in my young days.'

'You don't think it has to do with the introduction of natural gas?' asked the Senior Tutor.

'Natural gas? No such thing,' said the Dean. 'I agree with the Chaplain. Things have gone to pot.'

'Pot,' shouted the Chaplain. 'Did I hear somebody say pot?'

'I was merely saying . . .' began the Dean.

'At least nobody has suggested that young Zipser was on drugs,' interrupted the Bursar. 'The police made a very thorough investigation, you know, and they found nothing.'

The Dean raised his eyebrows. 'Nothing?' he asked. 'To the best of my knowledge they took away an entire sackful of . . . er . . . contraceptives.'

'I was talking of drugs, Dean. There was the question of motive, you understand. The police seemed to think Zipser was in the grip of an irrational impulse.'

'From what I heard he was in the grip of Mrs Biggs,'

said the Senior Tutor. 'I suppose you can call Mrs Biggs an irrational impulse. Certainly a very tasteless one. And as for the other things, I must admit I find a predilection for gas-filled contraceptives quite unaccountable.'

'According to the police, there were two hundred and fifty,' said the Bursar.

'No accounting for tastes,' said the Dean, 'though for my part I prefer . . . to regard the whole deplorable affair as being politically motivated. This fellow Zipser was clearly an anarchist. He had a lot of left-wing literature in his rooms.'

'I understood him to be doing research into pumpernickel,' said the Bursar. 'Its origins in sixteenth-century Germany.'

'He also belonged to a number of subversive societies,' the Dean continued.

'I'd hardly call the United Nations Association subversive, Dean,' the Bursar protested.

'I would,' said the Dean. 'All political societies are subversive. Must be. Stands to reason. Wouldn't exist if they weren't trying to subvert something or other.'

'Certainly a most extraordinary way of going about things,' said the Bursar. 'And it still doesn't explain the presence of Mrs Biggs.'

'I'm inclined to agree with the Dean,' said the Senior Tutor. 'Anyone who could go to bed with Mrs Biggs must have been either demented or motivated by a grossly distorted sense of social duty and to have launched two hundred and fifty lethal contraceptives on an unsuspecting world argues a fanaticism . . .'

'On the other hand,' said the Bursar, 'he had been to see you about his . . . er . . . compulsion for the good woman. You mentioned it at the time.'

'Yes, well, perhaps he did,' the Senior Tutor admitted, 'though I'd question your use of good as far as Mrs Biggs was concerned. In any case, I sent him on to the Chaplain.'

They looked at the Chaplain questioningly. 'Mrs Biggs good?' shouted the Chaplain. 'I should say so. Splendid woman.'

'We were wondering if Zipser gave you any hint as to his motives,' the Bursar explained.

'Motives?' said the Chaplain. 'Perfectly obvious. Good old-fashioned lust.'

'That hardly explains the explosive nature of his end,' said the Senior Tutor.

'You can't put new wine in old bottles,' said the Chaplain.

The Dean shook his head. 'Whatever his motives,' he said, 'Zipser has certainly made our own position extremely awkward. It is difficult to argue against the need for change when members of the College make such an exhibition of themselves. The meeting of the Porterhouse Society has been cancelled.'

The Fellows looked at him in amazement.

'But I understand the General had agreed to call it,'

said the Senior Tutor. 'He's surely not backing down now.'

'Cathcart has proved himself a broken reed,' said the Dean mournfully. 'He phoned me this morning to say that he thought we should wait until this whole affair had blown over. An unfortunate phrase but one sees his point. The College can hardly afford another scandal just yet.'

'Damn Zipser,' said the Senior Tutor. The Fellows finished their dinner in silence.

*

In the Master's Lodge Sir Godber and Lady Mary mourned the passing of Zipser more austerely over scrambled eggs. As was ever the case, tragedy had lent Lady Mary a fresh vitality, and the strange circumstances of Zipser's end had given a fillip to her interest in psychology.

'The poor boy must have had a fetish,' she said, peeling a banana with a dispassionate interest that reminded Sir Godber of his honeymoon. 'Just like that case of the boy who was found inside a plastic bag in the lavatory on a railway train.'

'Seems an odd place to be,' said Sir Godber, helping himself to some tinned raspberries.

'Of course, that was a much clearer case of the mother complex at work,' continued Lady Mary. 'The plastic bag was obviously a substitute placenta.'

Sir Godber pushed his plate away. 'I suppose you're going to tell me that filling contraceptives with gas is a sure indication that the poor fellow had penis envy,' he said.

'Boys don't have penis envy, Godber,' said Lady Mary austerely. 'That's a girls' complaint.'

'Is it? Well, perhaps the bedder suffered from it, then. I mean there's no indication that Zipser was actually responsible for stuffing them up the chimney. We know that he obtained the things, but for all we know Mrs Biggs filled them with gas and put them up the chimney.'

'And that's another thing,' Lady Mary said. 'The Dean's remarks about Mrs Biggs were in the worst of taste. He seemed to find the fact that the boy was having an affair with his bedder proof that Zipser was insane. A more glaring example of class prejudice it would be hard to imagine, but then I've always thought the Dean was a singularly common little man.'

Sir Godber looked at his wife with open admiration. The illogicality of her attitudes never ceased to amaze him. Lady Mary's egalitarianism stemmed from a sense of innate superiority which not even her marriage to Sir Godber had diminished. There were times when he wondered if her acceptance of his proposal had not been yet another political decision, a demonstration of her liberal pretensions. He brushed aside this domestic reverie and thought about the consequences of Zipser's death.

'It's going to be very difficult to quell the Dean now,'

he said thoughtfully. 'He's already maintaining that this whole affair is a result of sexual permissiveness.'

Lady Mary snorted. 'Absolute nonsense,' she snapped predictably. 'If there had been women in College this thing would never have happened.'

'In the Dean's view, it was precisely the presence of Mrs Biggs in Zipser's rooms that caused the disaster,' Sir Godber pointed out.

'The Dean,' said Lady Mary with feeling, 'is a male chauvinist pig. A sensible policy of coeducation would avoid the sexual repressions that result in fetishism. You must make the point at the next Council meeting.'

'My dear,' said Sir Godber wearily, 'you don't seem to understand the difficulty I am in. I can hardly resign the Mastership now. It would look as if I was admitting some responsibility for what has happened. As it is my time is going to be taken up raising money for the Restoration Fund. It's going to cost a quarter of a million to repair the Tower.'

Lady Mary regarded him sternly. 'Godber,' she said, 'you must not weaken now. You must not compromise your principles. You must stick to your guns.'

'Guns, my dear?'

'Guns, Godber, guns.'

Sir Godber raised his eyebrows doubtfully. What guns he had had, and, in the light of Lady Mary's pacifism, he doubted if the metaphor was morally appropriate, appeared to have been effectively spiked by Zipser's tragic act.

'I really can't see what I can do,' he said finally.

'Well, in the first place, you can see that contraceptives are freely available in the College.'

'I can what?' shouted Sir Godber.

'You heard me,' snapped his wife. 'King's College has a dispenser in the lavatory. So do some of the other colleges. It seems a most wholesome precaution.'

The Master shuddered. 'King's has them, eh? Well I daresay it needs them. The place is a hotbed of homosexuality.'

'Godber,' said Lady Mary warningly. Sir Godber stopped short. He knew Lady Mary's views on homosexuals. She held them in the same sort of esteem as foxes, and her views on foxhunting were intemperate to say the least.

'All I meant was that King's have them for a purpose,' he said.

'I hardly imagine that . . .' Lady Mary began when the French au pair girl brought in coffee.

'As I was saying . . .'

'Pas devant les domestiques,' said his wife.

'Oh quite,' said Sir Godber hastily. 'All I meant was that they have them pour encourager les autres.'

The girl went out and Lady Mary poured coffee.

'What others?' she asked.

'Others?' said Sir Godber, who by this time had lost the thread of the conversation.

'You were saying that King's had installed a dispenser to encourage the others.'

'Precisely. I know how you feel about homosexuality, my dear, but one can have enough of a good thing,' he explained.

'Godber, you are prevaricating,' said Lady Mary firmly. 'I insist that for once in your life you do what you say you're going to do. When I married you, you were filled with splendid ideals. Now when I look at you, I sometimes wonder what happened to the man I married.'

'My dear, you seem to forget that I have spent a lifetime in politics,' Sir Godber protested. 'One learns to compromise. It's a depressing fact but there it is. Call it the death of idealism if you will, at least it saves a lot of people's lives.' He took his coffee cup and went through to his study and sat morosely by the fire and wondered at his own pusillanimity.

He could remember a time when he had shared his wife's enthusiasm for social justice, but time had dimmed . . . or rather since Lady Mary remained vigorous over the years, not time itself but something had dimmed his zeal – if zeal could be dimmed. Sir Godber wondered about it and was struck by his preoccupation with the question. If not time then what? The intractability of human nature. The sheer inertia of Englishmen for whom the past was always sacred and inviolable and who prided themselves on their obstinacy. 'We didn't win the war,' thought Sir Godber, 'we just refused to lose it.' Stirred to a new belligerency, he reached for the poker and poked the fire angrily and watched the sparks fly upwards into the darkness. He was damned if he was going to be put upon by the Dean. He hadn't spent a lifetime in high office to be frustrated by an ageing academic with a taste for port. He got up and poured himself a stiff whisky and paced the room. Lady Mary was right. A dispenser would be a move in the right direction. He'd speak to the Bursar in the morning. He glanced out of the window towards the Bursar's rooms and saw the lights burning. It wasn't late. He'd pay him a social call now. He finished his drink and went out into the hall and put on his overcoat.

*

The Bursar lived out. He dined in College as frequently as possible, thanks to his wife's cooking, and it was only by chance that he had stayed on in his rooms after dinner. He had things to think about. The Dean's pessimism, for one thing, and his failure to solicit the help of Sir Cathcart. It might be as well, he thought, to consider transferring his tenuous loyalties to Sir Godber after all. The Master had already shown himself to be a man of some determination – the Bursar had not forgotten his ultimatum to the College Council – and properly handled might well reward him for services rendered. After all it had been the Bursar who had given him the information which Sir Godber had used to browbeat the Council. It was worth considering. He got up to put on his coat and go home when footsteps on the stairs suggested a late caller. The Bursar sat down at his desk again and pretended business. There was a knock on the door.

'Come in,' said the Bursar. Sir Godber peered round the door.

'Ah, Bursar,' he said. 'I hope I'm not disturbing you. I was crossing the Court when I saw your light and I thought I would pop up.'

The Bursar rose to greet him with warm obsequiousness. 'How good of you to come, Master,' he said, hurrying to take Sir Godber's coat. 'I was about to drop you a line asking if I could see you.'

'In that case, I am delighted to have saved you the trouble,' said Sir Godber.

'Do take a seat.' Sir Godber sat in an armchair by the fire and smiled genially. The warmth of the Bursar's welcome and the atmosphere of indigence in the furnishings of his rooms were to his taste. He looked round approvingly at the worn carpet and the second-rate prints on the walls, from an almanac by the look of them, and felt the broken spring in the chair beneath him. Sir Godber recognized the importunity of it all. His years in office had given him a nose for dependency, and Sir Godber was not a man to withhold favours.

'Would you care for a little something?' the Bursar asked, hovering uncertainly near a decanter of indifferent port. Sir Godber hesitated a moment. Port on top of whisky? He thrust the considerations of his liver aside in favour of policy.

'Just a small glass, thank you,' he said, taking out his

pipe and filling it from a worn pouch. Sir Godber was not an habitual pipe smoker; he found it burnt his tongue, but he had learnt the value of the common touch.

'A bad business about poor Zipser,' said the Bursar, bringing the port. 'It's going to be a costly business restoring the Tower.'

Sir Godber lit his lip. 'One of the topics I wanted to consult you about, Bursar. We'll have to set up a Restoration Fund, I imagine.'

'I'm afraid so, Master,' the Bursar said sadly.

Sir Godber sipped his port. 'In the ordinary way,' he said, 'and if the College were only less . . . er shall we say . . . less antiquated in its attitudes, I daresay I could use my influence in the City to raise a substantial sum, but as it is I find myself in an ambiguous position.' He trailed off airily, leaving the Bursar with a sense of infinite financial connections. 'No, we shall simply have to fall back on our own resources.'

'We have so few,' said the Bursar.

'We shall have to make what use we can of them,' Sir Godber continued, 'until such time as the College decides to give itself a more contemporary image. I'll do what I can of course, but I'm afraid it will be an uphill battle. If only the Council would see the importance of change.' He smiled and looked at the Bursar. 'But then I daresay you agree with the Dean?'

It was the moment the Bursar had been waiting for.

'The Dean has his own views, Master,' he said, 'and they are not ones I share.'

Sir Godber's eyebrows expressed encouragement with reservations.

'I have always felt that we were falling behind the times,' continued the Bursar, anxious to win the full approval of those eyebrows, 'but as Bursar I have been concerned with administration and it does tend to leave little time for policy. The Dean's influence is quite remarkable, you know, and of course there is Sir Cathcart.'

'I gather Sir Cathcart intends to call a meeting of the Porterhouse Society,' said Sir Godber.

'He's cancelled it since the Zipser affair,' the Bursar told him.

'That's interesting. So the Dean is on his own, is he?'

The Bursar nodded. 'I think some of the Council have had second thoughts too. The younger Fellows would like to see changes, but they don't carry much weight. So few of them too, but then we've never been noted for our Research Fellowships. We have neither the money nor the reputation to attract them. I have suggested . . . but the Dean . . .' He waved his hands helplessly.

Sir Godber gulped his port. In spite of it he was glad he had come. The Bursar's change of tune was encouraging and Sir Godber was satisfied. It was time to talk frankly. He knocked out his pipe and leant forward.

'Between ourselves I think we can circumvent the Dean,' he said, tapping the Bursar on the knee with a forefinger with a vulgar assurance. 'You mark my words. We'll have him where we want him.'

The Bursar stared at Sir Godber in startled fascination. The man's crudity, the change from an assumed urbanity to this backstair forcefulness took him by surprise, and Sir Godber noted his astonishment with satisfaction. The years of calling working men whom he despised 'Brother' had not been wasted. There was no doubting the menace in his grim bonhomie. 'He won't know his arse from his elbow by the time we've finished with him,' he continued. The Bursar nodded meekly. Sir Godber hitched his chair forward and began to outline his plans.

*

Skullion stood in the Court and wondered at the lights burning in the Bursar's room.

'He's staying late,' he thought. 'Usually home by nine, he is.' He walked through to the back gate and locked it, glancing hopefully at the spiked wall as he did so. Then he turned and made his way through the Fellows' Garden to New Court. He walked slowly and with a slight limp. The exertions of the chase had left him stiff and aching and he had still not recovered from the shock of the explosion in the Tower. 'Getting old,' he muttered and stopped to light his pipe, and as he stood in the shadow of a large elm the light in the

Bursar's room went out. Skullion sucked at his pipe thoughtfully and tamped the tobacco down with his thumb. He was about to leave the shelter of the elm when a crunch of gravel on the path caused him to hesitate. Two figures had emerged from New Court and were coming towards him deep in conversation. Skullion recognized the Master's voice. He moved back into the shadows and the two figures passed him.

'No doubt the Dean will object,' Sir Godber was saying, 'but faced with a *fait accompli* there won't be anything he can do about it. I think we can take it that the days of the Dean's influence are numbered.'

'Not before time,' said the Bursar. The two figures disappeared round the side of the Master's Lodge. Skullion emerged from the shadow and stood on the path peering after them, his mind furiously occupied. So the Bursar had gone over to Sir Godber. Skullion wasn't surprised. He had never had much time for the Bursar. The man wasn't out of the top drawer for one thing and for another he was responsible for the wages of the College servants. Skullion regarded him more as a foreman than a genuine Fellow, a paymaster, and a mean one at that, and held him responsible for the pittance he received. And now the Bursar had gone over to Sir Godber. Skullion turned and made his way into New Court with a fresh sense of grievance and some perplexity. The Dean should be told but Skullion knew better than to tell him. The Dean didn't approve of eavesdropping. He was a proper gentleman. Skullion wondered what a fate accomplee was. He'd have to think of some way of warning the Dean in the morning. He went through the Screens and across to the Porter's Lodge and made himself some cocoa. 'So the Dean's days are numbered, are they?' he thought bitterly. 'We'll see about that.' It would take more than Sir Godber Evans and the miserable Bursar to change things. There was always Sir Cathcart. He'd see they didn't get their way. He had great faith in Sir Cathcart. At midnight he got up and went outside to close the front gate. During the day the thaw had set in and the snow had begun to melt but the wind had changed during the evening and it had begun to freeze again. Skullion stood in the doorway for a moment and stared out into the street. A middle-aged man slipped on the pavement outside and fell. Skullion regarded his fall without interest. What happened outside Porterhouse was none of his affair. With a sudden wish that the Master would slip and break his neck, Skullion went back into the College and shut the door. Above him in the Tower the clock struck twelve.

11

On the towpath by the river the Dean stood huddled
in his overcoat against the wind. Behind him the
willows shuddered and shook and the hedgerow rustled.
In front the eights rowed through choppy water, each
with its coterie of coaches and supporters splashing
through the puddles on their bicycles and shouting
orders and encouragement. On every stroke the coxes
jerked backwards and the boats leapt forwards, each in
pursuit of the eight ahead and each in turn in flight
from the eight behind. Occasionally a sudden burst of
cheering signalled a bump as one eight touched the
boat in front and the two pulled into the side of the
river and the victors broke off a willow branch and
stuck it into the bow. There were gaps in the procession
where bumps had been achieved, spaces of empty water
and then another eight would appear round the bend
still trying desperately to catch the boat at least two
lengths ahead and overbump. Jesus. Porterhouse. Lady
Margaret. Pembroke. Trinity. St Catherine's. Christ's.
Churchill. Magdalene. Caius. Clare. Peterhouse. His-
toric names, hallowed names like so many prayers on a
rosary of racing boats to be repeated twice yearly at
Lent and after Easter. To the Dean the ritual was holy,

a sacred occasion to be attended, no matter how cold or wet the weather, in memory of the healthy athleticism of the past and the certainties of his youth . . . The Bumps were a time of renewal for him. Standing on the towpath he felt once more the innocence, the unquestioning innocence of his own rowing days and the fitness of things then. Yes, fitness, a fitness not simply of body, or even of mind, but of things in general, an acceptance of life as it was without the insidious subversion of questions or the dangerous speculations which had gained momentum since. A guiltless time, that, a golden age of assurance before the Great War when there was honey still for tea and a servant to bring it too. In memory of that time the Dean braved the wind and the cold and stood on the towpath while the bicycles splashed mud on to his shoes and the eights rowed by. When it was all over he turned and trudged back to the Pike and Eel where his car was parked. Behind him and in front, strung out along the path, old men like himself turned up the collars of their overcoats and headed home, their heads bent against the wind but with a new sprightliness in their step. The Dean had reached the railway bridge when he was aware of a familiar figure in front. 'Afternoon, Skullion. We rowed over again,' he said. Skullion nodded. 'Jesus never looked like catching us,' the Dean said, 'and we should bump Trinity tomorrow. It was the choppy water that stopped us today.'

They walked on in silence while the Dean recalled

other Bumps and famous crews and Skullion tried to
think of some way of broaching the subject of the
Bursar's treachery without offending the Dean's sense
of what was proper for College servants to say. It wasn't
easy even to walk beside the Dean. Not his place, and
presently Skullion gave up the unequal struggle with
his conscience and gradually fell back a pace or two
behind the old man. At the Pike and Eel the Dean, still
lost in thought, unlocked his car and climbed in.
Skullion fetched his bicycle and wheeled it across the
footbridge. Behind him the Dean sat in his car and
waited for the traffic to clear. He had forgotten Skullion. He had forgotten even the Bumps and the youth
they had recalled to him. He was thinking about Sir
Godber and the glibness of his modernity and the threat
to Porterhouse he represented. His feet were cold and
the joints in his knees ached. He was an old man, bitter
at the loss of his power. When the last of the other cars
had gone he started the engine and drove home through
the factory workers coming out of Pye's television
factory. Cars pulled out of the factory gates in front of
him. Men on bicycles ignored him and girls ran across
the road to catch their buses. The Dean eyed them
angrily. In the old days he would have blown his horn
and cleared them off the road. Now he had to sit and
wait. He found himself staring at an advertisement.
'Watch with Carrington on Pye', it said and a face
smiled at him from a television screen. A familiar face.
A face he knew. 'Carrington on Conservation. The

Nation's Heritage at Stake.' The Dean stared at the face and was suddenly conscious of new hope. Behind him someone hooted importunately and the Dean put his car in gear and moved forward. He drove steadily home, unaware now of the traffic and of the present.

He left his car in the garage behind Phipps Building and went up to his room and presently he was sitting at his desk checking the Porterhouse Register for Cornelius Carrington's name. There it was, 1935–8. The Dean closed the book and sat back contentedly. A nasty piece of work, Cornelius Carrington, but effective for all that. The Jeremiah of the BBC, they called him, and certainly his romantic Toryism was popular. Not even politically divisive, just good-hearted nostalgia for the best that was British and with immense family appeal. The Dean did not often watch television but he had heard of Cornelius Carrington's programmes. 'Jewels of the Empire' had been one such series, with the ubiquitous Carrington expatiating on the architectural treasures of Poona and Lucknow. Another programme had been devoted to the need to preserve the rum ration in the Royal Navy, and Carrington had made himself the spokesman for past privileges wherever they were threatened. He was, the Dean felt sure, capable of extolling the virtues of any subject you chose and certainly there was no doubting the effectiveness of his appearance. Elicit Cornelius Carrington's interest and you were sure of an audience. And the wretched fellow was a Porterhouse man. The Dean smiled to himself at the thought of Carrington's publicizing the threat that Sir Godber's innovations posed to the College. It was a nice thought. He would have to speak to Sir Cathcart about it. It would depend on the outcome of the College Council meeting in the morning.

*

Skullion was at his waterpipe in the boiler-room when the meeting began. With the usual interruptions from the central heating system he could hear much of what was said. Most of the discussion centred on the cost of repairing the damage done to the Tower by Zipser's experiment in the mass disposal of prophylactics. Sir Godber, it seemed, had very definite views on the subject.

'It is time,' he was saying, 'that the College recognized the need to act in accordance with the principles which appear to have motivated the members of this Council in the past. The changes which I proposed at our last meeting met with opposition on the grounds that Porterhouse is a self-sufficient and independent college, a self-governing body whose interests are internal and without reference to the world at large. For myself as you know, that view is without foundation, but I am prepared to accept it since it appears to represent the views of the majority of this Council.' The Master paused, evidently looking round the Fellows for approval. In the boiler-room Skullion tried to digest the import of his words without much success. It seemed too much to hope that Sir Godber had changed his mind.

'Are we to understand that you have conceded that there is no need for the changes you proposed at our last meeting?' the Dean asked.

'The point I am conceding, Dean,' continued the Master, 'is that the College is responsible for its own internal affairs. I am prepared to accept the views of the Council that we should not look for guidance or assistance from the public.'

'I should certainly hope not,' said the Senior Tutor fervently.

'That is all I am conceding and since that is the case the full responsibility for the recent tragic events must be borne by the College. In particular the cost of the repairs to the Tower must be met out of our own resources.'

A murmur of astonishment greeted the Master's statement.

'Impossible,' said the Dean angrily, 'out of the question. In the past we have had recourse to a Restoration Fund. There seems to be no good reason why we should not set up such a fund in this case.'

In the boiler-room Skullion followed the argument with difficulty. The Master's tactics evaded him.

'I must say, Dean, that I find your attitude a little difficult to understand,' Sir Godber continued. 'On the one hand you are opposed to any changes that would bring Porterhouse into line with contemporary stan-

dards of education . . .' There was an angry interjection
from the Dean. '. . . and on the other you seem only
too ready to appeal to public subscription to avoid the
necessary economies required to rebuild the Tower . . .'
At this point the central heating system interjected and
it was some time before Skullion could catch the drift
of the discussion again. By then they had got on to the
details of the economies Sir Godber had in mind. Not
surprisingly they seemed to embody just those changes
in College policy he had suggested at the previous
meeting but this time the Master was arguing less from
policy than from financial necessity.

Through the gurgles in the pipe Skullion caught the
words 'Self-service system in Hall . . . coeducation . . .
and the sale of College properties.' He was about to
climb down from his perch when Rhyder Street was
mentioned. Skullion lived in Rhyder Street. Rhyder
Street was College property. In the boiler-room Skullion's interest in the proceedings taking place above his
head took on a new and more personal touch.

'The Bursar and I have calculated that the cost of the
repairs can be met by the economies I have outlined,'
Skullion heard. 'The sale of Rhyder Street in particular
will provide something in the region of £150,000 at
today's inflated prices. It is slum property, I know, but
. . .' Skullion slid down the pipe and sat on the chair.
Slum property, he called it. Rhyder Street where he
lived in Number 41. Slum property. The Chef lived
there too. The street was filled with the houses of

College servants. They couldn't sell it. They'd got no right to. A new fury possessed Skullion, a bitterness against Sir Godber that was no longer a concern for the traditions of the College he had served so long but a sense of personal betrayal. He'd been going to retire to Rhyder Street. It had been one of the conditions of his employment. The College had provided a house at a nominal rent. Skullion hadn't worked for forty-five years at a pittance a week to be evicted from a house that had been sold over his head by Sir Godber. Without waiting to hear more he got up from the chair and lurched out of the boiler-room into the Old Court in search of the Chef. Above his head a new violence of debate had broken out in the Council Chamber. Sir Godber had announced the proposed installation of a contraceptive dispenser.

*

The Dean erupted from the meeting with a virulence that stemmed from the knowledge that he had been outmanoeuvred. The Master's appeal to principle had placed him in a false position and the Dean was conscious that his arguments against the Master's proposed economies had lacked the force of conviction. 'To cap it all,' he muttered to himself as he swept from the room, 'a damned contraceptive machine.' The Bursar's sudden change of allegiance had infuriated him too. With his support Sir Godber could manipulate the College finances as he pleased, and the Dean cursed the

Bursar viciously as he climbed the stairs to his room. There remained only Sir Cathcart and already he had shown himself pusillanimous in the matter of calling a meeting of the Porterhouse Society. Well, there were others who could be relied on to bring influence to bear. 'I'll see Sir Cathcart this afternoon,' he decided, and poured himself a glass of sherry.

*

Sir Godber left the meeting with the Bursar. He was feeling distinctly pleased with his morning's work.

'Why don't you lunch with us at the Lodge?' he said with a sudden generosity. 'My wife has been asking to meet you.'

'That's very kind of you,' said the Bursar, glad to escape the hostile reception he was likely to meet at High Table. They strolled across the lawn past a group of Fellows who were conferring at the entrance to the Combination Room. In the Screens they saw Skullion scowling darkly in the shadows.

'I must say I find Skullion's manner a trifle taciturn,' Sir Godber said when they were out of earshot. 'Even as an undergraduate I found him unpleasant to deal with, and age hasn't improved his manners.'

The Bursar sympathized with Sir Godber. 'Not a very likeable fellow but he's very conscientious and he is a great favourite of the Dean.'

'I can imagine that they get on well together,' said Sir Godber. 'All the same, Porterhouse may be the name of the College but it doesn't mean that the Head Porter is in charge. On the night of the ... er ... accident Skullion was distinctly disrespectful. I told him to open the main gates for the ambulancemen and he refused. One of these days I daresay I shall have to ask you to give him notice.'

The Bursar blanched at the thought. 'I think that would be most inadvisable, Master,' he said. 'The Dean would be most upset.'

'Well,' said Sir Godber, 'the next time I have any insolence from him out he goes and no mistake.' With the silent thought that it was time such relics of the past got their marching orders, the Master led the way into the Lodge.

Lady Mary was waiting in the drawing-room. 'I've asked the Bursar to lunch, my dear,' said Sir Godber, his voice a shade less authoritative in the presence of his wife.

'I'm afraid you'll just have to take pot luck,' Lady Mary told the Bursar. 'My husband tells me that you treat yourselves lavishly at High Table.'

The Bursar simpered apologetically. Lady Mary ignored these signs of submission. 'I find it quite deplorable that so much good money should be wasted on maintaining the ill-health of a number of elderly scholars.'

'My dear,' Sir Godber intervened, 'you'll be glad to hear that the Council has accepted our proposals.'

'And not before time,' said Lady Mary, studying the Bursar with distaste. 'One of the most astonishing things about the educational institutions of this country is the way they have resisted change. When I think how long we've been urging the abolition of private education I'm amazed. The public schools seem to go from strength to strength.'

To the Bursar, himself the product of a minor public school on the South Downs, Lady Mary's words verged on the blasphemous. 'You're surely not suggesting public schools should be abolished,' he said. From the table where Sir Godber was pouring sherry there came the sound of rattled glass. Lady Mary assumed a new hauteur.

'Am I to infer from that remark that you are in favour of private education?' she asked.

The Bursar groped for a conciliatory reply. 'Well, I think there is something to be said for it,' he mumbled finally.

'What?' asked Lady Mary.

But before the Bursar could think of anything to recommend the public school system without offending his hostess, Sir Godber had come to his rescue with a glass of sherry. 'Very good of you, Master,' he said gratefully and sipped his drink. 'And a very pleasant sherry, if I may say so.'

'We don't drink South African sherry,' Lady Mary said. 'I hope the College doesn't keep any in stock.'

'I believe we have some for the undergraduates,' said the Bursar, 'but I know the Senior Members don't touch the stuff.'

'Quite right too,' said Sir Godber.

'I was not thinking of the question of taste,' Lady Mary continued, 'so much as the moral objections to buying South African products. I have always made a point of boycotting South African goods.'

To the Bursar, long accustomed to the political opinions expressed at High Table by the Dean and the Senior Tutor, Lady Mary's views were radical in the extreme and the fact that they were expressed in a tone of voice which suggested that she was addressing a congregation of unmarried mothers unnerved him. He stumbled through the thorny problems of world poverty, the population explosion, abortion, the Nicaraguan earthquake, strategic arms limitation talks, and prison reform until a gong sounded and they went into lunch. Over a sardine salad that would have served as an *hors d'oeuvre* in Hall his discomfiture took a more personal turn.

'You're not by any chance related to the Shropshire Shrimptons?' Lady Mary asked.

The Bursar shook his head sorrowfully.

'My family came originally from Southend,' he said.

'How very unusual,' said Lady Mary. 'I only asked because we used to stay with them at Bognorth before the war. Sue Shrimpton was up with me at Somerville and we served together on the Needham Commission.'

The Bursar acknowledged Lady Mary's social distinction in silence. He would put his present humiliation to good use in the future. At sherry parties for years to come he would be able to say 'Lady Mary was saying to me only the other day . . .' or 'Lady Mary and I . . .' and establish his own superiority over lesser men and their wives. It was in such small achievements that the Bursar's satisfactions were found. Sir Godber ate his sardines in silence too. He was grateful to the Bursar for providing a target for his wife's conversation and moral rectitude. He dreaded to think what would happen if the injustices on which Lady Mary vented her moral spleen ever disappeared. 'The poor are always with us, thank God,' he thought and helped himself to a piece of Cheddar.

*

It was left to Skullion to represent the College on the towpath that afternoon. The Dean had driven over to Coft to see Sir Cathcart and Skullion stood alone in the biting wind watching Porterhouse row over for the second day running. The terrible sense of wrong that he had felt in the boiler-room when he heard the proposed sale of Rhyder Street had not left him. It had been augmented by the news Arthur had brought him from High Table after lunch.

'He's put the cat among the pigeons now, the Master has,' Arthur said breathlessly. 'He's got under their skin something terrible this time.'

'I don't wonder,' said Skullion, thinking bitterly of Rhyder Street.

'I mean you wouldn't want one in your own home, would you? Not one of them things.'

'What things?' Skullion asked, all too conscious of the fact that he was unlikely to have a home to put anything in if Sir Godber had his way.

'Well I don't rightly know what they're called,' Arthur said. 'Not exactly, that is. You put your money in and . . .'

'And what?' Skullion asked irritably.

'And you get these things out. Three I think. Not that I've ever had occasion to use them.'

'What things?'

'Frenchies,' said Arthur, looking round to make sure no one was listening.

'Frenchies?' said Skullion. 'What Frenchies?'

'The Frenchies that Zipser gentleman exploded himself with,' Arthur explained. Skullion looked at him in disgust. 'You mean to tell me they're going to bring one of those filthy things into the College?'

Arthur nodded. 'In the men's toilet. That's where it's going.'

'Over my dead body,' said Skullion. 'I'm not staying here as Head Porter with one of those things in the toilet. This isn't a bloody chemist's shop.'

'Some of the other colleges have them,' Arthur told him.

'Some of the other colleges may have them. Doesn't mean we've got to. It isn't right. Encourages immorality, French letters do. You'd have thought they'd have learnt that from what happened to that Zipser bloke. Preyed on his mind, all those FLs did.'

Arthur shook his head sorrowfully. ''Tisn't right,' he said, ''tisn't right, Mr Skullion. I don't know what the College is coming to. Senior Tutor is particularly upset. He says it will affect the rowing.'

Standing on the towpath Skullion agreed with the Senior Tutor. 'All this business about sex,' he muttered. 'It doesn't do anybody any good. It isn't right.'

When the Porterhouse VIII rowed past Skullion raised a feeble cheer and then stumped off after them. Around him bicycles churned the muddy puddles as they overtook him but, like the Dean the day before, Skullion was lost in thought and bitterness.

His anger, unlike the Dean's, was tainted with a sense of betrayal. The College whose servant he was and his ancestors before him had let him down. They had no right to let Sir Godber sell Rhyder Street. They should have stopped him. That was their duty to him, just as his duty to the College had been for forty-five years to sit in the Porter's Lodge all day and half the night for a miserable pittance a week, the guardian of privilege and of the indiscretions of the privileged young. How many drunken young gentlemen had Skullion helped to their rooms? How many secrets had he kept? How many insults had he suffered in his time? He could not begin to recall them but in the back of his mind the debits had balanced the credits and he had been secure in the knowledge that the College would always look after him now and in his old age. He had been proud of his servility, the Porter of Porterhouse, but what if the College's reputation was debased? What would he be then? A homeless old man with his memories. He wasn't having it. They'd got to see him right. It was their duty.

12

In the library at Coft Castle, the Dean put the same point to Sir Cathcart.

'It's our duty to see these damnable innovations are stopped,' he said. 'The man seems intent on changing the entire character of the College. For years, damn it for centuries, we've been famous for our kitchens and now he's proposing a self-service canteen and a contraceptive dispenser.'

'A what?' Sir Cathcart gasped.

'A contraceptive dispenser.'

'Good God, the man's insane!' shouted Sir Cathcart. 'Can't have one of those damned things in College. When I was an undergraduate you got sent down if you were caught riveting a dolly!'

'Quite,' said the Dean, who had a shrewd suspicion that in his time the General had been a steam-hammer if the imagery of his language was anything to go by. 'What you don't seem to appreciate, Cathcart,' he continued, before the General could indulge in any further mechanical memories, 'is that the Master is undermining something very fundamental. I'm not thinking simply of the College now. The implications are rather wider than that. Do you take my meaning?'

Sir Cathcart shook his head. 'No, I don't,' he said bluntly.

'This country,' said the Dean with a new intensity, 'has been run for the past three hundred years by an oligarchy.' He paused to see if the General understood the word.

'Quite right, old boy,' said Sir Cathcart. 'Always has been, always will be. No use denying it. Good thing.'

'An elite of gentlemen, Cathcart,' continued the Dean. 'Now don't mistake me, I'm not suggesting they started off as gentlemen. They didn't, half of them, they came from all walks of life. Take Peel, for instance, grandson of a mill hand, ended up a gentleman, though, and a damned fine Prime Minister. Why?'

'Can't think,' said Sir Cathcart.

'Because he had a proper education.'

'Ah. Went to Porterhouse, eh?'

'No,' said the Dean. 'He was an Oxford man.'

'Good God. And still a gentleman? Extraordinary.'

'The point I'm trying to make, Cathcart,' said the Dean solemnly, 'is that the two Universities have been the forcing-house of an intellectual aristocracy with tastes and values that had nothing whatever to do with their own personal backgrounds. How many of our Prime Ministers over the last hundred and seventy years have been to Oxford or Cambridge?'

'Good Lord, don't ask me,' said the General. 'Got no idea.'

'Most of them,' said the Dean.

'Quite right too,' said Sir Cathcart. 'Can't have any Tom, Dick or Harry running the affairs of state.'

'That is precisely the point I have been trying to make,' said the Dean. 'The business of the older Universities is to take Toms and Dicks and Harrys and turn them into gentlemen. We have been doing that very successfully for the past five hundred years.'

'Mind you,' said Sir Cathcart doubtfully, 'I knew some bounders in my time.'

'I daresay you did,' said the Dean.

'Used to duck 'em in the Fountain. Did them no end of good,' Sir Cathcart reminisced cheerfully.

'What Sir Godber proposes,' the Dean continued, 'means the end of all that. In the name of so-called social justice the man intends to turn Porterhouse into a run-of-the-mill college like Selwyn or Fitzwilliam.'

Sir Cathcart snorted.

'Take more than Godber Evans to do that,' he said. 'Selwyn! Full of religious maniacs in my time, and Fitzwilliam wasn't a college at all. A sort of hostel for townies.'

'And what do you think Porterhouse will be with a self-service canteen instead of Hall and a contraceptive dispenser in every lavatory? There won't be a decent family prepared to pay a penny towards the Endowment Fund, and you know what that means.'

'Oh come now, can't be as bad as that,' said Sir

Cathcart, 'I mean to say we've survived worse crises in the past. There was the business over the Bursar . . . what was his name?'

'Fitzherbert.'

'Enough to ruin another college, that was.'

'Enough to ruin us,' said the Dean. 'If it hadn't been for him we wouldn't be dependent on wealthy parents now.'

'But we got over it all the same,' Sir Cathcart insisted, 'and we'll get over this present nonsense. Just fashion, all this equality. Here today, gone tomorrow. Have a drink.' He got up and went over to the Waverley Novels. 'Scotch?' The Dean regarded the set in some bewilderment.

'Scott?' he asked. He had never regarded Sir Cathcart as a man with even remotely literary tastes and this sudden change in the conversation seemed unduly inconsequential.

'Or sherry? If you prefer,' said Sir Cathcart, indicating a handsomely bound copy of *Lavengro*. The Dean shook his head irritably. There was something extraordinarily vulgar about Sir Cathcart's travesty of a library.

'*Romany Rye* perhaps?' The Dean shook his head. 'Nothing, thank you,' he said. Sir Cathcart helped himself to *Rob Roy* and sat down.

'Proust,' he said, raising his glass. The Dean stared at him angrily. Sir Cathcart's flippancy was beginning to get on his nerves. He hadn't come out to Coft Castle to be regaled with the liquid contents of the library.

'Cathcart,' he said firmly, 'we have got to do something to stop the rot.'

The General nodded. 'Absolutely. Couldn't agree more.'

'It needs more than agreement to stop Sir Godber,' continued the Dean. 'It needs action. Public pressure. That sort of thing.'

'Difficult to get any public sympathy when you've got undergraduates running round blowing up buildings. Extraordinary thing to do really. Fill all those contraceptives with gas. Practical joke I suppose. Went wrong.'

'Very wrong,' said the Dean, who didn't want to get sidetracked.

'Mind you,' said Sir Cathcart, 'I can remember getting up to some pretty peculiar pranks. When I first went in the army, great thing was to fill a French letter with water and stick it down someone's bed when he was out. Top bunk, you follow. Comes back. Gets into bed. Puts his toe through the thing. Fellow below gets drenched.'

'Very amusing,' said the Dean grimly.

'That's only the beginning,' said the General. 'Fellow below thinks fellow on top has wet his bed. Gets up and clobbers him. Damned funny. Two fellows fighting like that.' He finished his whisky and got up to replenish his glass. 'Sure you won't change your mind,' he asked.

The Dean studied the shelves pensively. He was beginning to feel the need for some sort of restorative.

'A pink gin,' he said finally, with a malicious gleam in his eye.

'Zola,' said the General promptly and reached up for a copy of *Nana*. The Dean tried to collect his thoughts. Sir Cathcart's flippancy had begun to erode his fervour. He sipped his gin in silence while the General lit a cheroot.

'Trouble with you academic wallahs,' said Sir Cathcart finally, evidently sensing the Dean's confusion, 'is you take things too seriously.'

'This is a serious matter,' said the Dean.

'Didn't say it wasn't,' Sir Cathcart told him. 'What I said was you take it seriously. Bad mistake. Ever hear the joke Goering told his psychiatrist in the prison at Nuremberg?'

The Dean shook his head.

'About different nationalities. Very revealing,' Sir Cathcart went on. 'Take one German and what have you got?'

'And what have you got?'

'A good worker. Take two Germans and you've got a Bund. Three Germans and you've a war.'

The Dean smiled obediently. 'Very amusing,' he said, 'but I really don't see what this has to do with the College.'

'Haven't finished yet. Take one Italian and you've a tenor. Two Italians a retreat. Three Italians an unconditional surrender. Take one Englishman and you've an idiot. Two Englishmen a club and three Englishmen an Empire.'

'Very funny,' said the Dean, 'but a little out of date, don't you think? We seem to have mislaid the Empire en route.'

'Forgot to be idiots,' said Sir Cathcart. 'Great mistake. Did bloody well when we were chinless wonders. Done bloody badly since. The Sir Godbers of this world have upset the applecart. Look serious and are fools. Different in the old days. Looked fools and were serious. Confused the foreigners. Ribbentrop came over to London. Heil Hitlered the King. Went back to Germany convinced we were decadent. Got a thrashing for his pains in '40. Hanged for that slip-up. Should have looked a bit closer. Mind you, it wouldn't have helped him. Went on appearances.' Sir Cathcart chuckled to himself and eyed the Dean.

'You may be right at that,' said the Dean grudgingly. 'And certainly the Master is a fool.'

'Clever fellows often are,' Sir Cathcart said. 'Got one-track minds. Have to have, I suppose, to do so well. Great handicap, though. In life I mean. Get so carried away with what's going on inside their own silly heads they can't cope with what's going on outside. Don't know about life. Don't know about people. Got no nose for it.'

The Dean sipped his gin and tried to follow the train of Sir Cathcart's thoughts. A new mellowness had begun to steal over him and he had the feeling, it was no more than a mere glimmer, that somewhere in the General's rambling and staccato utterances there was a thread that was leading slowly to an idea. Something about the General's manner as he helped himself to a third whisky and the Dean to a second gin and bitters suggested it. Something like a sparkle of cunning in the bloodshot eyes and a twitch of his veined snout and the bristles of his ginger whiskers which reminded the Dean of an old animal, scarred but undefeated. The Dean began to suspect that he had underestimated Sir Cathcart D'Eath. He accepted one of the General's cheroots and puffed it slowly.

'As I was saying,' Sir Cathcart continued, settling once more into his chair, 'we've forgotten the natural advantages of idiocy. Puts the other fellow off you see. Can't take you seriously. Good thing. Then when he's off guard you give it to him in the goolies. Never fails. Out like a light. Want to do the same with this Godber fellow.'

'I really hadn't visualized going to quite such lengths,' said the Dean doubtfully.

'Shouldn't think he's got any,' said the General. 'Wife certainly doesn't look up to much. Scrawny sort of woman. Bad complexion. Not fond of boys, is he?'

The Dean shuddered. 'That at least we've been spared,' he said.

'Pity,' said Sir Cathcart. 'Useful bait, boys.'

'Bait?' asked the Dean.

'Bait the trap.'

'Trap?'

'Got to have a trap. Weak spot. Bound to have one. What?' said the General. 'Bleating of the sheep excites the tiger. *Stalky*. Great book.' He got up from his chair and crossed to the window and stared out into the darkness while the Dean, who had been trying to keep up with his train of thought, wondered if he should tell Sir Cathcart that *Lavengro* had nothing to do with Spain. On the whole he thought not. Sir Cathcart was too set in his ways.

'I forgot to mention it earlier,' he said at last, 'but the Master also intends to put Rhyder Street up for sale.'

Sir Cathcart, who had become immersed in his own reflection in the window, turned and stood glowering down at him. 'Rhyder Street?'

'He wants to use the money for the restoration of the Tower,' the Dean explained. 'It's old College property and rather run down. The College servants live there.'

The General sat down and fiddled with his moustache. 'Skullion live there?' he asked. The Dean nodded. 'Skullion, the Chef, the under-porter, the gardener, people like that.'

'Can't have that. Got to stable them somewhere,' said the General. He helped himself to a fourth whisky. 'Can't turn them out into the street. Old retainers. Wouldn't look good,' and his eyes which a moment before had been dark suddenly glittered. 'Not a bad idea either.'

'I must say, Cathcart,' said the Dean, 'I do wish you would not jump about so. What do you mean? "Wouldn't look good" and "Not a bad idea either". The two statements don't go together.'

'Looks bad for Sir Godber,' said the General. 'Bad publicity for a Socialist. Headlines. See them now. Wouldn't dare. Got him.'

Slowly and dimly, through the shrapnel of Sir Cathcart's utterances, the Dean perceived the drift of his thought.

'Ah,' he said.

The General winked a dreadful eye. 'Something there, eh?' he asked.

The Dean leant forward eagerly. 'Have you ever heard of a fellow called Carrington? Cornelius Carrington? Conservationist. TV personality.'

He was aware that the inflection of the General's staccato had finally taken hold of him but the thought was lost in the excitement of the moment. Sir Cathcart's eyes were gleaming brightly now and his nostrils were flared like those of a bronze warhorse.

'Just the fellow. An OP. Up his street. Couldn't do better. Nasty piece of work.'

'Right,' said the Dean. 'Can you arrange it?'

'Invite him up. Delighted to come. Snob. Give him the scent and off he'll go.'

The Dean finished his gin with a contented smile.

'It's just the sort of situation he likes,' he said, 'and although I deplore the thought of any more publicity – that wretched fellow Zipser gave us a lot of trouble in that direction you know – I rather fancy friend Carrington will give Sir Godber cause for thought. You definitely think he'll come?'

'Jump at the opportunity. I'll see to that. Same club. Can't think why. Should have been blackballed,' said the General. 'Fix it tomorrow.'

*

By the time the Dean left Coft Castle that evening he was a happier man. As he tottered out of his car in time for dinner and passed the Porter's Lodge he noticed Skullion sitting staring into the gas fire. 'Must ask him how we did,' the Dean muttered and went into the Porter's Lodge.

'Ah, Skullion,' he said as the porter got to his feet, 'I wasn't able to be at the Bumps this afternoon. How did it go?'

'Rowed over, sir,' said Skullion dejectedly.

The Dean shook his head sadly.

'What a pity,' he said. 'I was rather hoping we'd do better today. Still there is always a chance in May.'

'Yes, sir,' Skullion said, but without, it seemed to the Dean, the enthusiasm that had been his wont.

'Getting old, poor fellow,' the Dean thought as he stumbled past the red lanterns that guarded the fallen debris of Zipser's climacteric.

13

Cornelius Carrington travelled to Cambridge by train. It accorded with the discriminating nostalgia which was the hallmark of his programmes that he should catch the Fenman at Liverpool Street and spend the journey in the dining-car speculating on the suddenness of Sir Cathcart's invitation, while observing his fellow travellers and indulging in British Rail's high tea. As the train rattled past the tenements and factories of Hackney and on to Ponders End, Carrington recoiled from the harshness of reality into the world of his own choosing and considered whether or not to have a second toasted teacake. His was a soft world, fuzzy with private indecisions masked by the utterance of public verities which gave him the appearance of a lenient Jeremiah. It was a reassuring image and a familiar one, appearing at irregular but timely intervals throughout the year and bringing with it a denunciation of the present, made all the more acceptable by his approval of the recent past. If pre-stressed concrete and high-rise apartments were anathemas to Cornelius Carrington, to be condemned on social, moral and aesthetic grounds, his adulation of pebble-dash, pseudo-Tudor and crazy paving asserted the supreme virtues of the suburbs and reassured his viewers that all was well with the world in spite of the fact that nearly everything was wrong. Nor were his crusades wholly architectural. With a moral fervour which was evidently religious, without being in any way denominational, he espoused hopeless causes and gave viewers a vicarious sense of philanthropy that was eminently satisfying. More than one meths drinker had been elevated to the status of an alcoholic thanks to Carrington's intervention, while several heroin addicts had served an unexpected social purpose by suffering withdrawal symptoms in the company of Carrington, the camera crew, and several million viewers. Whatever the issue, Cornelius Carrington managed to combine moral indignation with entertainment and to extract from the situation just those elements which were most disturbing, without engendering in his audience a more than temporary sense of hopelessness which his own personality could render needless. There was about the man himself a genuinely comforting quality, epitomizing all that was sure and certain and humane about the British way of life. Policemen might be shot (and if his opinion was anything to go by they were being massacred daily across the country) but the traditions of the law remained unimpaired and immune to the rising tide of violence. Like some omniscient Teddy Bear, Cornelius Carrington was ultimately comforting.

As he sat in the dining car savouring the desultory landscape of Broxbourne, Carrington's thoughts turned from teacakes to the ostensible reasons for his visit. Sir

Cathcart's invitation had come too abruptly both in manner and in time to convince him that it was wholly ingenuous. Carrington had listened to the General's description of the recent events in Porterhouse with interest. His ties with his old college had been tenuous, to put it mildly, and he shared with Sir Godber some unpleasant memories of the place and his time as an undergraduate. At the same time he recognized that the changes Sir Cathcart regretted in other colleges and feared in Porterhouse might have a value for a series on Cambridge. Carrington on Cambridge. It was an excellent title and the notion of a personal view of the University by 'An Old Freshman' appealed to him. He had declined the General's invitation and had come unannounced to reconnoitre. He would visit Porterhouse, certainly, but he would stay more comfortably at the Belvedere Hotel. More comfortably and less fettered by obligation. No one should say that Cornelius Carrington had bit the hand that fed him.

By the time the train reached Cambridge, he had already begun to organize the programme in his mind. The railway station would make a good starting point and one that pointed a moral. It had been built so far from the centre of the town on the insistence of the University Authorities in 1845 who had feared its malign influence. Foresight or the refusal to accept change? The viewer could take his pick. Carrington was impartial. Then shots of college gateways. Eroded statues. Shields. Heraldic animals. Chapels and gilded towers. Gowns. Undergraduates. The Bridge of Sighs. It was all there waiting to be explored by Carrington at his most congenial.

He took a taxi and drove to the Belvedere Hotel. It was not what he remembered. The old hotel, charming in a quiet opulent way, was gone and in its place there stood a large modern monstrosity, as tasteless a monument to commercial cupidity as any he had ever seen. Cornelius Carrington's fury was aroused. He would definitely make the series now. Rejecting the anonymous amenities of the Belvedere, he cancelled his room and took the taxi to the Blue Boar in Trinity Street. Here too things had changed, but at least from the outside the hotel looked what it had once been, an eighteenth-century hostelry, and Carrington was satisfied. After all, it is appearances that matter, he thought as he went up to his room.

*

At any previous time in his life Skullion would have agreed with him but now that his house in Rhyder Street was up for sale, and the College's reputation threatened by the Master's flirtation with the commercial aspects of birth control, Skullion was less concerned with appearances. He skulked in the Porter's Lodge with a new taciturnity in marked contrast to the gruff deference he had accorded callers in the past. No longer did he appear at the door to greet the Fellows with a brisk 'Good morning, sir' and anyone calling for a parcel was likely to be treated to a surly indifference and a churlishness which defeated attempts at conversation. Even Walter, the under-porter, found Skullion difficult. He had never found him easy but now his existence was made miserable by Skullion's silence and his frequent outbursts of irritation. For hours Skullion would sit staring at the gas fire mulling over his grievances and debating what to do. 'Got no right to do it,' he would suddenly say out loud with a violence that made Walter jump.

'No right to do what?' he asked at first.

'None of your business,' Skullion snapped back and Walter gave up the attempt to discuss whatever it was that had put the Head Porter's back up. Even the Dean, never the most sensitive of men when it came to other people's feelings, noticed the change in Skullion when he called each morning to make his report. There was a hangdog look about the Porter that caused the Dean to wonder if it wasn't time he was put down before recalling that Skullion was after all a human being and that he had been misled by the metaphor. Skullion would sidle into the room with his hat in his hand and mutter, 'Nothing to report, sir,' and sidle out again leaving the Dean with a sense of having been rebuked in some unspoken way. It was an uncomfortable feeling after so many years of approval and the Dean felt aggrieved. If Skullion couldn't be put down, it was perhaps time he retired before this new churlishness tarnished his previously unspotted reputation for deference. Besides, the Dean had enough to worry about in Sir Godber's plans without being bothered with Skullion's private grievances.

If Skullion accorded the Dean scant respect, his attitude to the other Fellows was positively mutinous. The Bursar in particular suffered at his hands, or at least his tongue, whenever he had the misfortune to have to call in at the Porter's Lodge for some unavoidable reason.

'What do you want?' Skullion would ask in a tone that suggested he would like the Bursar to ask for a black eye. It was the only thing Skullion, it appeared, was prepared to give him. His mail certainly wasn't. It regularly arrived two days late and Skullion's inability on the telephone switchboard to put the Bursar's calls through to the right number exacerbated the Bursar's sense of isolation. Only the Master seemed happy to see him now and the Bursar spent much of his time in consultation with Sir Godber in the Master's Lodge, conscious that even here he was not wholly welcome, if Lady Mary's manner was anything to go by. Between the Scylla of Skullion and the Charybdis of Lady Mary, not to mention the dangers of the open sea in the shape of the Fellows at High Table, the Bursar led a miserable existence made no less difficult by Sir Godber's refusal to accept the limitations placed on his schemes by the financial plight of the College. It was during one of their many wrangles about money that the Bursar mentioned Skullion's new abruptness.

'Skullion costs us approximately a thousand pounds

a year,' he said. 'More if you take the loss of the house in Rhyder Street. Altogether the College servants mean an annual outflow of £15,000.'

'Skullion certainly isn't worth that,' said the Master, 'and besides I find his attitude decidedly obnoxious.'

'He has become very uncivil,' agreed the Bursar.

'Not only that but I dislike the proprietary attitude he takes to the College,' the Master said. 'Anyone would think he owns the place. He'll have to go.'

For once the Bursar did not disagree. As far as he was concerned Porterhouse would be a pleasanter place when Skullion no longer exercised his baleful influence in the Porter's Lodge.

'He'll be reaching retiring age in a few years' time,' he said. 'Do you think we should wait . . .'

But Sir Godber was adamant. 'I don't think we can afford to wait,' he said. 'It's a simple question of redundancy. There is absolutely no need for two porters, just as there is no point in employing a dozen mentally deficient kitchen servants where one efficient man could do the job.'

'But Skullion is getting on. He's an old man,' said the Bursar, who saw looming before him the dreadful task of telling Skullion that his services were no longer required.

'Precisely my point. We can hardly sack the under-porter, who is young, simply to satisfy Skullion, who, as you say yourself, will be retiring in a few years' time. We really cannot afford to indulge in sentimentality,

Bursar. You must speak to Skullion. Suggest that he look around for some other form of employment. There must be something he can do.'

The Bursar had no doubts on that score and he was about to suggest deferring Skullion's dismissal until they should see what the sale of Rhyder Street raised by way of additional funds when Lady Mary put a spoke in his wheel.

'I can't honestly see why the porter's job shouldn't be done by a woman,' she said. 'It would mark a significant break with tradition and really the job is simply that of a receptionist.'

Both Sir Godber and the Bursar turned and stared at her.

'Godber, don't goggle,' said Lady Mary.

'My dear . . .' Sir Godber began, but Lady Mary was in no mood to put up with argument.

'A woman porter,' she insisted, 'will do more than anything else to demonstrate the fact that the College has entered the twentieth century.'

'But there isn't a college in Cambridge with a female porter,' said the Bursar.

'Then it's time there was,' Lady Mary snapped. The Bursar left the Master's Lodge a troubled man. Lady Mary's intervention had ended once and for all his hopes of deferring the question of Skullion until the Porter had either made himself unpopular with the other Fellows by his manner or had come to his senses. The thought of having to tell the Head Porter that his services were no longer required daunted the Bursar. For a brief moment he even considered consulting the Dean but he was hardly likely to get any assistance from that quarter. He had burnt his bridges by siding with the Master. He could hardly change sides again. He entered his office and sat at his desk. Should he send Skullion a letter or speak to him personally? He was tempted by the idea of an impersonal letter but his better feelings prevailed over his natural timidity. He picked up the phone and dialled the Porter's Lodge.

'Best to get it over with quickly,' he thought, waiting patiently for Skullion to answer.

*

The summons to the Bursar's office caught Skullion in a rare mood of melancholy and self-criticism. The melancholy was not rare, but for once Skullion was not thinking of himself so much as of the College. Porterhouse had come down in the world since he had first come to the Porter's Lodge and in his silent commune with the gas fire Skullion had come to feel that he had been a little unjust in his treatment of the Dean and Fellows. They couldn't help what Sir Godber did. It was all the Master's fault. No one else was to blame. It was in this brief mood of contrition that he answered the phone.

'Wonder what he wants?' he muttered as he crossed the Court and knocked on the Bursar's door.

'Ah, Skullion,' said the Bursar with a nervous geniality, 'good of you to come.'

Skullion stood in front of the desk and waited. 'You wanted to see me,' he said.

'Yes, yes. Do sit down.' Skullion chose a wooden chair and sat down.

The Bursar shuffled some papers and then looked fixedly at the doorknob which he could see slightly to the left of the porter.

'I don't really know how to put this,' he began, with a delicacy of feeling that was wasted on Skullion.

'What?' said the Porter.

'Well to put the matter in perspective, Skullion, the College financial resources are not all that they should be,' the Bursar said.

'I know that.'

'Yes. Well, for some years now we've been considering the advisability of making some essential economies.'

'Not in the kitchen I hope.'

'No. Not in the kitchen.'

Skullion considered the matter. 'Wouldn't do to touch the kitchen,' he said. 'Always had a good kitchen the College has.'

'I can assure you that I am not talking about the kitchen,' said the Bursar, still apparently addressing the doorknob.

'You may not be talking about it but that's what the Master has in mind,' said Skullion. 'He's going to have a self-service canteen. Told the College Council, he did.'

For the first time the Bursar looked at Skullion. 'I really don't know where you get your information from . . .' he began.

'Never you mind about that,' said Skullion. 'It's true.'

'Well . . . perhaps it is. There may be something in what you say but that's not . . .'

'Right,' interrupted Skullion. 'And it's all wrong. He shouldn't be allowed to do it.'

'To be perfectly honest, Skullion,' said the Bursar, 'there are some changes envisaged on the catering side.'

Skullion scowled. 'Told you so,' he said.

'But I really didn't ask you here to discuss . . .'

'Could always raise money in the old days by asking the Porterhouse Society. Haven't tried that yet, have you?'

The Bursar shook his head.

'Lot of rich gentlemen still,' Skullion assured him. 'They wouldn't want to see changes in the kitchen. They'd chip in if they knew he was going to put a canteen in. You ask them before you do anything.'

The Bursar tried to think how to bring the conversation back to its original object.

'It isn't simply the kitchen, you know. There are other economies we have to make.'

'Like selling Rhyder Street I suppose,' said Skullion.

'Well, there's that and . . .'

'Wouldn't have done that in Lord Wurford's time. He wouldn't have stood for it.'

'We simply haven't got the money to do anything else,' said the Bursar lamely.

'It's always money,' Skullion said. 'Everything gets blamed on money.' He got up and walked to the door. 'Doesn't mean you've got the right to sell my home. Wouldn't have happened in the old days.' He went out and shut the door behind him. The Bursar sat at his desk and stared after him. He sighed. 'I'll simply have to write him a letter,' he thought miserably and wondered what it was about Skullion that was so daunting. He was still sitting there ten minutes later when there was a knock at the door and the Head Porter reappeared.

'Yes, Skullion?' the Bursar asked.

Skullion sat down again on the wooden chair. 'I've been thinking about what you said.'

'Really?' said the Bursar, trying to think what he had said. He had been under the impression that Skullion had done all the talking.

'I'm prepared to help the College,' Skullion said.

'Well, that's very good of you, Skullion,' said the Bursar, 'but . . .'

'It isn't very much but it's all I can do,' Skullion continued. 'You'll have to wait till tomorrow for it till I've been to the bank.'

The Bursar looked at him in astonishment.

'The bank? You don't mean . . .'

'Well, it's College property really. Lord Wurford left it to me in his will. It's only a thousand pounds but if it . . .'

'My dear Skullion, really this is . . . Well, it's extremely good of you but I . . . we couldn't possibly accept a gift from you,' the Bursar stuttered.

'Why not?' said Skullion.

'Well . . . well it's out of the question. You'll need it yourself. For your retirement . . .'

'I ain't retiring,' Skullion said firmly.

The Bursar stood up. The situation was getting quite beyond him. He must take a firm line.

'It's about your retirement that I wanted to see you,' he said with a determined harshness. 'It has been decided that it would be in your own interest if you were to seek other employment.' He stopped and stared out of the window. Behind him Skullion had sagged on the chair.

'Sacked,' he said, with a hiss of air that sounded as if he were expiring with disbelief.

The Bursar turned reassuringly.

'Not sacked, Skullion,' he said cheerfully. 'Not sacked, just . . . well . . . for your own sake, for everyone's sake it would be better if you looked around for another job.'

Skullion stared at him with an intensity that alarmed the Bursar. 'You can't do it,' he said, rising to his feet. 'You've got no right. No right at all.'

'Skullion,' the Bursar began warningly.

'You've sacked me,' Skullion roared, and his face which had been briefly pale flushed to a new and terrible red. 'After all these years I've given to the College you've sacked me.'

To the Bursar it seemed that Skullion had swollen to a fearful size which filled his office and threatened him. 'Now, Skullion,' he began, as the Porter loomed at him, but Skullion only stared a moment and then turned on his heel and rushed from the office slamming the door behind him. The Bursar subsided into his chair limp and exhausted.

*

To Skullion, stumbling blindly across the Court, the Bursar's words were impossible. Forty-five years. Forty-five years he had served the College. He reeled into the Screens and stood clutching the lintel of the Buttery counter for support. The sense of being needed, of being as much a support to the College as the stone lintel he clutched was to the wall above it, all this had left him or was leaving him as waves of realization swept over him and eroded his absolute conviction that he was still and would for ever be the Porter of Porterhouse. Breathing deeply Skullion heaved himself on down the steps into the Old Court and walked woodenly towards the Porter's Lodge and the consolation of his gas fire. There he brushed past Walter and sat slumped in his chair, unable even now to accept the enormity of the Bursar's words. There had been

Skullions at Porterhouse since the College was founded. He had Lord Wurford's word for it and with such a continuity of possession behind him, it was as though he stood upon the edge of the world with only an abyss before him. Skullion recoiled from the oblivion. It was impossible to conceive. In a state of numbed disbelief he heard Walter moving about the Lodge as if it were somehow distant.

'Gutterby and Pimpole,' Skullion muttered, invoking the saints of his calendar almost automatically in his agony.

'Yes, Mr Skullion?' said Walter. 'Did you say something?' But Skullion said nothing and presently Walter went out leaving the Head Porter muttering dimly to himself.

'Going off his head, old bugger,' he thought without regret. But Skullion was mad only in a figurative sense. As the full extent of his deprivation dawned on him, the anger which had been gathering in him since Sir Godber became Master broke through the barrier of his deference and swept like a flash flood down the arid watercourse of his feelings. For years, for forty-five years, he had suffered the arrogance and the impertinent assumptions of privileged young men and had accorded them in turn a quite unwarranted respect and now at last, released from all his obligations, the anger he had suppressed at so many humiliations added to the momentum of his present fury. It was almost as though Skullion welcomed the ruin of his pretensions, had secretly hoarded the memories of his afflictions against such an eventuality so that his freedom, when and if it came, should be complete and final. Not that it was or could be. The habits of a lifetime remained unaltered. An undergraduate came in for a parcel and Skullion rose obediently and brought it to the counter but without the rancour that had been the emblem of his servitude. His anger was all internal. Outwardly Skullion seemed subdued and old, shuffling about his office in his bowler hat and muttering to himself, but inwardly all was altered. The deep divisions in his mind, like the two separate lobes of his brain, his allegiance to the College and his self-interest, were sundered and Skullion's anger at his lot in life could run unchecked.

When Walter returned at six o'clock, Skullion put on his overcoat.

'Going out,' he said and left Walter dumbfounded. It wasn't his night on duty. Skullion went out of the gate and turned down Trinity Street towards the Round Church. On the corner he hesitated and looked down towards the Baron of Beef but it wasn't the pub for his present mood. He wanted something less tainted by change. He walked on down Sidney Street towards King Street. The Thames Boatman was better. He hadn't been there for some time. He went in and ordered a Guinness and sat at a table in the corner and lit his pipe.

14

Cornelius Carrington spent the day in rehearsal. With a cultivated eccentricity he wandered through the colleges singling out the architectural backdrops against which his appearance would be most effective. He adored King's College Chapel though only briefly. It was too well-known, hackneyed he thought and, more important, it dwarfed his personality. Conscious of his own limitations he sought the less demanding atmosphere of Corpus Christi and stood in the Old Court admiring its medieval charms. He pottered on through St Catherine's and Queens' over the wooden bridge and shuddered at the desecration of concrete that had been erected over the river. In Pembroke he lamented Waterhouse's library for its Victorian vulgarity before changing his mind and deciding that was an ornamental classic of its time. Glazed brick was preferable to concrete after all, he thought, as he made his way down Little St Mary's Lane towards the Graduate Centre.

He had morning coffee in the Copper Kettle, lunch in the Whim, and all the time his mind revolved around the question which had been bothering him since his arrival. The programme as he visualized it lacked the human touch. It was not enough to conduct a million viewers on a guided tour of Cambridge colleges. There had to be a moral in it somewhere, a human tragedy that touched the heart and raised the Carrington Programme from the level of aesthetic nostalgia to the heights of drama. He'd find it somewhere, somehow. He had a nose for the undiscovered miseries of life.

In the afternoon he continued his pilgrimage through Trinity and John's and fulminated at the huge new building there. He minced through Magdalene and it wasn't until half-past three that he found himself in Porterhouse. Here, if anywhere in Cambridge, time stood still. No hint of concrete here. The blackened walls of brick and clunch were as they had been in his day. The cobbled court with its chapel in the Gothic style, its lawns and the great Hall through whose stained-glass windows the winter sun glowed richly: all was as he remembered. And with the memory there came the uneasy feeling of his own inadequacy, which had been his mood in those days, and which, in spite of his renown, he had never wholly eradicated. Steeling himself against this recrudescence of inferiority he climbed the worn steps to the Screens and stood for a moment studying the notices posted in the glass cases there. Here too nothing had changed. The Boat Club. Rugger. Squash. Fixture lists. With a shudder Carrington turned away from this reminder that Porterhouse was a rowing college and stood in the archway looking down into New Court with astonishment. Here things had changed. Plastic sheeting covered the front of the

Tower and broken masonry lay heaped on the flags below. Carrington gaped at the extent of the destruction and was about to go down to make a closer examination when a small figure, heavily muffled in an overcoat, panted up the steps behind him and he turned to find himself face to face with the Dean.

'Good afternoon,' Carrington said, relapsing suddenly into a deference he thought he had outgrown. The Dean stopped and looked at him.

'Good afternoon,' he said, suppressing the glint of recognition in his eye. Carrington's face was familiar from the hoardings, but the Dean preferred to pretend to an infallible memory for Porterhouse men. 'We haven't seen you for a long time, have we?'

Carrington shrank a little at the supposition that his viewers, however numerous elsewhere, did not include the Senior Members of his old college.

'To my knowledge you haven't been back since . . . um . . . er,' the Dean fabricated a tussle with his memory, 'nineteen . . . er thirty-eight, wasn't it?'

Carrington agreed humbly that it was, and the Dean, secure now in his traditional role as the ward of an ineffable superiority, led the way towards his rooms.

'You'll join me for tea,' he asked and Carrington, already reduced to a submissiveness that infuriated him, thanked him for the offer.

'I'm told,' said the Dean as they climbed the narrow staircase, 'by those who know about these things, that you have made something of a name for yourself in the entertainment industry.'

Carrington found himself simpering a polite denial.

'Come, come, you're too modest,' said the Dean, rubbing salt into the wound. 'Your opinion matters, you know.'

Carrington doubted it.

'You must be one of the few distinguished members the College has produced in recent years,' the Dean continued, leading the way down the corridor from whose walls there stared the faces of Porterhouse men whose expressions left Carrington in little doubt that whatever they might think of him distinguished was not the word.

'You just sit down while I put the kettle on,' said the Dean and Carrington left for a moment tried hard to restore the dykes of his self-esteem. The room did not help. It was filled with reminders of past excellence in which he had no share. As an undergraduate Carrington had shone at nothing and even the knowledge that these peers of his youth who stared unwrinkled from their frames, singly or in teams, had failed to sustain the promise of their early brilliance did nothing to console him. They were probably substantial men, if hardly known, and Carrington for all his assumed arrogance was conscious of the ephemeral nature of his own reputation. He was not and would never be a substantial man, a man with Bottom, as the eighteenth

Tom Sharpe

century and no doubt the Dean would phrase it, and Carrington was enough of an Englishman to resent his inadequacy. It was probably this sense of having failed as a good fellow, a solid dependable sort of a chap, which gave to his practised nostalgia for the twenties and thirties its quality of genuine emotion as if he pined for a time as mediocre as himself. He was rescued from his self-pity by the Dean who emerged with a tray from his tiny kitchen.

'Harrison,' said the Dean of the photograph Carrington had been studying self-critically.

'Ah,' he agreed noncommittally.

'Brilliant scrum-half. Scored that try at Twickenham in . . . now when was it?'

'I've no idea,' said Carrington.

'Thirty-six? About your time. I'm surprised you don't remember.'

'I was never a great rugby man.'

The Dean looked at him critically. 'No, now I come to think of it you weren't, were you? Was it rowing you were interested in?'

'No,' said Carrington, uncomfortably aware that the Dean knew it already.

'You must have done something in your years in College. Mind you, a lot of the young fellows who come up these days don't do anything very much. I sometimes wonder what they come to University for. Sex, I suppose, though why they can't indulge their sordid appetites somewhere else I can't imagine.' He

212

shuffled into his kitchen and returned with a plate of rock cakes.

'I was looking at the damage to the Tower,' Carrington began when the Dean had poured tea.

'Come to make capital out of our misfortunes, I suppose,' said the Dean. 'You journalist fellows seem to be the carrion crows of contemporary civilization.' He sat back smiling at the happy alliteration of his insult.

'I wouldn't really regard myself as a journalist,' Carrington demurred.

'Wouldn't you? How very interesting,' said the Dean.

'I see myself more as a commentator.'

The Dean smiled. 'Of course. How stupid of me. One of the lords of the air. A maker of opinion. How very interesting.' He paused to allow Carrington to savour his indifference. 'Don't you often feel embarrassed at the amount of influence you wield? I know I should. But then of course nobody listens to what I have to say. I suppose you might say I lack the common touch. Do have some more tea.'

In his chair Carrington regarded the old man angrily. He had had enough of the Dean's hospitality, the polite insults and the delicate depreciation of everything he had achieved. Porterhouse had not changed. Not one iota. The place, the man, were anachronisms beyond the compassion of his nostalgia.

'One of the things that amazes me,' he said finally,

'is to find that in a University that prides itself on scholarship and research, Porterhouse remains so resolutely a sporting college. I was glancing at the notices just now. No mention of scholarships or academic work. Just the old rugby lists . . .'

'And what did you get? A double first, was it?' the Dean enquired sweetly.

'A two two,' said Carrington.

'And look where it's got you,' said the Dean. 'It speaks for itself really. Let's just say that we haven't succumbed to the American infection yet.'

'The American infection?'

'Doctoratitis. The assumption that a man's worth is to be measured by mere diligence. A man spends three years minutely documenting documents if you understand my meaning, anyway, investigating issues that have escaped the notice of more discriminating scholars, and emerges from the ordeal with a doctorate which is supposed to be proof of his intelligence. Than which I can think of nothing more stupid. But there you are, that's the modern fashion. It comes, I suppose, from a literal acceptance of the ridiculous dictum that genius is an infinite capacity for taking pains. These fellows seem to think that if you can demonstrate an appetite for indigestible and trivial details for three years you must be a genius. In my opinion, genius is by definition a capacity to jump the whole process of taking infinite pains, but then as I say, nobody listens to me. I mean there must be millions of people taking whatever these infinite pains are without a spark of intelligence let alone genius between them. And then again you have a silly fellow like Einstein who can't even count . . . it depresses me, it really does, but it's the fashion.'

The Dean waved his hands as if to exorcize the evil spirit of his time and Carrington ventured to intervene.

'But surely research does pay off . . .' he suggested.

'Pay?' said the Dean. 'I daresay it does. It certainly earns some colleges a great deal of money. Again you have this absurd assumption that provided you purchase enough sows' ears one of them is bound to turn into a silk purse. Utter nonsense, of course. It's the quality that counts not the quantity but then I don't expect you to sympathize with my old-fashioned point of view. When all's said and done it's quantity that's made your reputation, isn't it?'

'Quantity?'

'Megaviewers,' said the Dean. 'It seems an appropriate if nasty expression.'

By the time Cornelius Carrington left the Dean's rooms the erosion of his self-respect was almost complete and the comfortable acceptance of himself as the spokesman of a wholesome public concern quite gone. In the Dean's eyes he was clearly a parvenu, a jack in the box, he had suggested with a smile, and Carrington had found himself sharing the Dean's opinion. He walked out of Porterhouse envying the man his assurance and cursing himself for his inability to cope. What concrete and system-built housing was for him, he clearly was for the Dean, evidence of a facile and ugly commercialism. What had the Dean said? That he found the ephemeral distasteful, and there had been no doubt that of all ephemera he found television commentators the least to his liking. Carrington walked down Senate House Lane debating the source of the Dean's assurance. The man's lifetime spanned the coming of pebble-dash and the mock-Tudor suburbs Carrington found so appealing. He belonged to an earlier tradition. The Toby Jug Englishman, Squarsons and squires who didn't give a tuppenny damn what the world thought of them and bloodied the world's nose when it got in their way. In this mood of self-recrimination at his unalterable deference to such men, Carrington found himself in King Street. He wasn't at all sure how he had got there and at first found it difficult to recognize. King Street had changed more than any other part of Cambridge. The houses and shops that had stood huddled together down the narrow street were gone. A concrete multi-storeyed car park, a row of ugly brick arcades. And where were all the pubs? Walking down the street Carrington forgot his own demolition. Now it was bleak, impersonal and grim. A little further on he came to some remnants. An antique shop that had odds and ends of vases and bad paintings in its window. A coffee-shop cluttered with percolators and the more intricate jugs that undergraduates still evidently cultivated. But for the most part the developers had done their damnedest. Finally he came to the Thames Boatman and grateful to find it still standing he went inside.

'A pint of bitter, please,' he told the barman with his usual sense of place. Gin and tonic in a King Street pub would have been unthinkable. He took his beer to a table by the window.

'Seem to have been a lot of changes since I was here last,' he said, having taken a large swig from his beer glass. He didn't usually take large swigs. In fact he didn't usually drink beer at all, but beer in large swigs was, he remembered, customary in King Street.

'Knocking the whole street down,' said the barman laconically.

'Must be bad for business,' Carrington suggested.

''Tis and it isn't,' the barman agreed.

Carrington gave up the attempt to make conversation and turned his attention to the more responsive decorations of the bar-room.

A short time later a man in a bowler hat entered the bar and ordered a Guinness. Carrington studied his back and found a vague familiarity there. The dark overcoat, the highly polished shoes, the solid neck and above all the square set of the bowler hat, all these were tokens of a college porter. But it was the pipe, the jutting bulldog pipe, that woke his memory and told him this was Skullion. The porter paid for his Guinness and took it to the table in the corner and lit his pipe. A waft of blue smoke reached Carrington. He sniffed, and in that sniff the years receded and he was back in the Porter's Lodge in Porterhouse. Skullion. He had forgotten the man and his stiff, wooden, almost military ways. Skullion standing like some heraldic beast at the College gate or seen from his rooms above the Hall, a dark helmeted figure marching across the Court in the early morning, his attendant shadow jutting above the crenellations cast by the morning sunlight on the lawn. The pipe at the gates of dawn, Carrington had once called him, but there was nothing of the dawn about the Porter now. He sat over his Guinness and sucked his pipe and scowled unseeingly. Carrington studied the heavy features and was struck by the grim strength of the face below the brim of the bowler hat. If the Dean had prompted the thought of Toby Jugs, Skullion called to mind an older type than that. Something almost Chaucerian about the man, Carrington thought, relying for his assessment on vague memories of *The Prologue*. Certainly medieval. But above all it was the impressiveness of the man that struck him most. Impressive was the word for the face that stared out across the bar. Carrington drank his beer and ordered another. As he waited for it he crossed to the table where Skullion sat.

'It's Skullion, isn't it?' he asked. Skullion looked up at him doubtfully. 'What if it is?' he asked, adopting the impersonal pronoun as if to avoid an intrusion on his privacy.

'I thought I recognized you,' Carrington went on.

'You probably wouldn't remember me, Carrington. I was up at Porterhouse in the thirties.'

'Yes, I remember you. You had rooms over the Hall.'

'Let me get you another drink. Guinness, isn't it?' And before Skullion could say anything Carrington had returned back to the barman and was ordering a Guinness. Skullion regarded him morosely. He remembered Carrington all right. Bertie they used to call him. Flirty Bertie. Not a gentleman. He'd been something in the Footlights. Skullion hadn't approved of him.

Carrington brought the glasses across and sat down. 'I suppose you've retired now,' he asked presently.

'Not what you might call retired,' Skullion said grimly.

'You mean you're still Head Porter after all these years? My goodness, you have been there a long time.' He spoke with the affected eagerness of an interviewer, and indeed something about Skullion had awoken in him the feeling that there was a story here. Carrington had a nose for these things.

'Forty-five years,' said Skullion and drank his stout.

'Forty-five years,' echoed Carrington. 'Remarkable.'

Skullion grunted and lifted a bushy eyebrow. There was nothing remarkable about it to him.

'And now you've retired?' Carrington persisted. Skullion sucked his pipe slowly and said nothing. Carrington drank another mouthful of beer, and changed the subject.

'I don't suppose they have the King Street Run any more,' he said. 'Now that they've knocked down so many of the old pubs.'

Skullion nodded. 'Used to be fourteen and a pint in every one in half an hour. Took some doing.' He relapsed into silence. Carrington had caught the mood. The old ways were passed and with them the Head Porter. That partially explained the old man's grim expression but there was something more behind it. Carrington changed his tack.

'The College doesn't seem to have changed much anyway.'

Skullion's scowl deepened. 'Changed more than you know,' he grunted. 'Going to change out of recognition now.' He made a move as if to spit on the floor but turned back and smelt the bowl of his pipe.

'You mean the new Master?' Carrington enquired.

'Him and all the rest of them. Women in College. Self-service canteen in Hall. And what about us as served the College all our lives! Out on the street like dogs.' Skullion drank his beer and banged the glass down on the table. Carrington was silent. He sat still almost invisible with interest like a predator that sees its prey. Skullion lit his pipe and blew smoke.

'Forty-five years I've been a porter,' he said presently. 'A lifetime, wouldn't you say?' Carrington nodded solemnly. 'I've sat in that Lodge and watched the world go by. When I was a boy we used to wait at the Catholic church for the young gentlemen's cabs to come by from the station. "Carry your bags, sir," we'd shout and run beside the horses all the way to the College and carry their trunks up to their rooms for sixpence. That's how we earned some money in those days. Running a mile and carrying trunks into College. For sixpence.' Skullion smiled at the memory and for a moment it seemed to Carrington that the intensity had gone out of him. But there was something more than mere memory there, a sense of wrong that Carrington could sense and which in a remote way matched his own feelings. And his own feelings? It was difficult to define them, to say precisely what it was that he had found so monstrous in the Dean's delicate contempt. Except an insufferable arrogance that viewed him distantly as if he had been a microbe squirming convulsively upon a slide. Carrington acknowledged his own infirmity of spirit but his anger remained. He turned to Skullion as to an ally.

'And now they've turned you out?' he asked.

'Who said they had?' Skullion asked belligerently. Carrington prevaricated. 'I thought you said something about being made redundant,' he murmured.

'Got no right to do it,' he said almost to himself. 'They wouldn't have done it in the old days.'

'I seem to remember in my day that the College had rather a good reputation among the servants.'

Skullion looked at him with new respect. 'Yes, sir,' he said, 'Porterhouse was known for its fairness.'

'That's what I thought,' said Carrington, adopting

the lordly manner which was evidently what Skullion required of him.

'Old Lord Wurford wouldn't have dreamt of turning the Head Porter into the streets,' Skullion continued. 'When he died he left me a thousand pounds. Offered it to the Bursar, I did, to help the College out. Turned me down. Would you believe it? Turned my offer down.'

'You offered him a thousand pounds to help the College out?' Carrington asked.

Skullion nodded. 'I did that. "Oh no," he says, "wouldn't dream of taking it," and the next second he gives me notice. It's not credible, is it?'

To Carrington credibility hardly mattered. The story was enough.

'They're selling Rhyder Street too,' Skullion went on.

'Rhyder Street?'

'Where all the College servants live. Turning us all out.'

'Turning you out? They can't do that.'

'They are,' Skullion said. 'Chef, the head gardener, Arthur, all of us.'

Carrington finished his beer and bought two more. He had the human touch he had been seeking and with it the knowledge that his visit had not been wasted after all. He had his story now.

15

The Dean smiled. He had enjoyed his tea with Carrington. It was seldom nowadays that he had the opportunity to put his gifts for malice to good use. 'Nothing like a goad for making a man prove himself,' he thought, recalling his happy days as coach to the Porterhouse crew, and the insults he had used to drive the VIII to victory. And Carrington had suffered the gibes in silence. They would fester in him and give him the edge that was needed. He would do the programme on Porterhouse. His coming to Cambridge had proved his interest in the College in spite of his refusal of Sir Cathcart's invitation. And that refusal was an advantage too. Nobody could say now that he had been put up to it. As for the content of the programme, the Dean felt secure in the knowledge that Carrington was the high priest of nostalgia. Sir Godber's plans would be the bait. Tradition sullied. The old and proven ways under threat. The curse of modernism. The Dean could hear the clichés now, rolling off Carrington's tongue to stir the millions hungry for the good old days. And what of Sir Godber himself? Carrington would make mincemeat of the man's pretensions. The Dean helped himself to sherry with the air of a man well content, if not with the world, at least with that corner of it over which he was guardian. He went down to dinner in high spirits. They were having Caneton à l'Orange and the Dean was fond of duck. He entered the Combination Room and was surprised to find the Master already there talking to the Senior Tutor. The Dean had forgotten that Sir Godber dined in Hall occasionally.

'Good evening, Master,' he said.

'Good evening, Dean,' Sir Godber replied. 'I have just been discussing this business of the restoration fund with the Senior Tutor. It seems that we've had an offer for Rhyder Street from Mercantile Properties. They've offered one hundred and fifty thousand. I must say I'm inclined to accept. What's your opinion?'

The Dean grasped his gown and frowned. His objections to the sale of Rhyder Street were tactical. He opposed what Sir Godber proposed on principle but now it was useful that the Master should commit himself to an act whose lack of charity Cornelius Carrington could emphasize.

'Opinion? Opinion?' he said finally. 'I have no opinions on the matter. I regard the sale of Rhyder Street as a betrayal of our trust to the College servants. That is not an opinion. It is a matter of fact.'

'Ah well,' said Sir Godber, 'we shall just have to differ, won't we?'

The Senior Tutor was conciliatory. 'It's a hard

decision to make. I do see that,' he said. 'On the one hand the servants have to be considered and on the other there is no doubt that the restoration fund needs the money. A difficult decision.'

'Not one that I apparently am called to make,' said the Dean. They trooped into Hall and in the absence of the Chaplain, whose deafness had in no way improved since the explosion in the tower, the Dean said grace. They ate in silence for a while, Sir Godber munching his duck and congratulating himself on the change in the Senior Tutor's attitude, due possibly to the poor showing of the College in the Bumps, and one or two unfortunate remarks by the Dean. Eager to exploit the rift, Sir Godber set out to cultivate the Senior Tutor. He passed the salt without being asked for it. He told two amusing stories about the Prime Minister's secretary and finally, when the Senior Tutor ventured the opinion that he thought such goings-on were due to the entry into the Common Market, launched into a detailed account of an interview he had once had with de Gaulle. Throughout it all the Dean remained patently uninterested, his eyes fixed on tables where the undergraduates sat talking noisily, and his mind entertained by the fuse that had been lit in Cornelius Carrington. Towards the end of the meal the Master, having exhausted the eccentricities of de Gaulle, turned the monologue to matters nearer home.

'My wife is most anxious that you should dine with

us one evening,' he fabricated. 'She is concerned to know your views on the question of lady tutors for our female undergraduates.'

'Lady tutors?' said the Senior Tutor. 'Lady tutors?'

'Naturally as a coeducational college we shall require some female Fellows,' the Master explained.

'Charming,' said the Dean nastily.

'This comes as something of a shock, Master,' said the Senior Tutor.

Sir Godber helped himself to Stilton. 'There are some matters, Senior Tutor, that are essentially feminine if you see what I mean. You would hardly want a young woman coming to you for advice about an abortion.'

The Senior Tutor disengaged himself from a mango precipitately. 'Certainly not,' he spluttered.

'It's an eventuality we have to consider, you know,' continued Sir Godber. 'These things do happen, and since they do it would be as well to have a Lady tutor.'

Down the table the Dean smiled happily. 'And possibly a resident surgeon?' he suggested.

The Master flushed. 'You find the topic amusing, Dean?' he enquired.

'Not the topic, Master, so much as the contortions of the liberal conscience,' said the Dean, settling back in his chair with relish. 'On the one hand we have an overwhelming urge to promote the equality of the sexes. We admit women to a previously all-male college on the grounds that their exclusion is clearly discriminatory. Having done so much we find it necessary to provide a contraceptive dispenser in the Junior lavatory and an abortion centre doubtless in the Matron's room. Such a splendid prospect for parents to know that the welfare of their daughters is so well provided for. No doubt in time there will be a College crèche and a clinic.'

'Sex is not a crime, Dean.'

'In my view pre-marital intercourse comes into the category of breaking and entering,' said the Dean. He pushed back his chair and they stood while he said grace.

*

As he walked back through the Fellows' Garden the Master felt again that sense of unease which dining in Hall always seemed to give him. There had been a confidence about the Dean that he distrusted. Sir Godber couldn't put his finger on it exactly but the feeling persisted. It wasn't simply the Dean's manner. It had something to do with the Hall itself. There was something vaguely barbarous about the Hall, as if it were a shrine to appetite and hallowed by the usage of five hundred years. How many carcasses had been devoured within its walls? And what strange manners had those buried generations had? Pre-Renaissance men, pre-scientific men, medieval men had sat and shouted and thought ... Sir Godber shuddered at the superstitions they had entertained as if he could undo the thread of time that linked him to their animality. He willed his separation from them. He was a rational man. The contradiction in the phrase alarmed him suddenly. A rational man, free of the absurd and ignorant restrictions that had limited those men whose speculations on the nature of angels and devils, on alchemy and Aristotle, seemed now to verge on the insane. Sir Godber halted in the garden, astonished at the idea that he was the product of such a strange species. They were as remote to him as prehistoric animals and yet he inhabited buildings which they had built. He ate in the same Hall in which they had eaten and even now was standing on ground where they had walked. Alarmed at this new apprehension of his pedigree, Sir Godber peered around him in the darkness and hurried down the path to the Master's Lodge. Only when he had closed the door and was standing in the hall beneath the electric light did he feel reassured. He went into the drawing-room where Lady Mary was watching a film on television about the problems of senility. Sir Godber allowed himself to be conducted through several geriatric wards before becoming uncomfortably aware that his simple equation of progress with improvement did not apply to the ageing process of the human body. With the silent thought that if that was what the future held in store for him he would prefer to return to the past, he took himself up to bed.

Skullion returned from the Thames Boatman at

closing time. He had had no supper and eight pints of Guinness had done nothing to improve his opinion that he had been shamefully treated. He staggered into the Porter's Lodge and, ignoring Walter's protest that his wife had been expecting him home for supper at seven o'clock and it was now eleven and what was he supposed to tell her, stumbled through to the back room and lay on the bed. It was a long time since he had had eight pints of anything and it was this more than his innate sense of duty that got him off the bed to close the front gate at twelve o'clock. In the intervals between tottering through to the lavatory Skullion lay in the darkness, while the room revolved around him, trying to sort out what he should do from what that television chap had said to him. Go and see the General in the morning. Appear on the box with Carrington. Programme on Cambridge. Finally he got to sleep and woke late for the first time in forty-five years. It no longer mattered. His days as Head Porter of Porterhouse were over.

By the time Walter arrived Skullion had made up his mind. He took his coat down from the hook and put it on. 'Going out,' he told the astonished under-porter (Skullion hadn't been known to go out in the morning since he had been his assistant) and fetched his bicycle. The thaw had set in and this time as Skullion pedalled out to Coft the fields around him were piebald. Head bent against the wind, Skullion concentrated on what he was going to say and failed to notice the Dean's car

as it swept past him. By the time he reached Coft
Castle the bitterness that had been welling in him since
his interview with the Bursar had bred in him an
indifference to etiquette. He left his bicycle beside the
front door of the house and knocked heavily on the
door knocker. Sir Cathcart answered the door himself
and was too astonished to find Skullion glowering at
him from the doorstep to remind him that he was
expected to use the kitchen door. Instead he found
himself following the Porter into his drawing-room
where the Dean, already ensconced in an armchair in
front of the fire, had been telling him the news about
Cornelius Carrington. Skullion stood inside the door
and stared belligerently at the Dean while Sir Cathcart
wondered if he should ring for the cook to bring a
kitchen chair.

'Skullion, what on earth are you doing here?' asked
the Dean. There was nothing hangdog about the Porter
now.

'Come to tell the General about being sacked,' said
Skullion grimly.

'Sacked? What do you mean? Sacked?' The Dean
rose to his feet, and stood with his back to the fire. It
was a good traditional stance for dealing with truculent
servants.

'What I say,' said Skullion, 'I've been sacked.'

'Impossible,' said the Dean. 'You can't have been
sacked. Nobody's told me anything about this. What for?'

'Nothing,' said Skullion.

'There must be some mistake,' said the General. 'You've got hold of the wrong end of . . .'

'Bursar sent for me. Told me I'd got to go,' Skullion insisted.

'Bursar? He's got no authority to do a thing like that,' said the Dean.

'Well, he's done it. Yesterday afternoon,' Skullion continued. 'Told me to find other employment. Says the College can't afford to keep me on. Offered him money too, to help out. Wouldn't take it. Just gave me the sack.'

'This is scandalous. We can't have College servants treated in this high-handed fashion,' said the Dean. 'I'll have a word with the Bursar when I get back.'

Skullion shook his head sullenly. 'That won't do any good. The Master put him up to it.'

The Dean and Sir Cathcart looked at one another. There was in that glance a hint of triumph which grew as Skullion went on. 'Turned out of my own house. Sacked after all the years I've given to the College. It isn't right. Not standing for it, I'm not. I'm going to complain.'

'Quite right,' said the General. 'Absolutely scandalous behaviour on the part of the Master.'

'I want my job back now or else,' Skullion muttered. The Dean turned and warmed his hands at the fire. 'I'll put in a good word for you, Skullion. You need have no fear on that score.'

'I'm sure the Dean will do his best for you, Skullion,'

said Sir Cathcart, opening the door for him. But Skullion stood his ground.

'Going to need more than words,' he said defiantly. The Dean turned round sharply. He wasn't used to being spoken to in that tone of voice by servants.

'You heard what I said, Skullion,' he said peremptorily. 'We'll do what we can for you. Can't promise more than that.'

Still Skullion stood where he was.

'Got to do better than that,' he muttered.

'I beg your pardon, Skullion,' said the Dean. But Skullion was not to be intimidated.

'It's my right to be Porter,' he maintained. 'I've not done anything wrong. Forty-five years . . .'

'Yes, we know all that, Skullion,' said the Dean.

'I'm sure this is just a misunderstanding,' interposed Sir Cathcart. 'The Dean and I will see what we can do to put the matter right. I'll see the Master personally if necessary. Can't have this sort of thing going on in a college like Porterhouse.'

Skullion looked at him gratefully. The General would see him right. He turned to the door and went out. The General followed him into the hall. 'Ask Cook to give you some tea before you go,' he said, reverting to his old routine, but Skullion had already gone. Planting his bowler hat firmly on his head he mounted his bicycle and pedalled off down the drive.

Sir Cathcart went back into the drawing-room. 'What price Sir Godber now?' he said.

The Dean rubbed his hands happily. 'I think we've got the rod we need,' he said. 'The Master is going to rue the day he sacked Skullion. That's one of the nice things about these damned Socialists. The first people to get hurt by their rage for social justice are the working classes.'

'He's certainly got old Skullion's back up,' said Sir Cathcart. 'Well, I suppose we had better get in touch with the Bursar and see what we can do.'

'Do? My dear Cathcart, we do precisely nothing. If Sir Godber is fool enough to have the Bursar sack Skullion, I for one am not going to rescue him from his folly.'

Sir Cathcart stared uneasily at the receding figure of the Porter. Seen through the glass of the mullioned window Skullion had assumed a new amorphous aspect, dwindling but at the same time unsettling. He wondered briefly how much the Dean knew about Skullion's amendment of the examination process. It seemed a question better left unasked. Doubtless the whole business would blow over.

'After all, Cathcart,' said the Dean, 'you were the one who said the bleating of the sheep excites the tiger. Carrington is going to love this. He's staying at the Blue Boar. I think I'll drop in and have a word with him on the way back. Invite him to dine in Hall.'

General Sir Cathcart D'Eath sighed. It was one of the few good things about the affair that he didn't have to share his house with Cornelius Carrington.

16

Cornelius Carrington spent the morning in his room organizing his thoughts. It was one of his characteristics as a spokesman for his times that he seldom knew what to think about any particular issue. On the other hand he had an unerring instinct about what not to think. It was for instance unthinkable to approve of capital punishment, of government policy, or of apartheid. These were always beyond the pale and on a par with Stalin, Hitler and the Moors murderers. It was in the middle ground that he found most difficulty. Comprehensive schools were terrible but then so was the eleven-plus. Grammar schools were splendid but he despised their products. The unemployed were shiftless unless they were redundant. Miners were splendid fellows until they went on strike, and the North of England was the heart of Britain to be avoided at all costs. Finally Ireland and Ulster. Cornelius Carrington's mind boggled when he tried to find an opinion on the topic. And since his existence depended upon his capacity to appear to hold inflexible opinions on nearly every topic under the sun without at the same time offending more than half his audience at once, he spent his life in a state of irresolute commitment.

Even now, faced with the simple case of Skullion's sacking, he needed to decide which side the angels were on. Skullion was irrelevant, the object of an issue and superbly telegenic, but otherwise unimportant. He would be paraded before the cameras, encouraged to say a few inarticulate but moving sentences, and sent home with his fee to be forgotten. It was the issue that bothered Carrington. Who to blame for the injustice done to the old retainer? What aspect of Cambridge life to deplore? The old or the new? Sir Godber, who was evidently doing his best to turn Porterhouse into an academic college with modern amenities in an atmosphere of medieval monasticism? Or the Dean and Fellows, whose athletic snobbery Carrington found personally so insufferable? On the surface, Sir Godber was the culprit but there was much to be said for lambasting the Dean without whose obstinacy the economies which necessitated sacking the Head Porter could have been avoided. He would have to see Sir Godber. It was necessary in any case to get his permission to do the programme. Carrington picked up the phone and dialled the Master's Lodge.

'Ah, Sir Godber,' he said when the Master answered, 'my name is Carrington, Cornelius Carrington.' He paused and listened to the Master's voice change tone from indifference to interest. Sir Godber was evidently a man who knew his media, and rose accordingly in Carrington's estimation.

'Of course. Come to lunch. We can have it here or

in Hall as you prefer,' Sir Godber gushed. Carrington said he'd be delighted to. He left the Blue Boar and walked towards Porterhouse.

Sir Godber sat in his study invigorated. A programme on Porterhouse by Cornelius Carrington. It was an unexpected stroke of luck, a chance for him to appear once more in the public eye, and a golden opportunity to propound his philosophy of education. Come to think of it, he cut a good figure on television. He rather doubted if the Dean would come across as well, always supposing the old fool was prepared to appear on anything quite so new fangled. He was still engrossed in composing an unrehearsed account of the changes he had in mind for the College when the doorbell rang and the au pair girl announced Cornelius Carrington. The Master rose to greet him.

'How very nice of you to come,' he said warmly and led Carrington into the study. 'I had no idea you were an old Porterhouse man and to be perfectly honest I still find it hard to believe. I don't mean that in any derogatory sense, I assure you. I'm a great admirer of yours. I thought that thing you did on epilepsy in Flintshire was excellent. It's just that I've come to associate the College with a rather less concerned approach to contemporary problems.' Conscious that he was perhaps being a little too effusive, the Master offered him a drink. Carrington looked round the room appreciatively. There were no photographs here to remind him of the insignificance of his own youth and

Sir Godber's adulation came as a pleasant change from
the Dean's polite asperity.

'This programme of yours on the College is a splendid idea,' Sir Godber continued when they were seated.
'Just the sort of thing the College needs. A critical look
at old traditions and an emphasis on the need for
change. I imagine you have something of that sort in
mind?' Sir Godber looked at him expectantly.

'Quite,' said Carrington. Sir Godber's generalities
left every option open. 'Though I don't imagine the
Dean will approve.'

Sir Godber looked at him keenly. The hint of
malice he detected was most encouraging. 'A wonderful
character, the Dean,' he said, 'though a trifle hidebound.'

'A genuine eccentric,' agreed Carrington drily. It was
evident from his manner that the Dean did not com-
mand his loyalty. Reassured, the Master launched into
an analysis of the function of the college system in the
modern world while Carrington toyed with his glass
and considered the invincible gullibility of all politicians. Sir Godber's faith in the future was almost as
insufferable as the Dean's condescension and Carrington's erratic sympathies veered back towards the past.
Sir Godber had just finished describing the advantages
of coeducation, a subject that Carrington found personally distasteful, when Lady Mary arrived.

'My dear,' said Sir Godber, 'I'd like you to meet
Cornelius Carrington.'

Carrington found himself gazing into the arctic depths of Lady Mary's eyes.

'How do you do?' said Lady Mary, her sympathies strained by the evident ambiguities of Carrington's sexual nature.

'He's thinking of doing a programme on the College,' Sir Godber said, pouring the driest of sherries.

'How absolutely splendid,' Lady Mary barked. 'I found your programme on spina bifida most invigorating. It really is time we put some backbone into those people at the Ministry of Health.'

Carrington shivered at the forcefulness of Lady Mary's enthusiasm. It filled him with that nostalgia for the nursery that was the hidden counterpart of his own predatory nature. The nursery with Lady Mary as the nanny. Even the thin mouth thrilled him, and the yellow teeth.

'Of course it's the same with the dental service,' Lady Mary snarled telepathically. 'We should put some teeth into it.' She smiled and Carrington glimpsed the dry tongue.

'I imagine you must find this a great change from London,' he said.

'It's quite extraordinary,' said Lady Mary still blossoming under the warmth of his asexual attention. 'Here we are only fifty miles from London and it seems like a thousand.' She pulled herself together. He was still a man for all that.

'What sort of thing were you thinking of doing on the College?' she asked. On the sofa Sir Godber blended with the loose cover.

'It's really a question of presentation,' Carrington said vaguely. 'One has to show both sides, naturally . . .'

'I'm sure you'll do that very well,' said Lady Mary.

'And leave it to the viewers to make up their own minds,' Carrington went on.

'I think you'll have difficulty persuading the Dean and the Fellows to cooperate. You've no idea what a reactionary lot they are,' Lady Mary said. Carrington smiled.

'My dear,' said Sir Godber. 'Carrington is a Porterhouse man himself.'

'Really,' said Lady Mary, 'in that case I must congratulate you. You've come out of it very well.' They went in to lunch and Lady Mary talked enthusiastically about her work with the Samaritans over a pilchard salad while Carrington slowly wilted. By the time he left the Lodge carrying with him their benediction on the programme Carrington had begun to feel he understood the Master's longing for a painless, rational and fully automated future free from disease, starvation and the miseries of war and personal incompatibility. There would be no place in it for Lady Mary's terrifying philanthropy.

He dawdled throughout the College grounds, gazed at the goldfish in the pond, patted the busts in the Library, and posed in front of the reredos in the Chapel.

Finally he made his way to the Porter's Lodge to reassure himself that Skullion was still agreeable to stating his grievances before three million viewers. He found the Porter less pessimistic than he'd hoped.

'I told them,' he said, 'I told them they'd got to do something.'

'Told whom?' Carrington asked, grammatically influenced by his surroundings.

'Sir Cathcart and the Dean.'

Carrington breathed a sigh of relief. 'They should certainly see that you're reinstated,' he said, 'but just in case they don't, you can always find me at the Blue Boar.'

He left the office and made his way to the hotel. There was really nothing to worry about. An appeal by the Dean to Sir Godber's better feelings was hardly likely to advance the Porter's cause but, just in case, Carrington phoned the *Cambridge Evening News* and announced that the Head Porter of Porterhouse had been dismissed for objecting to the proposed installation of a contraceptive dispenser in the Junior lavatory. 'You can confirm it with the Domestic Bursar,' he told the sub-editor, and replaced the receiver.

A second call to the Students Radical Alliance announcing the victimization of a college servant for joining a trade union, and a third to the Bursar himself, conducted this time in pidgin English, and complaining that the UNESCO expert on irrigation in Zaire expected his diplomatic immunity to protect him from

being ejected with obscenities by the guardian of the
Porterhouse gate, completed the process of ensuring
that Skullion's dismissal should become public knowledge, the centre of left-wing protest, and irrevocable.
Feeling fully justified, Carrington lay back on his bed
with a smile. It had been a long time since he had been
ducked in the fountain in New Court but he had never
forgotten it. In the Bursar's office the telephone rang
and rang again. The Bursar answered, refused to comment, demanded to know where the sub-editor had got
his information, denied that a contraceptive dispenser
had been installed in the Junior lavatory, admitted that
one was going to be, refused to comment, denied any
knowledge of sexual orgies, agreed that Zipser's death
had been caused by the explosion of gas-filled prophylactics, asked what that had to do with the Head
Porter's dismissal, admitted that he had been sacked
and put the phone down. He was just recovering when
the Students Radical Alliance phoned. This time the
Bursar was brief and to the point. Having relieved his
feelings by telling the Radical Students what he thought
of them he replaced the receiver with a bang only to
hear it ring again. The ensuing conversation with the
delegate from Zaire, marked as it was by frequent
references to the Secretary of State for Foreign Affairs
and the Race Relations Board and punctuated by apol-
ogies from the Bursar and the assurance that the porter
in question had been dismissed, completed his demoralization. He put the phone down, picked it up again and

sent for Skullion. He was waiting for him when the Dean entered.

'Ah, Bursar,' he said, 'just wanted a word with you. What's all this I hear about Skullion being sacked?' The Bursar looked at him vindictively. He had had about all he could take of Skullion for one afternoon.

'It would appear that you have been misinformed,' he said with considerable restraint, 'Skullion has not been sacked. I have merely suggested to him that it is time he looked around for other employment. He's getting on and he's due for retirement shortly. If he can find another job in the meantime it would be sensible for him to take it.' He paused for a moment to allow the Dean to digest this version before continuing. 'However, that was yesterday. What has happened today puts the matter in an entirely different light. I have sent for Skullion and I do intend to sack him.'

'You do?' said the Dean, who had never before seen the Bursar so forthright.

'I have just received a complaint from a diplomat from Zaire who says that he was thrown out of the College by Skullion, who, if I understood him aright, called him among other things a nigger.'

'Quite right and proper,' said the Dean, who had been trying to figure out where Zaire was. 'The College is private property and Skullion doubtless had good reasons for chucking the blighter out. Probably committing a public nuisance.'

'He called him a nigger,' said the Bursar.

'If the man is a nigger, I see no reason why Skullion shouldn't call him one.'

'The Race Relations Board might not view the matter quite so leniently.'

'Race Relations Board? What the devil has it got to do with them?' asked the Dean.

'The fellow said he was going to complain to them. He also mentioned the Foreign Secretary.'

The Dean capitulated. 'Dear me,' he muttered, 'we can't have the College involved in a diplomatic incident.'

'We certainly can't,' said the Bursar. 'Skullion will just have to go.'

'I suppose you're right,' said the Dean, and took his leave. Outside in the Court he found the Porter waiting in the rain.

'This is a bad business, Skullion,' he said mournfully. 'A very bad business. There's nothing I can do for you now I'm afraid. A bad business,' and still shaking his head he made his way across the lawn to his staircase. Behind him Skullion stood in the falling dusk with a new and terminal sense of betrayal. There was evidently no point in seeing the Bursar. He turned and plodded back to the Porter's Lodge and began to pack his odds and ends.

The Bursar sat on in his office waiting. He phoned the Porter's Lodge but there was no reply. Finally he typed a letter to Skullion and posted it on the way home.

*

It was still raining when Skullion left the Porter's Lodge with his few belongings in a battered suitcase. The rain gathered in his bowler and flecked his face so that it was difficult even for him to know if there were tears running down his nose or not. If there were they were not for himself but for the past whose representative he had ceased to be. He stopped every now and then to make sure that none of the labels on the suitcase had come off in the rain. The bag had belonged to Lord Wurford and the stickers from Cairo and Cawnpore and Hong Kong were like relics from some Imperial pilgrimage. He crossed the Market Square, where the stalls were empty for the night. He went down Petty Curie and through Bradwell's Court and across Christ's Piece towards Midsummer Common. It was already dark and his feet squelched in the mud of the cycle track. Like the wind that blew in his face, swerved to left and right and suddenly propelled him forward, Skullion's feelings seemed to have no fixed direction. There was no calculation in them; the years of his subservience had robbed him of self-interest. He was a servant with nothing left to serve. No Master, no Dean, not even an undergraduate to whom he could attach himself, grudgingly, rudely, to disguise from himself the totality of his dependence. Above all, no College to protect him from the welter of experience. It wasn't the physical college that mattered. It was the idea and that had gone with his dismissal and the betrayal it represented.

Skullion crossed the iron footbridge and came to Rhyder Street. A tiny street of terraced houses hidden among the large Victorian villas of Chesterton so that even here Skullion could feel himself not far removed from the boathouses and the homes of professors. He went inside and took off his coat and put the suitcase on the kitchen table. Then he sat down and took his shoes off. He made a pot of tea and sat at the kitchen table wondering what to do. He'd go and see the bank manager in the morning about his legacy from Lord Wurford. He fetched a tin of boot polish and a duster and began to polish the toecaps of his shoes. And slowly, as each toecap began to gather lustre under the gentle circling of his finger, Skullion lost the sense of hopelessness that had been with him since the Dean had left him standing in New Court. Finally, taking a clean duster, he gave a final polish to the shoes and held them up to the light and saw reflected in their brilliance something remote that he knew to be his face. He got up and put the duster and the tin of polish away and made himself some supper. He was himself again, the Porter of Porterhouse, and with this restoration of his own identity there came a new stubbornness. He had his rights. They couldn't turn him out of his own home and his job. Something would happen to stop them. As he moved about the house his mind became obsessed with Them. They had always been there hedged with respect and carrying an aura of authority and trust so that he had felt himself to be safe from Them but it was different now. The old loyalty was gone and Skullion had lost all sense of obligation to Them. Looking back over the years since the war he could see that there'd been a steady waning of respect. There'd been no real gentlemen since then, none that he'd had much time for, but if each succeeding year had disillusioned him a little more with the present, it had added a deal of deference to the more distant past. It was as though the war had been the fulcrum of his regard. Lord Wurford, Dr Robson, Professor Dunstable, Dr Montgomery, they had gained in lustre out of sheer contrast with the men who had come after them. And Skullion himself had been exalted with them because he had known and served them.

At ten o'clock he went to bed and lay in the darkness unable to sleep. At midnight he got up and shuffled downstairs almost automatically and opened the front door. It had stopped raining and Skullion shut the door again after peering up and down the street. Then, reassured by this act of commemoration, he lit the gas fire in the front room and made himself a pot of tea. At least he had still got his legacy. He'd go to the bank in the morning.

*

The bank manager saw Skullion at ten o'clock. 'Shares?' he said. 'We have an investment department and we could advise you of course.' He looked down at the details of Skullion's deposit account. 'Yes, five thousand pounds is quite sufficient but don't you think it would be wiser to put the money into something less speculative?'

Skullion shifted his hat on his knees and wondered why no one seemed to listen to what he said. 'I don't want to buy any shares. I want to buy a house,' he said.

The manager looked at him approvingly. 'A much better idea. Put your money in property especially in these days of inflation. You have a property in mind?'

'It's in Rhyder Street,' said Skullion.

'Rhyder Street?' The manager raised his eyebrows and pursed his mouth. 'That's a different matter. It's being sold as a lot, you know. You can't buy individual houses in Rhyder Street, and quite frankly I don't suppose your five thousand would match some of the other bids.' He permitted himself a chuckle. 'In fact it's doubtful if five thousand would get you anything in Cambridge. You'd have to raise a mortgage, and at your age that's not an easy matter.'

Skullion produced the envelope containing his shares. 'I know that,' he said. 'That's why I want to sell these shares. There are ten thousand. I think they're worth a thousand pounds.'

The manager took the envelope. 'We must just hope they're worth a little more than that,' he said. 'Now then . . .' His condescendingly cheerful tone stuttered out. 'Good God!' he said, and stared at the sheaf of shares before him. Skullion shifted guiltily on his chair, as if he personally took the blame for whatever it was about the pieces of paper that caused the manager to stare in such amazement. 'Amalgamated Universal Stores. But this is quite extraordinary. How many did you say?' The manager was on his feet now twittering.

'Ten thousand,' said Skullion.

'Ten thousand?' The manager sat down again. He picked up the phone and rang the investment department. 'Amalgamated Universal Stores. What's the current selling price?' There was a pause while the manager studied Skullion with a new incredulous respect. 'Twenty-five and a half?' He put the phone down and stared at Skullion.

'Mr Skullion,' he said at last, 'this may come as something of a shock to you. I don't quite know how to put it, but you are worth a quarter of a million pounds.'

Skullion heard the words, but they had no visible effect upon him. He sat unmoved upon his chair and stared numbly at the bank manager. It was the manager himself who seemed most affected by the sudden change in Skullion's status. He laughed nervously and with a slight hysteria.

'I don't think there's much doubt that you can make a bid for Rhyder Street now,' he said at last but Skullion wasn't listening. He was a rich man. It was something he had never dreamed of being.

'There must have been dividends,' said the manager. Skullion nodded. 'In the building society.' He got up and put the chair back against the wall. He looked at the shares which represented his fortune. 'You'd better put them back into the safe,' he said.

'But . . .' began the manager. 'Now Mr Skullion, sit down and let's discuss this matter. Rhyder Street? There's no need to think of Rhyder Street now. We can sell these shares and . . . or at least some of them and you can purchase a decent property and settle down to a new life.'

Skullion considered the suggestion. 'I don't want a new life,' he said grimly. 'I want my old one back.'

He left the manager standing behind his desk and went out into Sydney Street. In his office the bank manager sat down, his mind crowded with cheap images of wealth, cruises and cars and bright suburban bungalows, ideas he had thought disreputable before. To Skullion, standing on the pavement, such things meant nothing. He was a rich man and the knowledge did nothing to ease his resentment. If anything it increased it. He had been cheated somehow. Cheated by his own ignorance and the loyalty he had given Porterhouse. The Master, the Dean, even General Sir Cathcart D'Eath, were the legatees of his new bitterness. They had misused him. He was free now, without the fear of dismissal or unemployment to mitigate his hatred. He went down Green Street towards the Blue Boar.

17

During the next two days Cornelius Carrington was intensely busy. His dapper figure trotted across lawns and up staircases with a retinue of cameramen and assistants. Corners of Porterhouse that had remained obscure for centuries were suddenly illuminated by the brightest of lights as Carrington adorned his commentary with architectural trimmings. Everyone cooperated. Even the Dean, convinced that he was heaping coals of fire on the Master's head, consented to discuss the need for conservatism in the intellectual climate of the present day. Standing beneath a portrait of Bishop Firebrace, Master 1545–52, who had, as Carrington was at some pains to point out in his added commentary, played a notable role in suppressing Kett's Rebellion, the Dean launched into a ferocious attack on permissive youth and extolled the celibacy of previous generations of undergraduates. In contrast, the Chaplain was driven to admit that what many supposed to have been a nunnery before it was burnt down in 1541 had in fact been a brothel during the fifteenth century. The camera dwelt at length on foundations of the 'nunnery' still visible in parts in the Fellows' Garden while Carrington expressed surprise that a college like Porterhouse should have allowed such sexual laxity so many centuries before. The Senior Tutor was filmed cycling along the towpath by Fen Ditton coaching an eight, and was then interviewed in Hall on the dietary requirements of athletes. Carrington wheedled out of him the fact that the annual Feast cost over £2,000 and then went on to ask if the College made any contribution to Oxfam. At this point, forgetful of his electronic audience, the Senior Tutor told him to mind his own business and stalked out of the Hall trailing the broken lead of his throat microphone. Sir Godber was treated more gently. He was allowed to stroll across New Court and through the Screens discoursing on the need for a progressive and humanitarian role for Porterhouse. Pausing to look far-sightedly across the thirty feet that separated him from the end wall of the Library, the Master spoke of the emotional–intellectual symbiosis that was a part of university experience, he lowered his head and addressed a crocus on the catharsis of sexual union, he raised his eyes to a fifteenth-century chimney and esteemed the compassion of the young, their energetic concern and the rightness of their revulsion at the outmoded traditions that . . . He waxed eloquent on meaningful relationships and urged the abolition of exams. Above all he praised youth. The elderly, by which he evidently meant anyone over thirty-five, must not stand in the way of young men and women whose minds and bodies were open . . . Even Sir Godber faltered at this point and Carrington steered him back to the subject of social compassion, which he saw as the true benefit of a university education. The Master agreed that a sense of social justice was indeed the hallmark of the educated mind. Carrington stopped the cameras and Sir Godber made his way back to the Master's Lodge, certain that he had ended on the right note. Carrington thought so too. While his cameramen took close-ups of the heraldic beasts on the front of the main gate and panned along the spikes that guarded the back wall, Carrington drove over to Rhyder Street and spent an hour closeted with Skullion. 'All I want you to do is to come back to the College and talk about your life as Head Porter,' he told him. Skullion shook his head. Carrington tried again. 'We'll take some shots of you outside the main gate and then you can stand in the street and I'll ask you a few questions. You don't have to go into the College itself.' Skullion remained adamant.

'You'll do me in London or you won't do me at all,' he insisted.

'In London?'

'Haven't been to London for thirteen years,' said Skullion.

'We can take you up to London for a day if you like but it would be much better if we filmed the interview here. We can do it here in your own home.' Carrington looked round the dingy kitchen approvingly. It had just that element of pathos he required.

'Wouldn't look good,' said Skullion. Under his breath Carrington cursed the old fool.

'I'm not having myself on film either,' Skullion continued.

'Not having yourself on film?'

'I want to go out live,' said Skullion.

'Live?'

'In a studio. Like they do on *Panorama*. Always wanted to see what it was like in a studio,' Skullion went on. 'It's more natural, isn't it?'

'No,' said Carrington, 'it's extremely unnatural. It's hot and you have large cameras . . .'

'That's the way I want it,' Skullion said, 'I'm not doing it any other way. Live.'

'All right,' Carrington said finally, 'if you insist. We'll have to rehearse it first, of course. I'll put questions to you and you'll reply. We'll run through it so that there aren't any mistakes.' He left the house in some annoyance, troubled by Skullion's persistence and conscious that without Skullion the programme would lack dramatic impact. If Skullion wanted to go to London and if, in his superstitious way, he objected to being 'put on film' he would have to be placated. In the meantime the cameramen could film Rhyder Street and at least the exterior of the Head Porter's home. He drove back to Porterhouse and collected the camera crew. Only one interview left now, that with General Sir Cathcart D'Eath at Coft Castle.

*

A week later Carrington and Skullion travelled to London together. Carrington had spent the week editing the film and adding his commentary but all the time he had been harassed by a nagging suspicion that there was something wrong, not with the programme as he had finally concocted it but with Skullion. The petulance that had attracted Carrington to him in the first place had gone out of him. In its stead there was a stillness and an impression of strength. It was as though Skullion had gained in stature since his dismissal and was pursuing interests he knew to be his own and no one else's. Carrington did not mind the change. In its own way it would heighten the effect Skullion would have on the millions who would watch him. Carrington had even found reason to congratulate himself on the Porter's insistence that he appear live in the studio. His rugged face, with its veined nose and heavy eyebrows, would stand out against the artificiality of the studio and give his appearance a sense of immediacy that was lacking in the interviews filmed in Cambridge. Above all, Skullion's inarticulate answers would stir the hearts of his audience. Across the country men and women would sit forward in their chairs to listen to his pitiable story, conscious that they were witnessing an authentic human drama. Coming after the radical platitudes of Sir Godber and the reactionary vehemence of the Dean, Skullion's transparent honesty would emphasize the homely virtues in which they and Cornelius Carrington placed so much faith. And finally there would come the master-stroke. From the gravel drive in front of Coft Castle, General Sir Cathcart D'Eath would offer Skullion a home and the camera would pan to a bungalow where the Head Porter could see his days out in peace. Carrington was proud of that scene. Coft Castle was suburbia inflated and transplanted to the countryside and the General himself the epitome of a modern English gentleman. It had taken a good deal of editing to achieve that result, but Carrington's good sense had prevailed over Sir Cathcart's wilder flights of abuse. He had to admit that the Sealyham had helped to inject a note of sympathy into Sir Cathcart's conversation. Carrington had spotted the dog playing on the lawn and had asked the General if he was fond of dogs.

'Always been fond of 'em,' Sir Cathcart had replied. 'Loyal friend, obedient, go anywhere with you. Nothing to touch 'em.'

'If you found a stray you'd give him a home?'

'Certainly,' said Sir Cathcart. 'Glad to. Couldn't leave him to starve. Plenty of room here. Have the run of the place. Decent quarters.'

Since in the edited version Sir Cathcart's hospitality appeared to refer to Skullion, Carrington felt that he could congratulate himself on a brilliant performance. All it had needed had been the substitution of 'If Skullion needed a place to live you'd offer him a home?' for 'If you found a stray you'd give him a home?' The

General was unlikely to deny his invitation. The consequences to his image as a public benefactor would be too enormous.

As they drove to London Carrington coached Skullion in his role. 'Remember to look straight into the camera. Just answer my questions simply.' In the darkness Skullion nodded silently.

'I'll say, "When did you first become a porter?" and you'll say, "In 1928." You don't have to elaborate. Do you understand?'

'Yes,' said Skullion.

'Then I'll say, "You've been the Head Porter of Porterhouse since 1945?" and you'll say "Yes."'

'Yes,' said Skullion.

'Then I'll go on, "So you've been a College servant for forty-five years?" and you'll say, "Yes." Is that clear?'

'Yes,' said Skullion.

'Then I'll say, "And now you've been sacked?" and you'll say, "Yes." I'll say, "Have you any idea why you've been sacked?" What will you say to that?'

'No,' said Skullion. Carrington was satisfied. The General might just as well have been talking about Skullion when he said that dogs were obedient. Carrington relaxed. It was going to go well.

They crossed London to the studio and Skullion was shepherded by an assistant to the entertainment room in the basement while Carrington disappeared into a lift. Skullion looked around him suspiciously. The room looked like a rather large air-raid shelter.

'Do sit down, Mr Skullion,' said the young man. Skullion sat on the plastic sofa and took off his bowler hat, while the young man unlocked what looked like a built-in wardrobe and wheeled out a large box. Skullion scowled at the box.

'What's that?' he enquired.

'It's a sort of portable bar. It helps to have a drink before one goes up to the studio.'

'Ah,' said Skullion and watched the young man unlock the box. A formidable array of bottles gleamed in the interior.

'What would you care for? Whisky, gin?'

'Nothing,' said Skullion.

'Really,' twittered the young man. 'That's most unusual. Most people need a drink especially if they're going on live.'

'You have one if you want one,' Skullion said. 'Mind if I smoke?' He took out his pipe and filled it slowly. The young man looked doubtfully at the portable bar.

'Are you sure you wouldn't care for a drink?' he asked. 'It does help, you know.'

Skullion shook his head. 'Have one afterwards,' he said, and lit his pipe. The young man locked the bar and put it back into the wardrobe.

'Is this your first time?' he asked, evidently anxious to put Skullion at his ease.

Skullion nodded and said nothing.

He was still saying nothing when Cornelius Carrington came down to collect him. The room was filled with the acrid smoke from Skullion's pipe and the young man was sitting at the far end of the plastic sofa in a state of considerable agitation.

'He won't drink anything,' he whispered. 'He won't say anything. He just sits there smoking that filthy pipe.' Carrington looked at Skullion with some alarm. Visions of Skullion drying up in the middle of the interview began to seem a distinct possibility.

'Are you all right?' he asked.

Skullion looked at him sourly. 'Never felt better,' he said. 'But I can't say I like the company.' He glowered at the young man.

Carrington escorted him out into the corridor. 'Poofter,' said Skullion as they went up in the lift. Carrington shuddered. There was something disturbing about the Head Porter's new attitude. He lacked the eagerness to please that seemed to affect most people who came to be interviewed, a nervous geniality that made them pliable and stimulated in Carrington a dominance he was unable to satisfy outside the artificial environs of the studio. If anyone was likely to dry up, he admitted to himself, it seemed more likely to be Cornelius Carrington than Skullion. He ushered the Porter into the brilliantly lit studio and sat him in the chair before hurrying out and having two quick slugs of whisky. By the time he had returned Skullion was telling a young make-up woman to keep her paws to herself.

Carrington took his seat and smiled at Skullion. 'One thing you must try to avoid is kicking the mike,' he said. Skullion said he'd try not to. The cameras moved round him. Young men came and went. In the next room behind a large darkened window the producer and the technicians arranged themselves at the console. Carrington on Cambridge was on the air. 9.25. Peak-hour viewing.

*

In Porterhouse dinner was over. It had, for a change, been an equable affair without any of the verbal infighting that usually occurred whenever the Fellows were gathered together. Instead a strange goodwill prevailed. Even the Master dined in Hall and the Dean sitting on his right managed to refrain from being offensive. It was as though a truce had been declared.

'I've done my best to see that more influential members of the Porterhouse Society have been informed about the programme,' he told the Master.

'Excellent,' said Sir Godber. 'I'm sure we all owe you a debt of gratitude, Dean.' The Dean forbore from sniggering. 'One does one's best,' he said. 'After all it's for the good of the College. We should get one or two fairly healthy subscriptions for the restoration fund as a result of young Carrington's efforts.'

'I found him a most sympathetic man,' said Sir Godber. 'Unusually perceptive, I thought, for . . .' He was about to say an old Porterhouse man but thought better of it.

'Flirty Bertie, they used to call him, when he was an undergraduate,' shouted the Chaplain.

'Ah well, he seems to have changed a good deal since those days,' said Sir Godber.

'They ducked him in the fountain,' the Chaplain continued. It was the only ominous remark of the whole meal.

Afterwards they sat in the Combination Room over coffee and cigars, glancing occasionally at the large colour television set that had been installed for the occasion. At nine they switched it on and watched the news, while Arthur, the waiter, was told to bring some more brandy. Sir Cathcart arrived at the invitation of the Dean and when *The Carrington Programme* began all those who had some part in it were present in the Combination Room. All except Skullion, who sat in the studio with the suggestion of a smile softening imperceptibly the harsh lines of his face.

In the Combination Room Cornelius Carrington's voice broke through the last bars of the Eton Boating Song which had accompanied the opening shots of the Backs and King's College Chapel. 'To many people Cambridge is one of the great centres of learning, the birthplace of science and of culture. Here the great English poets had their education. Milton was a scholar of Christ's College.' The interior of Milton's room appeared upon the screen. 'Wordsworth and Tennyson, Byron and Coleridge were all Cambridge men.' The camera skipped briefly from an upper window in St John's to Trinity and Jesus, before settling on the seated figure of Tennyson in Trinity Chapel. 'Here, Newton,' Newton's statue glowed on the screen, 'first discovered the laws of gravity, and Rutherford, the father of the atom bomb, first split the atom.' A corner of the Cavendish Laboratory, discreetly photographed to avoid any sign of modernity, appeared.

'I must say friend Carrington has a way of leaping the centuries fairly rapidly,' said the Dean.

'What's the Eton Boating Song got to do with King's?' asked Sir Cathcart.

Carrington continued. Cambridge was the Venice of the Fens. Shots of the Bridge of Sighs. Punts. Grantchester. Undergraduates pouring out of the lecture rooms in Mill Lane. Carrington's emollient voice proclaimed the glory that was Cambridge.

'But tonight we are going to look at a college that is unique even in the unchanging world of Cambridge.'

The Master sat forward and stared at the College crest on the tower above the main gate. Around him the Fellows stirred uneasily in their chairs. The invasion of their privacy had begun. And it continued. Carrington asked his audience to consider the anachronism that was his old college. The balm had left his voice. A new strident note of alarm had crept in suggesting to his audience that what they were about to see might well shock and surprise them. There was an implication that Porterhouse was something more than a mere college and that the crisis which had developed there was somehow symbolic of the choice that confronted the country. In the Combination Room the Fellows gaped at the screen in amazement. Even Sir Godber shivered at the new emphasis. Malaise was hardly a word he'd expected to hear applied to the condition of the College and when, after floating through Old Court and the Screens, the camera zoomed in on the plastic sheeting of the Tower there was a unanimous gasp in the Combination Room.

'What drove a brilliant young scholar to take his life and that of an elderly woman in this strange fashion?' Carrington asked, and proceeded to describe the circumstances of Zipser's death in a manner which fully justified his earlier warning that viewers must expect to be shocked and surprised.

'Good God,' shouted Sir Cathcart, 'what's the bastard trying to do?' The Dean closed his eyes and Sir Godber took a gulp of brandy.

'I asked the Dean his opinion,' Carrington continued and the Dean opened his eyes to peer at his own face as it appeared on the screen.

'It's my opinion that young men come up today with their heads filled with anarchist nonsense. They seem to think they can change the world by violent means,' the Dean heard himself telling the world.

'He did nothing of the sort,' shouted the Dean. 'He never mentioned Zipser!'

Carrington issued his denial. 'So you see this as an act of self-destructive nihilism on the part of a young man who had been working too hard?' he asked.

'Porterhouse has always been a sporting college. In the past we have tried to achieve a balance between scholarship and sport,' the Dean replied.

'He never put that question to me,' yelled the real Dean. 'He's taking my words out of context.'

'You don't see this as an act of sexual aberration?' Carrington interrupted.

'Sexual promiscuity plays no part in college life,' the Dean asserted.

'You've certainly changed your tune, Dean,' shouted the Chaplain. 'The first time I've heard you say that.'

'I didn't say that,' screamed the Dean. 'I said . . .'

'Hush,' said Sir Godber, 'I'm trying to hear what you did say.'

The Dean turned purple in the darkness as Carrington continued.

'I interviewed the Chaplain of Porterhouse in the Fellows' Garden,' he told the world. The Dean and Bishop Firebrace had disappeared to be replaced by the rockeries and elms and two tiny figures walking on the lawn.

'I never realized the Fellows' Garden was so large,' said the Chaplain, peering at his remote figure.

'It's distorted by the wide-angle lens . . .' Sir Cathcart began to explain.

'Distorted?' snarled the Dean. 'Of course it's distorted, the whole bloody programme's a distortion.'

The camera zoomed in on the Chaplain.

'The College used to have a brothel, you know. People like to pretend it was a nunnery but it was actually a whorehouse. In the fifteenth century it was quite the normal thing,' the Chaplain's voice echoed across the lawn. 'Burnt down in 1541. A great pity really. Mind you I'm not saying there weren't nuns. The Catholics have always been broadminded about such things.'

'So much for the ecumenical movement,' muttered the Senior Tutor.

'So you don't agree with the Dean that . . .' Carrington began.

'Agree with the Dean, dear me no,' the Chaplain shouted. 'Never did. Peculiar fellow, the Dean. All those photographs of young men in his room. And he's getting on in years now. We all are. We all are.' The camera moved away slowly, leaving the Chaplain a distant figure in a landscape with his voice growing fainter like the distant cawing of rooks.

The Chaplain turned to the Senior Tutor. 'That was rather nice. Seeing oneself on the screen like that. Most enlightening.' In the corner a strangled sound issued from the Dean. The Senior Tutor was breathing hard too, and staring at the river at Fen Ditton. An eight was swinging round Grassy Corner and an aged youth in a blazer and cap cycled busily after them. As the eight approached and disappeared the screen filled with the perspiring face of the Senior Tutor. He stopped and dismounted his bicycle. Carrington's voice interrupted his panting.

'You've been coach now for twenty years and in that time you must have seen some extraordinary changes in Porterhouse. What do you think of the type of young man coming up to Cambridge today?'

'I've seen some lily-livered swine in my time,' the Senior Tutor bawled, 'but nothing to equal this. A more disgraceful exhibition of gutlessness I've never seen.'

'Would you put this down to pot-smoking?' Carrington enquired.

'Of course,' said the Senior Tutor, and promptly disappeared from the screen.

In the Combination Room the Senior Tutor was speechless with rage. 'He didn't ask me any questions like that. He wasn't even there,' he managed to gasp. 'He told me they were simply going to film me on the river.'

'It's poetic licence,' said the Chaplain, and relapsed into silence as Carrington and the Senior Tutor reappeared in Hall and strolled between the tables. The camera focused on the several portraits of obese Masters before returning to the Senior Tutor.

'Porterhouse has enjoyed a long reputation for good living,' Carrington said. 'Would you say that the sort of expense involved in providing caviar and truffled duck pâté was really necessary for scholastic achievement?'

'I think much of our success has been due to the balanced diet we provide in Porterhouse,' said the Senior Tutor. 'You can't expect people to do well unless they are adequately fed.'

'But I understand that you spend fairly large sums on the annual Feast. Would you say that £2,000 on a single meal was a fair estimate?' Carrington enquired.

'We do have an endowed kitchen,' the Senior Tutor admitted.

'And I suppose the College makes a large contribution to Oxfam,' said Carrington.

'That's none of your damned business,' shouted the Senior Tutor. The camera followed his figure out of Hall.

As the devastating disclosures continued the Fellows sat dumbfounded in the Combination Room. Carrington waxed eloquent on Porterhouse's academic shortcomings, interviewed several undergraduates who sat with their backs to the camera to preserve their anonymity and claimed that they were afraid they would be sent down if their identities were known to the Senior Members of the College. They accused the College authorities of being hidebound and violently reactionary in their politics, and . . . On and on it went. Sir Godber put his case for social compassion as the hallmark of the educated mind and suddenly the scene changed. The images of Cambridge disappeared and the Fellows found themselves staring lividly at Skullion who sat firmly in his seat in the studio. The camera switched to Carrington. 'In the interviews we have already shown tonight we have heard a good deal to justify, and some would say to condemn, the role of institutions such as Porterhouse. We have heard the old traditions defended. We have heard privilege attacked by the progressive young and we have heard a great deal about social compassion, but now we have in the studio a man who more than any other has an intimate knowledge of Porterhouse and whose knowledge extends over four decades. Now you, Mr Skullion, have been for some forty years the Porter of Porterhouse.'

Skullion nodded. 'Yes,' he said.

'You first became a porter in 1928?'

'Yes.'

'And in 1945 you were made Head Porter?'

'That's right.'

'So really you've been in the College long enough to have seen some quite remarkable changes?' Skullion nodded obediently.

'And now I understand you've been sacked?' said Carrington. 'Have you any idea why this has happened?'

Skullion paused while the camera moved in for a close-up.

'I have been dismissed because I objected to the installation of a contraceptive dispenser in the College for the use of the young gentlemen,' Skullion told three million viewers. There was a pause while the camera swung back to Carrington, who was looking suitably shocked and surprised.

'A contraceptive dispenser?' he asked. Skullion nodded. 'A contraceptive dispenser. I don't think it's right and proper for Senior Members of a college like Porterhouse to encourage young men to behave like that.'

'Oh my God,' said the Master. Beside him the Senior Tutor was staring at the screen with bulging eyes while the Dean appeared to be in the throes of some appalling paroxysm. Throughout the Combination Room the Fellows gazed at Skullion as if they were seeing him for the first time, as if the caricature that they had known had suddenly come alive by virtue of the very apparatus which separated him from them. Skullion's presence filled the room. Even Sir Cathcart took note of the change and sat rigidly to attention. Beside him the Bursar whimpered. Only the Chaplain remained unmoved. 'Skullion's remarkably fluent,' he said, 'and making some interesting points too.'

Carrington too seemed to have shrunk to a less substantial role. 'You think the attitude of the authorities is wrong?' he asked lamely.

'Of course it's wrong,' said Skullion. 'Young people shouldn't be taught to think that they've a right to do what they want. Life isn't like that. I didn't want to be a porter. I had to be one to earn my living. Just because a man's been to Cambridge and got a degree doesn't mean life's going to treat him any different. He's still got to earn a living, hasn't he?'

'Quite,' said Carrington, desperately trying to think of some way of getting the discussion back to the original topic. 'And you think—'

'I think they've lost their nerve,' said Skullion. 'They're frightened. They call it permissiveness. It isn't that. It's cowardice.'

'Cowardice?' Carrington had begun to dither.

'It's the same all over. Give them degrees when they haven't done any work. Let them walk about looking like unwashed scarecrows. Don't send them down when they take drugs. Let them come in at all hours of the night and have women in their rooms. When I first started as a porter they'd send an undergrad down as soon as look at him and quite right too, but now, now they want them to have an FL machine in the gents to keep them happy. And what about queers?' Carrington blanched.

'You ought to know about that,' said Skullion. 'Used to duck them in the fountain, didn't they? Yes, I remember the night they ducked you. And quite right too. It's all cowardice. Don't talk to me about permissiveness.' Carrington gazed frantically at the programme controller behind the dark glass but the programme remained on the air.

'And what about me?' Skullion asked the camera in front of him. 'Worked for a pittance for forty years and they sack me for nothing. Is that fair? You want permissiveness? Well, why can't I be permitted to work? A man's got a right to work, hasn't he? I offered them money to keep me on. You ask the Bursar if I didn't offer him my savings to help the College out.'

Carrington grasped at the straw. 'You offered the Bursar your life savings to help the College out?' he asked with as much enthusiasm as the recent revelations about his sex life had left him.

'He said they couldn't afford to keep me on as Porter,' Skullion explained. 'He said they were having to sell Rhyder Street to pay for the repairs to the Tower.'

'And Rhyder Street is where you live?'

'It's where all the College servants live. They've got no right to turn us out of our own homes.'

In the Combination Room the Master and Fellows of Porterhouse watched the reputation of the College disintegrate as Skullion pressed on with his charges. This was no longer Carrington on Cambridge. Skullion had taken over with a truer and more forceful nostalgia. While Carrington sat pale and haggard beside him, Skullion ranged far and wide. He spoke of the old virtues, of courage and loyalty, with an inarticulate eloquence that was authentically English. He praised gentlemen long dead and castigated men still alive. He asserted the value of tradition in college life against the shoddy innovations of the present. He expressed his admiration for scholarship and deplored research. He extolled wisdom and refused to confuse it with knowledge. Above all he claimed the right to serve and with it the right to be treated fairly. There was no petulant whine about Skullion's appeal. He held a mirror up to a mythical past and in a million homes men and women responded to the appeal.

By the time the programme ended, the switchboard at the BBC was jammed with calls from people all over the country supporting Skullion in his crusade against the present.

18

In the Combination Room the Fellows sat looking at the blank screen long after Skullion's terrible image had disappeared and the Bursar had switched the set off. It was the Chaplain who finally broke the appalled silence.

'Very interesting point of view, Skullion's,' he said, 'though I must admit to having some doubts about the effect on the restoration fund. What did you think of the programme, Master?'

Sir Godber suppressed a torrent of oaths. 'I don't suppose,' he said with a desperate attempt at composure, 'that many people will take much note of what a college porter has to say. The public have very short memories, I'm glad to say.'

'Damned scoundrel,' snarled Sir Cathcart. 'Ought to be horsewhipped.'

'What? Skullion?' asked the Senior Tutor.

'That swine Carrington,' shouted the General.

'It was your idea in the first place,' said the Dean.

'Mine?' screamed Sir Cathcart. 'You put him up to this.'

The Chaplain intervened. 'I always thought it was a mistake to duck him in the fountain,' he said.

'I shall consult my solicitor in the morning,' said the Dean. 'I think we have adequate grounds for suing. There's such a thing as slander.'

'I must say I can hardly see any justification for going to law,' said the Chaplain. Sir Godber shuddered at the prospect.

'He deliberately fabricated questions to answers I had already given,' said the Senior Tutor.

'He may have done that,' the Chaplain agreed, 'but I think you'll have difficulty in proving it. In any case if I were asked I should have to say that he did manage to convey the spirit of our opinions if not the actual letter. I mean you do think the modern generation of undergraduates are . . . what was the expression?. . . a lot of lily-livered swine. The fact that you have now said it in public may be regrettable but at least it's honest.'

They were still fulminating an hour later when the Master, exhausted by the programme and by the terrible animosity it had provoked among his colleagues, finally left the Combination Room and made his way across the Fellows' Garden to the Master's Lodge. As he stumbled across the lawn he was still uncertain what effect the programme would have. He tried to console himself with the thought that public opinion was essentially progressive and that his record as a reforming politician would carry him safely through the outcry that was bound to follow. He tried to recall what it was about his own appearance on the screen that had so alarmed him. For the first time in his life he had seen himself as others saw him, an old man mouthing clichés with a conviction that was wholly unconvincing. He went into the Lodge and shut the door.

Upstairs in the bedroom Lady Mary disembarked from her corset languidly. She had watched the programme by herself and had found it curiously stimulating. It had confirmed her opinion of the College while at the same time she had been aroused once again by the warm hermaphroditism of Cornelius Carrington himself. Age and the Rubicon of menopause had stimulated Lady Mary's appetite for such men and she found herself moved by his vulnerable mediocrity. As ever with Lady Mary's affections, distance lent enchantment to the view, and for one brief self-indulgent moment she saw herself the intimate patroness of this idol of the media. Sir Godber, she had to admit, was a spent force whereas Carrington was still an influence. She smothered the impulse with cold cream but there was enough vivacity left to surprise Sir Godber when he came to bed.

'I thought it went rather well, didn't you?' she asked as the Master wearily untied his shoes. Sir Godber lifted his head balefully.

'Well of course there was that awful creature at the end,' Lady Mary conceded. 'I can't imagine why he had to appear.'

'I can,' said Sir Godber.

'Otherwise I enjoyed it. It showed the Dean up in a very foolish light.'

'It showed us all up in a perfectly terrible light,' said Sir Godber.

'He gave you fair warning,' Lady Mary pointed out. 'He said he had to show both sides of the problem.'

'He didn't say he had to show it from underneath,' Sir Godber snapped. 'He made us all look like complete idiots and as for Skullion, anybody would think we had done the damned man an injustice.'

'Aren't you being a bit extreme?' Lady Mary said. 'After all anyone could see he was a dreadful oaf.'

Sir Godber went through to the bathroom and did his teeth while Lady Mary settled down comfortably wth the latest statistics on juvenile crime.

*

At Shepherd's Bush Skullion sat on smoking his pipe and drinking whisky while Carrington screamed at the programme producer.

'You had no right to let him continue,' he shouted. 'You should have cut him off.'

'It's your programme, sweetie,' said the producer. The telephone rang. 'Anyway I don't know what you're worried about,' said the producer, 'the public loved him. The phone's been ringing non-stop.' He listened for a moment and turned to Carrington. 'It's Elsie. She wants to know if he's available for an interview.'

'Elsie?'

'Elsie Controp. The *Observer* woman,' said the producer.

'No, he isn't,' shouted Carrington.

'Yes, he is still here,' the producer said into the phone. 'If you come over now you'll probably get him.' He put the phone down.

'Do you realize he is likely to involve us in a legal action,' Carrington asked. The phone rang. 'Yes,' said the controller. He turned to Carrington. 'They want him for *Talk-In* on Monday. Is that all right?'

'For God's sake,' shouted Carrington.

'He says that's fine,' said the producer.

*

Skullion sat in the entertainment room with Elsie Controp. It was past eleven but Skullion was not feeling tired. His appearance had invigorated him and the whisky was helping. 'You mean the College authorities accept candidates who have taken no entrance examination and who have no A-levels?' Miss Controp asked. Skullion drank some more whisky and nodded.

'And their parents subscribe to an Endowment Fund?' Skullion nodded again. Miss Controp's pencil flitted across her pad.

'And this is quite a normal procedure at Porter-house?' she asked. Skullion agreed that it was.

'And other colleges admit candidates in the same way?'

'If you're rich enough you can usually get into a college,' Skullion told her. 'I don't say they subscribe to any funds like in Porterhouse but they get in all the same.'

'But how do they get degrees if they can't pass the exams?'

Skullion smiled. 'Oh, they fail the Tripos. Then they give them pass degrees. College recommends someone for a pass degree and they get it. It's a fiddle.'

'You can say that again,' said Miss Controp fervently. Skullion spent the night in a hotel in Bayswater. On Saturday he went to the Zoo and on Sunday he stayed in bed reading the *News of the World* and then went down to Greenwich to look at the *Cutty Sark*.

*

Sir Godber came down to breakfast on Sunday to find Lady Mary engrossed in the *Observer*. He could see from her expression that a disaster had struck some part of the world.

'Where is it this time?' he asked wearily. Lady Mary did not reply. 'It must be a simply appalling catastrophe,' Sir Godber thought and helped himself to toast. He sat munching noisily and looking out of the window. Saturday had been an unpleasant day. There had been a number of calls from old Porterhouse men who wanted to say how much they resented the sacking of Skullion and who hoped that the Master would think again before making any changes to the College. He had been asked for his opinions by several leading

London papers. He had been approached by the BBC to appear on *Talk-In*. He had even received a phone call from the League of Contraception complimenting him on his stand. Altogether the Master was in no mood to face Lady Mary's sympathy for some wretched population stricken by disease, destitution, or natural disaster at the other end of the globe. He could have done with some sympathy himself.

He looked up from a piece of toast to find her regarding him with unusual severity.

'Godber,' she said, 'this is simply dreadful.'

'I rather imagined it must be,' said the Master.

'You've got to do something about it immediately.'

Sir Godber put down his piece of toast. 'My dear,' he said, 'my capacity for doing anything about the inhumanity of man to man or of nature to man or of man to nature is strictly limited. That much I have learnt. Now whatever it is that's causing you such exquisite pain and suffering for the plight of mankind this morning, I am not in any position to do anything about it. I have enough trouble trying to do something about this College—'

'I am talking about the College,' Lady Mary interrupted. She thrust the paper across the table to him and Sir Godber found himself staring at headlines that read, CAMBRIDGE COLLEGE SELLS DEGREES. PORTER ALLEGES CORRUPTION, by Elsie Controp. A photograph of Skullion appeared below the headlines and several columns were devoted to an analysis of Porterhouse's financial affairs. The Master breathed deeply and read.

'Porterhouse College, one of Cambridge's socially more exclusive colleges, has been in the habit of selling pass degrees to unqualified sons of wealthy parents, according to the College Porter, Mr James Skullion.'

'Well?' said Lady Mary before Sir Godber could read any further.

'Well what?' said the Master.

'You've got to do something about it. It's outrageous.'

The Master peered vindictively at his wife. 'If you would give me time to read the article I might be able to think of something to do about it. As it is I have had time neither to digest its import nor what little break-fast—'

'You must issue a press statement denying the allegations,' said Lady Mary.

'Quite,' said Sir Godber. 'Which, since as far as I have been able to read, seem to be perfectly true, would do nobody, least of all me, any good whatsoever. I suppose Skullion might benefit by being awarded damages for being called a liar.'

'Are you trying to tell me that you've been condoning the sale of degrees?'

'Condoning?' shouted the Master. 'Condoning? What the hell do you—'

'Godber,' said Lady Mary threateningly. The Master lapsed into a stricken silence and tried to finish the article while Lady Mary launched into a sermon on the iniquities of bribery and corruption, public schools and the commercial ethics, or lack of them, of the middle classes. By the end of breakfast the Master was feeling like a battered baby.

'I think I'll take a walk,' he said, and left the table. Outside the sun was shining and in the Fellows' Garden the daffodils were out. So were the pickets. Outside the main gate several youths were sitting on the pavement with placards which read REINSTATE SKULLION. The Master walked past them with his head lowered and headed for the river wondering why it was that his well-meaning efforts to effect a radical change should always provoke the opposition of those in whose interests he was acting. Why should Skullion, whose ideas were archaic in the extreme and who would have chased those long-haired youths away from the main gate, elicit their sympathy now? There was something perverse about English political attitudes that defeated logic. Looking back over his lifetime Sir Godber was filled with a sense of injustice. 'It's the Right wot gets the power. It's the Left wot gets the blame,' he thought. 'Ain't it all a blooming shame?' He wandered on along the path across Sheep's Green towards Lammas Land, dreaming of a future in which all men would be happy and all problems solved. Lammas Land. The land of the day that would never come.

The Dean didn't read the *Observer*. He found its emphasis on the malfunction of the body politic and the body physical not at all to his taste. In fact none of the Sunday papers appealed to him. He preferred his agnosticism straight and accordingly attended morning service in the College Chapel where the Chaplain could be relied upon to maintain the formalities of religious observance in a tone loud enough to make good the deficiency of his congregation and with an irrelevance to the ethical needs of those few who were present that the Dean found infinitely reassuring. He was therefore somewhat surprised to find that the Chaplain had chosen his text from Jeremiah 17:11. 'As the partridge sitteth on eggs, and hatcheth them not; so he that getteth riches, and not by right, shall leave them in the midst of his days, and at his end shall be a fool.' Fortunately for the Dean, he was so preoccupied with the problem of the continuing existence of partridges in spite of their evident shortcomings as parents that he missed a great deal of what the Chaplain had to say. He awoke from his reverie towards the end of the sermon to find the Chaplain in a strangely outspoken way criticizing the college for admitting undergraduates whose only merit was that they belonged to wealthy families. 'Let us remember our Lord's words, "It is easier for a camel to go through the eye of a needle, than for a rich man to enter into the Kingdom of God",' shouted the Chaplain. 'We have too many camels in Porterhouse.' He climbed down from the pulpit and the service ended with 'As pants the hart . . .' The Dean and the Senior Tutor left together.

'A most peculiar service,' said the Dean. 'The Chaplain seemed obsessed with various forms of wild life.'

'I think he misses Skullion,' said the Senior Tutor.

They walked down the Cloisters with a speculative air. 'After that dreadful programme I would hardly go so far as to say that I missed him,' the Dean said, 'though I daresay he's a great loss to the College.'

'In more ways than one,' said the Senior Tutor. 'I dined in Emmanuel last night.' He shuddered at the recollection.

'Very commendable,' said the Dean. 'I try to avoid Emmanuel. I had some cutlets there once that disagreed with me.'

'I hardly noticed the food,' said the Senior Tutor. 'It was the conversation I found disagreeable.'

'Carrington, I suppose?'

'There was some mention,' said the Senior Tutor. 'I did my best to play it down. No, what I really had in mind was something old Saxton there told me. Apparently there is a not unsubstantial rumour going around that Skullion's assertion that he offered the College his life savings was not without foundation.'

The Dean waded through the morass of double negatives towards some sort of assertion. 'Ah,' he said finally, uncertain how far to commit himself.

'I understood Saxton to say he had it on the highest authority that Skullion was worth a good deal more than one might have supposed.'

'I always said Skullion was invaluable,' said the Dean.

'The sum mentioned was in the region of a quarter of a million pounds,' said the Senior Tutor.

'Out of the question to accept ... What?' said the Dean.

'A quarter of a million pounds.'

'Good God!'

'Lord Wurford's legacy to him,' explained the Senior Tutor.

'And the bloody Bursar turned it down,' stuttered the Dean.

'It puts a rather different complexion on the matter, doesn't it?'

It had certainly put a different complexion on the Dean who stood in the Cloister trying to get his breath.

'My God, a quarter of a million pounds. And the Master sacked him,' he gasped. The Senior Tutor helped him down the Cloisters.

'Come and have a little something in my rooms,' he said. They passed the main gate where a youth was holding a placard.

'Reinstate Skullion,' said the Dean. 'For once I think the protestors are right.'

'The danger is that some other college will bag him before we get the chance,' said the Senior Tutor.

'Do you really think so?' asked the Dean anxiously. 'The dear old fellow was ... is such a loyal College servant.' Even to the Dean's ears the word 'servant' had a hollow ring to it now.

In the Senior Tutor's rooms the bric-à-brac of a

rowing man hung like ancient weapons on the walls, an arsenal of trophies. The Dean sipped his sherry pensively.

'I blame Carrington entirely,' he said. 'The programme was a travesty. Cathcart should never have invited him.'

'I had no idea he had,' said the Senior Tutor. The Dean changed direction.

'As a matter of fact I found myself agreeing with a great deal of what Skullion had to say. Most of his accusations applied only to the Master. And Sir Godber is entirely responsible for the whole disgraceful affair. He should never have been nominated. He has done irreparable damage to the reputation of the College.'

The Senior Tutor stared out of the window at the damage done to the Tower. The animosity he had felt for the Dean, an antagonism which had taken the place of the transitory attachments of his youth, had quite left him. Whatever the Dean's faults, and over the years the Senior Tutor had catalogued them all meticulously, no one could accuse him of being an intellectual. Together, though never in unison, they had steered Porterhouse away from the academic temptations to which all other Cambridge colleges had succumbed and had preserved that integriy of ignorance which gave Porterhouse men the confidence to cope with life's complexities which men with more educated sensibilities so obviously lacked. Unlike the Dean, whose lack of scholarship was natural and unforced, the Senior

Porterhouse Blue

Tutor had once possessed a mind and it had only been by the most rigorous discipline that he had suppressed his academic leanings in the interests of the College spirit. His had been an intellectual decision founded on his conviction that if a little knowledge was a dangerous thing, a lot was lethal. The damage done to the Tower by Zipser's researches confirmed him in his belief.

'Has it occurred to you,' he said, at last turning from his contemplation of the dangers of intellectualism, 'that it might be possible to turn this affair of Carrington's programme and Skullion's sacking to some advantage?'

The Dean agreed that he had hoped it might unnerve the Master. 'It's too late for that now,' he said. 'We have been exposed to ridicule. All of us. It may be College policy to suffer fools gladly but I am afraid the public has other views about university education.'

The Senior Tutor shook his head. 'I think you may be unduly pessimistic,' he said. 'My reading of the situation differs from yours. We have certain advantages on our side. For one thing we have Skullion.' The Dean began to protest but the Senior Tutor held up his hand. 'Hear me out, Dean, hear me out. However ludicrous we may have been made to appear by friend Carrington, Skullion made an extremely favourable impression.'

'At our expense,' the Dean pointed out.

'Certainly, but the fact remains that public sympathy is on his side. Let us assume for a moment that we – and by we I mean the College Council – all excepting

285

the Master, agree to demand Skullion's reinstatement. Sir Godber would naturally resist and would be seen to resist such a move. We should appear as the champions of the underdog and the Master would find himself in an extremely difficult position. If further we present a reasoned case for our admissions policy—'

'Impossible,' said the Dean. 'No one is going to—'

'I haven't finished,' said the Senior Tutor. 'There is a sound case to be made for admitting candidates without suitable academic qualifications. We provide a natural outlet for those without apparent ability. No other college performs such a necessary function. Only the clever people get in to King's or Trinity. Certainly New Hall admits candidates under, to put it mildly, peculiar circumstances, but that's a women's college.'

The Dean sniffed disparagingly.

'Quite,' said the Senior Tutor. 'My point is this: that a properly articulated appeal on behalf of the scholastically crippled might win a great deal of public support. Couple it to demands on our part for Skullion's reinstatement and we could well turn what appears to be defeat into victory.' The Senior Tutor fetched the decanter and poured more sherry while the Dean considered his words.

'There may be something in what you say,' he admitted. 'It has always seemed to me to be decidedly inequitable that only the intelligent minority should be allowed to benefit from a university education.'

'My point exactly,' said the Senior Tutor. 'We cease

to be the college of privilege, we become the college of the intellectually deprived. It is simply a question of emphasis. What is more, since we are not dependent on grant-assisted undergraduates, it is self-evident that we are saving public money. The question remains how to present this new image to the public. I confess the problem baffles me.'

'The first essential is to call an urgent meeting of the College Council and get some degree of unanimity about reinstating Skullion,' said the Dean.

The Senior Tutor picked up the telephone.

19

The College Council met at ten on Monday morning. Several Fellows were unable to attend but signified their readiness to vote by proxy through the Dean. Even the Master, who was not fully informed of the agenda, welcomed the meeting. 'We must thrash this affair out once and for all,' he told the Bursar, as they made their way to the Council Chamber. 'The allegations in yesterday's *Observer* have made it essential to make a clean break with the past.'

'They've certainly made things very awkward for us,' said the Bursar.

'They've made it a damned sight more awkward for the old fogeys,' said Sir Godber.

The Bursar sighed. It was evidently going to be an acrimonious meeting.

It was. The Senior Tutor led the attack.

'I am proposing that we issue a statement rescinding the dismissal of Skullion,' he told the Council when the preliminaries had been dealt with.

'Out of the question,' snapped the Master. 'Skullion has chosen to draw the attention of the public to facts about College policy which I am sure we all agree have put the reputation of Porterhouse in jeopardy.'

'I can't agree,' said the Dean.

'I certainly don't,' said the Senior Tutor.

'But the whole world knows now that we sell degrees,' Sir Godber insisted.

'That portion of the world that happens to read the *Observer*, perhaps,' said the Senior Tutor, 'but in any case allegations are not facts.'

'In this case they happen to be facts,' said the Master. 'Unadulterated facts. Skullion was speaking no more than the truth.'

'In that case I can't see why you should object to his reinstatement,' said the Senior Tutor.

They argued for twenty minutes but the Master remained adamant.

'I suggest we put the motion to the vote,' said the Dean finally. Sir Godber looked round the table angrily.

'Before we do,' he said, 'I think you should consider some further matters. I have been examining the College statutes over the past few days and it appears that as Master I am empowered, should I so wish, to take over admissions. In the light of your refusal to agree to a change in College policy regarding the sort of candidates we admit, I have decided to relieve the Senior Tutor of his responsibilities in this sphere. From now on I shall personally choose all Freshmen. It also lies within my power to select College servants and to dismiss those I consider unsatisfactory. I shall do just that. However you may vote in Council, I shall not, as Master, reinstate Skullion.'

In the Council Chamber a momentary silence followed the Master's announcement. Then the Senior Tutor spoke.

'This is outrageous,' he shouted. 'The statutes are out of date. The position of the Master is a purely formal one.'

'I admire your consistency,' snapped the Master. 'As the upholder of outmoded traditions you should be the first to congratulate me for reassuming powers that are a legacy of the past.'

'I am not prepared to stand by and see College traditions flouted,' shouted the Dean.

'They are not being flouted, Dean,' said Sir Godber, 'they are being applied. As to your standing by, if by that you mean that you wish to resign your fellowship, I shall be happy to accept your resignation.'

'I did not say anything . . .' stuttered the Dean.

'Didn't you?' interrupted the Master. 'I thought you did. Am I to understand that you withdraw your—'

'He never made it,' the Senior Tutor was on his feet now. 'I find your behaviour quite unwarranted. We, sir, are not some pack of schoolboys that you can dictate to—'

'If you behave like schoolboys, you may expect to be treated like schoolboys. In any case the analogy was yours not mine. Now if you would be so good as to resume your seat the meeting may continue.' The Master looked icily at the Fellows and the Senior Tutor sat down.

'I shall take this opportunity, gentlemen,' said Sir Godber after a long pause, 'to enlighten you on my views about the function of the College in the modern world. I must confess that I am astonished to find that you seem unaware of the changes that have taken place in recent years. Your attitude suggests that you regard the College as part of a private domain of which you are custodians. Let me disabuse you of that notion. You are part of the public realm, with public duties, public obligations and public functions. The fact that you choose to ignore them and to conduct the affairs of the College as though they are your personal property indicates to me that you are acting in abuse of your powers. Either we live in a society that is free, open and wholly equalitarian or we do not. As Master of this College I am determined that we shall extend the benefits of education to those who merit it by virtue of ability, irrespective of class, sex, financial standing or race. The days of rotten boroughs are over.' Sir Godber's voice was strident with idealism and threat. Not since the days of the Protectorate had the Council Chamber of Porterhouse known such vehemence, and the Fellows sat staring at the Master as at some strange animal that had assumed the shape of a man. By the time he had exhausted his theme he had left them in no doubt as to his intentions, Porterhouse would never be the same again. To the long catalogue of changes he had proposed at earlier meetings, he had now added the creation of a student council, with executive powers

Tom Sharpe

to decide College appointments and policy. He left the
Council Chamber emotionally depleted but satisified
that he had made his point. Behind him the Fellows sat
aghast at the crisis they had precipitated. It was a long
time before anyone spoke.

'I don't understand,' said the Dean pathetically, 'I
simply don't understand what these people want.' It
was clear that in his mind Sir Godber's eloquence had
elevated or possibly debased him from an individual to
a class.

'Their own way,' said the Senior Tutor bitterly.

'The Kingdom of Heaven,' shouted the Chaplain.

The Bursar said nothing. His multiple allegiances left
him speechless.

*

Lunch was a mournful occasion. It was the end of
term and the Fellows at High Table ate in a silence
made all the more noticeable by the lack of conversation from the empty tables below them. To make
matters worse, the soup was cold and there was cottage
pie. But it was the knowledge of their own dispensabil-
ity that cast gloom over them. For five hundred years
they and their predecessors had ordained at least some
portion of the elite that had ruled the nation. It had
been through the sieve of their indulgent bigotry that
young men had squeezed to become judges and lawyers, politicians and soldiers, men of affairs, all of them
imbued with a corporate complacency and an intellec-

tual scepticism that desiccated change. They were the guardians of political inertia and their role was done. They had succumbed at last to the least effectual of politicians.

'A student council to run the College. It's monstrous,' said the Senior Tutor, but there was no hope in his protest. Despite his cultivated mediocrity of mind, the Senior Tutor had seen change coming. He blamed the sciences for reestablishing the mirage of truth, and still more the pseudomorph subjects like anthropology and economics whose adepts substituted inapplicable statistics for the ineptness of their insights. And finally there was sociology with its absurd maxim, The Proper Study of Mankind is Man, which typically it took from a man the Senior Tutor would have rejected as unfit to cox the rugger boat. And now with Sir Godber triumphant, and the Senior Tutor, at least privately, admitted the Master's victory, Porterhouse would lose even the semblance of the College he had loved. Sickly unisex would replace the healthy cheerful louts who had helped to preserve the inane innocence and the athleticism that were his only safeguards against the terrors of thought.

'There must be something we can do,' said the Dean.

'Short of murder I can think of nothing,' the Senior Tutor answered.

'Is he really entitled by statute to take over admissions?'

The Senior Tutor nodded. 'Tradition has it so,' he answered mournfully.

*

'There's only one thing they can do now,' said Sir Godber to Lady Mary over coffee.

'And what is that, dear?'

'Surrender,' said the Master. Lady Mary looked up. 'How very martial you do sound, Godber,' she said, invoking the ancient spirit of Sir Godber's pacifism. The Master resisted the call.

'I sounded a good deal more belligerent in the Council,' he said.

'I'm sure you did, dear,' Lady Mary parried.

'I should have thought you would have approved,' Sir Godber said. 'After all, if they had their way the College would continue to sell degrees, and exclude women.'

'Oh, don't think for a moment I am criticizing you,' said Lady Mary. 'It's just that power changes one.'

'It has been said before,' Sir Godber replied wearily. His wife's insatiable dissatisfaction subdued him. Looking into her earnest face he sometimes wondered what she saw in him. It must be something pretty harrowing, he thought. They'd been happily married for twenty-eight years.

'I'll leave you to your little victory,' Lady Mary said, getting up and putting her cup on the tray. 'I shan't be in this evening for dinner. It's my night as a Samaritan.'

She went out and Sir Godber poked the fire lethargically. He felt depressed. As usual there had been something in what his wife had said. Power did change one, even the power to dominate a group of elderly Fellows in a fourth-rate college. And it was a little victory after all. Sir Godber's humanity prevailed. It wasn't their fault that they opposed the changes that he wanted. They were creatures of habit, comfortable and indulgent habits. Bachelors too – he was thinking of the Dean and the Senior Tutor – without the goad of an empty marriage to spur them to attainment. Good-hearted in their way. Even their personal animosities and petty jealousies sprang from a too constant companionship. When he examined his own motives he found them rooted in inadequacy and personal pique. He would go and speak to the Senior Tutor again and try to establish a more rational ground for disagreement. He got up and carried the coffee cups through to the kitchen and washed up. It was the au pair's day off. Then he put on his coat and went out into the spring sunshine.

*

Skullion lay in bed and stared at the pale blue ceiling of his hotel room. He felt uncomfortable. For one thing the bed was strange and the mattress too responsive to his movements. It wasn't hard enough for him. There was something indefinite about the whole room which left him feeling uneasy and out of place. It wasn't anything he could put his finger to but it reminded him of a whore he'd once had in Pompey. Too eager to please so that what had started out as a transaction, impersonal and hard, had turned into an encounter with his own feelings. It was the same with this room. The carpet was too thick. The bed too soft. There was too much hot water in the basin. There was nothing to grumble about and in the absence of anything particular to assert himself against, Skullion's resentment was turned in on himself. He was out of place.

His tour of monuments had unsettled him too. He wasn't interested in the *Cutty Sark* or even in *Gypsy Moth*. They too were out of place, set high and dry for kids to run about on and pretend that they were sailors. Skullion had no such romantic illusions. He couldn't pretend even for a moment that he was other than he was, a college servant out of work. The knowledge that he was a rich man only aggravated his sense of loss. It seemed to justify his dismissal by robbing him of his right to feel hard done by. Skullion even regretted his appearance on *The Carrington Programme*. They'd said how good he was but who were they? A lot of brown-hatters and word-merchants he had no time for, giggling and squeaking and rushing about like blue-arsed flies. They could keep their bleeding compliments to themselves, Skullion didn't need them.

He got out of bed and went through to the bathroom and shaved. They had even bought him a new razor and aerosol of shaving foam and the very ease with which he shaved robbed him of his own ritual in the matter. He put on his collar and tie and did up his waistcoat. He'd had enough. He'd said his piece and he'd been inside a television studio. That was sufficient, he decided. He'd go back to Cambridge. They could have their talk-in without him. He collected his things together and went down to the desk and paid his bill. Two hours later Skullion was sitting in the train smoking his pipe and looking out at the flat fields of Essex. The monotony of the landscape pleased him and reminded him of the Fens. He could buy a bit of land in the Fens now if he wanted to, and grow vegetables like his stepfather had done. Skullion considered the idea only to reject it. He didn't want a new life. He wanted his old one back.

When the train stopped at Cambridge Station Skullion had made up his mind. He would make one last appeal, this time not to the Dean or Sir Cathcart. He'd speak to the Master himself. He walked out of the station and down Station Road wondering why he hadn't thought of it before. He had his pride, of course, and he'd put his trust in the Dean but the Dean had let him down. Besides, he despised Sir Godber, according him only that automatic respect that went with the Mastership. At the corner of Lensfield Road he hesitated under the spire of the Catholic church. He could turn right across Parker's Piece to Rhyder Street or left to Porterhouse. It was only twelve o'clock and he hadn't eaten. He'd walk into town and have a bite to eat in a pub and think about it. Skullion trudged on down Regent Street and went into the Fountain and ordered a pint of Guinness and some sandwiches. Sitting at a table by the door he drank his beer and tried to imagine what the Master would say. He could only turn him down. Skullion considered the prospect and decided it was worth trying even if it meant risking his self-respect. But was he risking it? All he was asking for was his rights and besides he had a quarter of a million pounds to his name. He didn't need the job. Nobody could accuse him of grovelling. It was simply that he wanted it, wanted his good name back, wanted to go on doing what he had always done for forty-five years, wanted to be the Porter of Porterhouse. Buoyed by the good sense of his own argument Skullion finished his beer and left the pub. He threaded his way through the shoppers towards the Market Hill, his mind still mulling over the wisdom of his action. Perhaps he should wait a day or two. Perhaps they had already changed their mind and a letter was waiting for him at home offering him his job back. Skullion dismissed the idea. And all the time there was the nagging fear that he was putting in jeopardy his self-respect by asking. He silenced the fear but it remained with him, as constant as the natural tendency of his steps to lead towards Porterhouse. Twice he decided to go home and twice changed his mind, postponing the decision by walking down Sydney Street towards the Round Church instead of going on down Trinity Street. He tried to fortify his resolve by

thinking about Lord Wurford's legacy but the idea of
all that money was as unreal to him as the experience
of the past few days. There was no consolation to be
found in money. It couldn't replace the cosiness of his
Porter's Lodge with its pigeonholes and switchboard
and the sense that he was needed. The sum was almost
an affront to him, its fortuity robbing his years of
service of their sense. He needn't have been a porter.
He could have been anything he wanted, within reason.
The realization increased his sense of purpose. He
would speak to the Master. He hesitated at the Round
Church. He wouldn't go in the Main Gate, he'd knock
at the Master's Lodge. He turned and went back the
way he'd come.

*

The Master's sudden decision to seek some ground of
understanding with the Senior Tutor left him almost as
soon as he had crossed the Fellows' Garden. Any sort
of overture now would be misinterpreted, he realized,
taken as evidence of weakness on his part. He had
established his authority. It would not do to weaken it
now. But having come out he felt obliged to continue
his walk. He went into town and browsed in Heffer's
for an hour before buying Butler's *Art of the Possible*. It
was not a maxim with which he had much sympathy.
It smacked of cynicism but Sir Godber was sufficient of
a politician still to appreciate the author's sense of
irony. He wandered on debating his own choice of a

title for his autobiography. *Future Perfect* was probably the most appropriate, combining as it did his vision with a modicum of scholarship. Catching sight of his reflection in a shop window he found it remarkable that he was as old as he looked. It was strange that his ideals had not altered with his appearance. The methods of their attainment might mellow with experience but the ideals remained constant. That was why it was so important to see that the undergraduates who came up to Porterhouse should be free to form their own judgements, and more important still that they should have some judgements to form. They should rebel against the accepted tenets of their elders and, in Sir Godber's opinion, their worse. He stopped at the Copper Kettle for tea and then made his way back to Porterhouse and sat in his study reading his book. Outside the sky darkened, and with it the College. Out of term it was empty and there were no room lights on to brighten the Court. At five the Master got up and pulled the curtains and he was about to sit down again when a knock at the front door made him stop and go down the corridor into the hall. He opened the door and peered out into the darkness. A dark familiar shape stood on the doorstep.

'Skullion?' said Sir Godber as if questioning the existence of the shape. 'What are you doing here?'

To Skullion the question emphasized his misery. 'I'd like a word,' he said.

Sir Godber hesitated. He didn't want words with

Skullion. 'What about?' he asked. It was Skullion's turn to hesitate. 'I've come to apologize,' he said finally.

'Apologize? What for?' Skullion shook his head. He didn't know what for. 'Well, man? What for?'

'It's just that . . .'

'Oh, for goodness' sake,' said Sir Godber, appalled at Skullion's inarticulate despair. 'Come on in.' He turned and led the way to his study with Skullion treading gently behind him.

'Well now, what is it?' he asked when they were in the room.

'It's about my dismissal, sir,' Skullion said.

'Your dismissal?' Sir Godber sighed. He was a sympathetic man who had to steel himself with irritation. 'You should see the Bursar about that. I don't deal with matters of that sort.'

'I've seen the Bursar,' said Skullion.

'I don't see that I can do anything,' the Master said. 'And in any case I really don't think that you can expect much sympathy after what you said the other night.'

Skullion looked at him sullenly. 'I didn't say anything wrong,' he muttered. 'I just said what I thought.'

'It might have paid you to consider what you did think before . . .' Sir Godber gave up. The situation was most unfortunate. He had better things to do with his time than argue with college porters. 'Anyway there's nothing more to be said.'

Skullion stirred resentfully. 'Forty-five years I've been a porter here,' he said.

Sir Godber's hand brushed the years aside. 'I know. I know,' he said. 'I'm aware of that.'

'I've given my life to the College.'

'I daresay.'

Skullion glowered at the Master. 'All I ask is to be kept on,' he said.

The Master turned his back on him and kicked the fire with his foot. The man's maudlin appeal annoyed him. Skullion had exercised a baleful influence on the College ever since he could remember. He stood for everything Sir Godber detested. He'd been rude, bullying and importunate all his life and the Master hadn't forgotten his insolence on the night of the explosion. Now here he was, cap in hand, asking to be taken back. Worst of all he made the Master feel guilty.

'I understand from the Bursar that you have some means,' he said callously. Skullion nodded. 'Enough to live on?'

'Yes.'

'Well then, I really can't see what you're complaining about. A lot of people retire at sixty. Haven't you got a family?' Skullion shook his head. Again Sir Godber felt a tremor of unreasonable disgust. His contempt showed in his face, contempt as much for his own vulnerable sensibilities as for the pathetic man before him. Skullion saw that contempt and his little eyes darkened. He had swallowed his pride to come and ask but it rode up in him now in the face of the Master's scorn. It rose up out of the distant past when he'd been a free man and it overwhelmed the barriers of his reference. He hadn't come to be insulted even silently by the likes of Sir Godber. Without knowing what he was doing he took a step forward. Instinctively Sir Godber recoiled. He was afraid of Skullion and, like his contempt a moment before, it showed. He'd been afraid of Skullion all his life, the little Skullions who lived in drab streets he'd had to pass to go to school, who chased him and threw stones and wore grubby clothes.

'Now look here,' he said with an attempt at authority, but Skullion was looking. His bitter eyes stared at Sir Godber and he too was in the grip of the past and its violent instincts. His face was flushed and unknown to him his fists were clenched.

'You bastard!' he shouted and lunged at the Master. 'You bloody bastard!' Sir Godber staggered backwards and tripped against the coffee table. He fell against the mantelpiece and clutched at the edge of the armchair and the next moment he had fallen back into the fireplace. Beneath his feet a rug gently slid away and Sir Godber subsided on to the study floor. His head had hit the corner of the iron grate. Above him Skullion stood dumbfounded. Blood oozed on to the parquet. Skullion's fury ebbed. He stared down at the Master for a moment and turned and ran. He ran down the passage and out the front door into the street. It was empty. Skullion turned to the right and hurried along the

Tom Sharpe

pavement. A moment later he was in Trinity Street. People passed him but there was nothing unusual about a college porter in a hurry.

*

In the Master's Lodge Sir Godber lay still in the flickering light of his fire. The blood running fast from his scalp formed in a pool and dried. An hour passed and Sir Godber still bled, though more slowly. It was eight before he recovered consciousness. The room was blurred and distant and clocks ticked noisily. He tried to get to his feet but couldn't. He knelt against the fireplace and reached for the armchair. Slowly he crawled across the room to the telephone. He'd got to ring for help. He reached up and pulled the phone down on to the floor. He started to dial emergency but the thought of scandal stopped him. His wife? He put the receiver back and reached for the pad with the number of the Samaritans on it. He found it and dialled. While he waited he stared at the notice Lady Mary had pinned on the pad. 'If you are in Despair or thinking of Suicide, Phone the Samaritans.'

The dialling tone stopped. 'Samaritans here, can I help you?' Lady Mary's voice was as stridently concerned as ever.

'I'm hurt,' said Sir Godber indistinctly.

'You're what? You'll have to speak up.'

'I said I'm hurt. For God's sake come . . .'

'What's that?' Lady Mary asked.

'Oh God, oh God,' Sir Godber moaned feebly.

'All right now, tell me all about it,' said Lady Mary with interest. 'I'm here to help you.'

'I've fallen in the grate,' Sir Godber explained.

'Fallen from grace?'

'Not grace,' said Sir Godber desperately. 'Grate.'

'Great?' Lady Mary enquired, evidently convinced she was dealing with a disillusioned megalomaniac.

'The hearth. I'm bleeding. For God's sake come . . .' Exhausted by his wife's lack of understanding Sir Godber fell back upon the floor. Beside him the phone continued to squeak and gibber with Lady Mary's exhortations.

'Are you there?' she asked. 'Are you still there? Now there's no need to despair.' Sir Godber groaned. 'Now don't hang up. Just stay there and listen. Now you say you've fallen from grace. That's not a very constructive way of looking at things, is it?' Sir Godber's stentorian breathing reassured her. 'After all what is grace? We're all human. We can't expect to live up to our own expectations all the time. We're bound to make mistakes. Even the best of us. But that doesn't mean to say we've fallen from grace. You mustn't think in those terms. You're not a Catholic, are you?' Sir Godber groaned. 'It's just that you mentioned bleeding hearts. Catholics believe in bleeding hearts, you know.' Lady Mary was adding instruction to exhortation now. It was typical of the bloody woman, Sir Godber thought helplessly. He tried to raise himself so that he could replace the receiver and shut out for ever the sound of Lady Mary's implacable philanthropy but the effort was too much for him.

'Get off the line,' he managed to moan. 'I need help.'

'Of course you do and that's what I'm here for,' Lady Mary said. 'To help.'

Sir Godber crawled away from the receiver, spurred on by her obtuseness. He had to get help somehow. His eye caught the trays of drinks near the door. Whisky. He crawled towards it and managed to get the bottle. He drank some and still clutching the bottle reached the side door. Somehow he opened it and dragged himself out into the Fellows' Garden. If only he could reach the Court, perhaps he could call out and someone would hear him. He drank some more whisky and tried to get to his feet. There was a light on in the Combination Room. If only he could get there. Sir Godber raised himself on his knees and fell sideways on to the path.

20

It was Sir Cathcart's birthday and as usual there was a party at Coft Castle. On the gravel forecourt the sleek cars bunched in the moonlight like so many large seals huddled on the foreshore. Inside the animal analogy continued. In the interests of several royal guests and uninhibited debauchery, masks were worn if little else. Sir Cathcart typically adopted the disguise of a horse, its muzzle suitably foreshortened to facilitate conversation and his penchant for fellatio. Her Royal Highness the Princess Penelope sought anonymity as a capon and deceived no one. A judge from the Appellate Division was a macaw. There was a bear, two gnus, and a panda wearing a condom. The Loverley sisters sported dildos with stripes and claimed they were zebras and Lord Forsyth, overzealous as a Labrador, urinated against a standard lamp in the library and had to be resuscitated by Mrs Hinkle, who was one of the judges at Cruft's. Even the detectives mingling with the crowd were dressed as pumas. Only the Dean and the Senior Tutor came as humans, and they were not invited.

*

'Cathcart's the only man I know who could do it,' the Dean had said suddenly during dinner in the empty Hall.

'Do what?' asked the Senior Tutor.

'See the PM,' said the Dean. 'Get him to rescind the Master's nomination.'

The Senior Tutor lacerated a shinbone judiciously and wiped his fingers. 'On what grounds?'

'General maladministration,' said the Dean.

'Difficult to prove,' said the Senior Tutor.

The Dean helped himself to devilled kidneys and Arthur replenished his wine glass. 'Let us review the facts. Since his arrival the College has seen the deaths of one undergraduate, a bedder, the total destruction of a building classified as a national monument, charges of peculation and a scandal involving the admission of unqualified candidates, the sacking of Skullion and now, to cap it all, the assumption of dictatorial powers by the Master.'

'But surely—'

'Bear with me,' said the Dean. 'Now you and I may know that the Master is not wholly responsible, but the general public thinks otherwise. Have you seen today's *Telegraph*?'

'No,' said the Senior Tutor, 'but I think I know what you mean. *The Times* has three columns of letters, all of them supporting Skullion's statement on the box.'

'Exactly,' said the Dean. 'The *Telegraph* also has a leading article calling for a stand against student indiscipline and a return to the values Skullion so eloquently advocated. Whatever the merits of *The Carrington Programme*, it has certainly provoked a public reaction against the dismissal of Skullion. Porterhouse may have been blackguarded but it is Sir Godber who takes the blame.'

'As Master, you mean?'

'Precisely,' continued the Dean. 'He may claim—'

'As Master he must accept full responsibility,' said the Senior Tutor.

'Still, I don't see that the Prime Minister would willingly dismiss him. It would reflect poorly on his own judgement in the first place.'

'The Government's position is not a particularly healthy one just at the moment,' said the Dean. 'It only needs a nudge . . .'

'A nudge? From whom?'

The Dean smiled and signalled to Arthur to make himself scarce. 'From me,' he said when the waiter had shuffled off into the darkness of the lower hall.

'You?' said the Senior Tutor. 'How?'

'Have you ever heard of Skullion's Scholars?' the Dean asked. His bloated face glowed in the light of the candles.

'That old story,' said the Senior Tutor. 'An old chestnut surely?'

The Dean shook his head. 'I have the names and the dates and the sums involved,' he said. 'I have the names of the graduates who wrote the papers. I have even some examples of their work.' He put the tips of his fingers together and nodded. The Senior Tutor stared at him.

'No,' he muttered.

'Yes,' the Dean assured him.

'But how?'

The Dean withdrew a little. 'Let's just say that I have,' he said. 'There was a time when I disapproved of the practice. I was young in those days and full of foolishness but I changed my mind. Fortunately I did not destroy the evidence. You see now what I mean by a nudge?'

The Senior Tutor gulped some wine in his amazement. 'Not the PM?' he muttered.

'Not,' admitted the Dean, 'but one or two of his colleagues.' The Senior Tutor tried to think which ministers were Porterhouse men.

'I have some eighty names,' said the Dean, 'some eighty *eminent* names. I think they're quite sufficient.'

The Senior Tutor mopped his forehead. There was no doubt in his mind about the sufficiency of the Dean's information. It would bring the Government down. 'Could you rely on Skullion to substantiate?' he asked.

The Dean nodded. 'I hardly think it will come to that,' he said, 'and if it does I am prepared to stand as scapegoat. I am an old man. I no longer care.'

They sat in silence. Two old men together in the

isolated candlelight under the dark rafters of the Hall. Arthur, standing obediently by the green baize door, watched them fondly.

'And Sir Cathcart?' asked the Senior Tutor.

'And Sir Cathcart,' agreed the Dean.

They stood up and the Dean said grace, his voice tremulous in the vastness of the silent Hall. They went out into the Combination Room and Arthur shuffled softly up to the High Table and began to collect the dishes.

*

Half an hour later they drove out of the College car park in the Senior Tutor's car. Coft Castle was blazing with Edwardian brilliance when they arrived.

'It seems an inopportune moment,' said the Senior Tutor doubtfully surveying the shoal of cars.

'We must strike while the iron is hot,' said the Dean. Inside they were accosted by a puma.

'Do we look like gatecrashers?' the Dean asked severely. The puma shook his head.

'We have urgent business with General Sir Cathcart D'Eath,' said the Senior Tutor. 'Be so good as to inform him that the Dean and Senior Tutor have arrived. We shall wait for him in the library.'

The puma nodded dutifully and they pushed their way through a crush of assorted beasts to the library.

'I must say I find this sort of thing extremely

distasteful,' said the Dean. 'I am surprised that Cathcart allows such goings on at Coft Castle. One would have thought he had more taste.'

'He always did have something of a reputation,' said the Senior Tutor. 'Of course he was before my time but I did hear one or two rather unsavoury stories.'

'Youthful excess is one thing,' said the Dean, 'but mutton dressed as lamb is another.'

'They say the leopard doesn't change its spots,' said the Senior Tutor. He sat down in a club easy while the Dean idly examined a nicely bound copy of Stendhal. It contained, as he had expected from the title, a bottle of liqueur.

Outside the puma stalked Sir Cathcart. He found it extremely difficult. He tried the billiard-room without success. In the kitchen he asked the cook if she had seen him.

'I wouldn't know him if I had,' the cook said primly. 'All I know is that he's gone as a horse.'

The detective went back into the menagerie and asked several guests who were wearing horsey masks if they were Sir Cathcart. They weren't. He helped himself to champagne and tried again. Finally he ran Sir Cathcart to ground in the conservatory with a well-known jockey. The detective surveyed the scene with disgust.

'Two gentlemen to see you in the library,' he said. Sir Cathcart got to his feet.

'What do you mean?' he said indistinctly. 'What are

they doing there? I said nobody was to go in the library.' He staggered off down the passage and into the library where the Dean had just discovered a copy of *A Man and A Maid* inside an early edition of *Great Expectations.*

'What the hell . . .?' Sir Cathcart began before realizing who they were.

'Cathcart?' enquired the Dean, staring doubtfully at the General.

'Who?' said Sir Cathcart.

'We are waiting to speak to Sir Cathcart D'Eath,' said the Dean.

'Isn't here. Gone to London,' said the General, slurring his voice deliberately and hoping that his mask was a sufficient proof against identity. The Dean was unpersuaded. He recognized the General's fetlocks.

'I am prepared to accept the explanation,' he said grimly. 'We have not come here to pry.' He returned the copy of *Great Expectations* to its place. 'We simply wanted to inform Sir Cathcart that the matter of Skullion's Scholars is about to receive a public airing.'

'Damnation,' shouted the General, 'how the hell did . . .?' He stopped and regarded the Dean bitterly.

'Quite,' said the Dean. He sat down behind the desk and the General sank into a chair. 'The matter is urgent, otherwise we shouldn't be here. We have no desire to abuse your hospitality, if that were possible, any longer than we have to. Let us assume that Sir Cathcart is in London for the moment.'

The General nodded his agreement with this tactful proposition. 'What do you want?' he asked.

'Things have reached a crisis,' said the Senior Tutor rising from his club easy. 'We simply want the Prime Minister to be informed that Sir Godber's Mastership must be rescinded.'

'Must?' said the General. The word had an authoritarian ring about it that he was unused to.

'Must,' said the Dean.

Sir Cathcart inside his mask looked doubtful. 'It's a tall order.'

'No doubt,' said the Dean. 'The alternative is possibly the fall of the Government. I am prepared to place my information in the hands of the press. I think you follow the likely consequences.'

Sir Cathcart did. 'But why, for God's sake?' he asked. 'I don't understand. If this got out it would ruin the College.'

'If the Master stays there will be no College to ruin,' said the Dean. 'There will be a hostel. I have some eighty names, Cathcart.'

Sir Cathcart peered through his mask bitterly. '*Eighty*? And you're prepared to put their reputations at risk?'

The Dean's mouth curved upwards in a sneer. 'In the circumstances I find that question positively indecent,' he said.

'Oh, come now,' said the General. 'We all have our little peccadilloes. A fellow's entitled to a little fun.'

On the way out they were importuned by a fowl. 'These gentlemen are just leaving,' said Sir Cathcart hurriedly.

'Before me?' cackled the capon. 'It's against protocol.'

They drove back to Porterhouse in silence. What they had just witnessed had left them with a new sense of disillusionment.

*

'The whole country is going to the dogs,' said the Senior Tutor as they crossed New Court. As if in answer there was a low moan from the Fellows' Garden.

'What on earth was that?' said the Dean. They turned and peered into the darkness. Under the elms a shadow darker than the rest struggled to its feet and collapsed. They crossed the lawn cautiously and stood staring down at the figure on the ground.

'A drunk,' said the Senior Tutor. 'I'll fetch the Porter,' but the Dean had already struck a match. In the small flare of light they looked down into the ashen face of Sir Godber.

'Good God,' said the Dean, 'it's the Master.'

They carried him slowly and with difficulty down the gravel path to the Master's Lodge and laid him on the sofa.

'I'll get an ambulance,' said the Senior Tutor, and picked the phone off the floor and dialled. While they waited the Dean sat staring down into the Master's face. It was evident Sir Godber was dying. He struggled to speak but the words wouldn't come.

'He's trying to tell us something,' said the Senior Tutor softly. There was no bitterness now. In extremis the Master had regained the Senior Tutor's loyalty.

'He must have been drunk,' said the Dean, who could smell the whisky on Sir Godber's feeble breath.

The Master shook his head. An indefinite future awaited him now in which he would only be a memory. It must not be sullied by false report.

'Not drunk,' he managed to mutter, gazing pitifully into the Dean's face. 'Skullion.'

The Dean and Senior Tutor looked at one another. 'What about Skullion?' the Senior Tutor asked but the Master had no answer for him.

*

They waited for the ambulance before leaving. It had been impossible to contact Lady Mary. She was on the phone to a depressive who was threatening to end his life. On the way back through the Fellows' Garden the Dean retrieved the whisky bottle.

'I don't think we need mention this to the police,' he said. 'He was obviously drunk and fell into the fireplace. A tragic end.'

The Senior Tutor was lost in thought. 'You realize what he's done?' he asked.

'Only too well,' said the Dean. 'I'll phone Sir Cathcart and tell him to cancel the ultimatum. There's no need for it now. We shall have to elect a new Master. Let us see to it that he has the true interests of the College at heart. We mustn't make another mistake.'

The Senior Tutor shook his head. 'There can be no question of an election, Dean,' he said. 'The Master has already nominated his own successor.'

In the darkness the two old men stared at one another digesting the extraordinary import of Sir Godber's last word. It was unthinkable but yet . . .

*

They went into the Combination Room to deliberate. The ancient panelled walls, the plaster ceiling decorated with heraldic devices and grotesque animals, the portraits of past Masters, and the silver candlesticks all combined to urge considerations of the past upon their present dilemma.

'There are precedents,' said the Senior Tutor. 'Thomas Wilkins was a pastrycook.'

'He was also an eminent theologian,' said the Dean.

'Dr Cox began his career as a barber,' the Senior Tutor pointed out. 'He owed his election to his wealth.'

'I take your point,' said the Dean. 'In the present circumstances it is one that cannot be ignored.'

'There is also the question of public opinion to consider,' the Senior Tutor continued. 'In the present climate it would not be an unpopular appointment. It would disarm our critics entirely.'

'So it would,' said the Dean. 'It would indeed. But the College Council—'

'Have no say in the matter,' said the Senior Tutor. 'Tradition has it that the Master's dying words constitute an unalterable decision.'

'If uttered in the presence of two or more of the Senior Fellows,' agreed the Dean. 'So it is up to us.'

'There is little doubt that he would be malleable,' the Senior Tutor continued after a long pause. The Dean nodded. 'I confess to finding the argument unanswerable,' he said. They rose and snuffed the candles.

*

Skullion sat in the darkness of his kitchen, shivering. It was a cold night but Skullion was unconscious of the cold. His tremors had other causes. He had threatened the Master. He had in all probability killed him. The memory of Sir Godber lying in a pool of blood in the fireplace haunted Skullion. He could not think of sleep. He sat there at the kitchen table shivering with fright. He couldn't begin to think what to do. The law would find him. Skullion's innate respect for authority rejected the possibility that his crime would go undetected. It was almost as monstrous a thought as the knowledge that he was a murderer. He was still there when the Dean and the Senior Tutor knocked on his door at eight o'clock. They had brought the Praelector with them. As usual his was a supernumerary role.

Skullion listened to the knocking for some minutes

before his instincts as a porter got the better of him. He got up and went down the dingy hall and opened the door. He stood blinking in the sunlight, his face purple with strain but with a solemnity that befitted the occasion.

'If we could just have a word with you, Mr Skullion,' the Dean said. To Skullion the addition of the title had the effect of confirming his worst fears. It suggested the polite formalities of the hangman. He turned and led the way into his front parlour where the sun, shining through the lace curtains, dappled the antimacassars with a fresh embroidery.

The three Fellows removed their hats and sat awkwardly on the Victorian chairs. Like most of the furniture in the house they had been salvaged from the occasional refurbishment of Porterhouse.

'I think it would be better if you sat down,' said the Dean when Skullion continued to stand before them. 'What we are about to tell you may come as something of a shock.'

Skullion sat down obediently. Nothing that they could tell him would come as a shock, he felt sure. He had prepared himself for the worst.

'We have come here this morning to tell you that the Master has died,' said the Dean. Skullion's face remained impassively suffused. To the three Fellows his evident self-control augured well for the future.

'On his deathbed Sir Godber named you as his successor,' said the Dean slowly. Skullion heard the words but his expectations deprived them of their meaning. What had seemed unthinkable to the Dean and Senior Tutor at first hearing was inconceivable to Skullion. He stared uncomprehendingly at the Dean.

'He nominated you as the new Master of Porterhouse,' continued the Dean. 'We have come here this morning on behalf of the College Council to ask you to accept this nomination.' He paused to allow the Porter to consider the proposal. 'Naturally we understand that this must come as a very great surprise to you, as indeed it did to us, but we would like to know your answer as soon as possible.'

In the silence that followed this announcement, Skullion underwent a terrible change. A tremor ran down his body and his face, already purple, became darker still. He wrestled with the terrible inconsequentiality of it all. He had murdered the Master and they were offering him the Mastership. There were no just rewards in life, only insane inversions of the scheme of things in which he had trusted. It seemed for a moment that he was going mad.

'We must have your answer,' said the Dean. Skullion's body acted uncontrollably as he went into apoplexy. His head nodded frantically.

'Then we may take it that you accept?' asked the Dean. Skullion's head nodded without stop.

'Then let me be the first to congratulate you, Master,' said the Dean and seizing Skullion's hand shook it convulsively. The Praelector and the Senior Tutor followed suit.

*

'The poor fellow was quite overcome,' said the Dean as they climbed back into the car. 'It seemed to leave him speechless.'

'Hardly surprising, Dean,' said the Praelector, 'I find it difficult to voice my feelings even now. Skullion as the Master of Porterhouse. That it should come to this.'

'At least we shan't have any speeches at the Feast,' said the Senior Tutor.

'I suppose there is that to be said for it,' said the Praelector.

*

In the front parlour of his old home the new Master of Porterhouse lay still in his chair and stared calmly at the linoleum. A new peace had come to Skullion out of the chaos of the last few minutes. There were no contradictions now between right and wrong, master and servant, only a strange inability to move his left side.

Skullion had suffered a Porterhouse Blue.

21

'A stroke of luck really,' said the Dean at lunch after the formal ceremony in the Council Chamber at which the new Master had presided before being wheeled back by Arthur to the Master's Lodge.

'I must say I don't follow you, Dean,' said the Praelector with distaste. 'If you are referring to the Master's affliction—'

'I was merely trying to draw your attention to the advantages of the situation,' said the Dean. 'The Master is not without his comforts after all, and we . . .'

'Enjoy the administration of policy?' the Senior Tutor suggested.

'Precisely.'

'I suppose that is one way of looking at it. Certainly Sir Godber's reforms have been frustrated. I thought Lady Mary behaved extremely badly.'

The Dean sighed. 'Liberals tend to overreact, in my experience. There seems to be something inherently hysterical about progressive opinion,' he said. 'Still, there was no excuse whatsoever for accusing the police of incompetence. Nothing could be more absurd than her suggestion that Sir Godber had been murdered. For one moment I thought she was going to accuse the Senior Tutor and myself.'

'I suppose he was drunk,' said the Praelector.

'Not according to the coroner,' said the Bursar.

The Dean sniffed. 'I have never placed much faith in expert opinion,' he said. 'I smelt the fellow's breath. He was as drunk as a lord.'

'It's certainly the only rational explanation of his choice of Skullion,' said the Praelector. 'To my knowledge he loathed the man.'

'I'm afraid I have to agree with you,' said the Bursar. 'Lady Mary—'

'Accused us of lying,' said the Dean and the Senior Tutor simultaneously.

'As you said yourself, Dean, she was hysterical,' said the Praelector. 'She wasn't herself.'

The Dean scowled down the table. Lady Mary's accusation still rankled. 'Damned woman,' he said, 'she's a disgrace to her sex.' He took his irritation out on the new waiter. 'These potatoes are burnt.'

'Now you come to mention it,' said the Senior Tutor, 'what went wrong at the crematorium? There seemed an inordinately long delay.'

'There was a power cut,' the Dean said, 'on account of the strike.'

'Ah, was that it?' said the Senior Tutor. 'A sympathy strike no doubt.'

They finished their meal and took coffee in the Combination Room.

'There's still the question of Sir Godber's portrait to be considered,' said the Senior Tutor. 'I suppose we should decide on a suitable artist.'

'There's only Bacon,' said the Dean, 'I can think of no one else who could portray a more exact likeness.'

The Fellows of Porterhouse had regained their vivacity.

*

In the Master's Lodge Skullion's life followed its inexorable pattern. He was wheeled from room to room to catch the sun so that it was possible to tell the time of day from his position at the windows, and every afternoon Arthur would take him out through the Fellows' Garden and across New Court to the main gate. Occasionally late at night the wheel chair, with its dark occupant wearing his bowler hat, could be seen in the shadows by the back gate waiting and watching with an implacable futility of purpose the spiked wall over which the undergraduates no longer climbed. But if Skullion's horizons were limited to the narrow confines of the College they were celestial in time. Each corner of Porterhouse held memories for him that made good the infirmities of the present. It was as if his stroke had sutured the gaps in his memory so that in his immobility he was left free at last to haunt the years as once he had patrolled the courtyards and the corridors of Porterhouse. Sitting in New Court he would recall the occupants of every room, their names and faces, even the counties they came from, so that the Court assumed a new dimension, at once recessional and mute. Each staircase was a warren in his mind alive with men no longer living who had once conferred the honour of their disregard upon him. 'Skullion,' they had shouted, and the shouts still echoed in his mind with their call to a service he would never know again. Instead they called him Master now and Skullion suffered their respect in silence.

*

Around him the life of the College went on unaltered. Lord Wurford's legacy helped to restore the Tower and Skullion had signed the papers with his thumbprint unprotestingly. As a sop to scholarship there were a few research fellows, mainly in law and the less controversial sciences, but apart from these concessions, little changed. The undergraduates kept later hours, grew longer hair and sported their affectations of opinion as trivially as ever they had once seduced the shopgirls. But in essentials they were just the same. In any case, Skullion discounted thought. He'd known too many scholars in his time to think that they would alter things. It was the continuity of custom and character that counted. What men were, not what they said, and looking round him he was reassured. The faces that he saw and the voices he heard, though now obscured by hair and the borrowed accents of the poor, had still the recognizable attributes of class, and if the old unfeeling

Tom Sharpe

arrogance had been replaced by a kindliness and gentle quality that he despised, it was still Them and Us even in the privilege of sympathy. And when an undergraduate would offer to wheel the Master for a walk, he would be deterred by the glint in Skullion's eyes which betrayed a contempt that made a mockery of his dependence.

Occasionally the Senior Tutor would smother his revulsion for the physically inadequate and visit the Master for tea to tell him how the VIII was doing or what the rugger XV had won, and every day the Dean would waddle to the Master's Lodge to report the day's events. Skullion did not enjoy this strange reversal of roles but it seemed to afford the Dean some little satisfaction. It was as if this mock subservience assuaged his sense of guilt.

'We owe it to him,' he told the Senior Tutor who asked him why he bothered.

'But what do you find to say to him?'

'I ask after his health,' said the Dean gaily.

'But he can't reply,' the Senior Tutor pointed out.

'I find that most consoling,' said the Dean. 'And after all no news is good news, isn't it?'

*

On Thursday nights the Master dined in Hall, wheeled in by Arthur at the head of the Fellows to sit at the end of the table and watch the ancient ritual of grace and the serving of the dishes with a critical eye. While the

326

Fellows gorged themselves, Skullion was fed a few, choice morsels by Arthur. It was his worst humiliation. That, and the fact that his shoes lacked the brilliance that his patient spit and polish had once given them.

It was left to the Dean, unfeeling to the end, to say the last word in the Combination Room after one such meal. 'He may not have been born with a silver spoon in his mouth, but by God he's going to die with one.'

In his corner by the fire the Master was seen to twitch deferentially at this joke at his own expense, but then Skullion had always known his place.

Ancestral Vices

Tom Sharpe

'Savage and side-splitting'
Daily Express

'A novelist who has broken out of the pack, established a wholly
distinctive style . . . such a keen eye for the ridiculous and
marvellous ability to puncture it'
Scotsman

'An immense gift for social satire . . . the action is unflagging'
Daily Telegraph

'There's almost no-one funnier'
Observer

arrow books

Blott on the Landscape

Tom Sharpe

'Confirms that he has inherited the mantle of the late
P. G. Wodehouse. This is deliciously English comedy'
Guardian

Extremely funny . . . Mr Sharpe's dialogue is nifty, imaginative,
enjoyable'
Peter Ackroyd, *Spectator*

'I laughed out loud, I really did . . . Tom Sharpe is nowhere more
buoyant than when mounting catastrophic scenes of hilarious
mayhem'
Statesmen

'A very funny writer indeed . . . Tom Sharpe's comedy lies as much
in his language and the pace of the dialogue as in the outrageous
muddles and confusions of his comic situations'
The Times

'This exuberant novel will cheer all those who dislike bureaucracy'
Daily Telegraph

arrow books